PRAISE FOR TRACY

TRAIL

OF

DESTRUCTION

OTHER TITLES BY TRACY BUCHANAN:

TRAIL
OF
DESTRUCTION

Tracy Buchanan

LAKE UNION
PUBLISHING

Published by Lake Union Publishing, Seattle

www.apub.com

Amazon, the Amazon logo, and Lake Union Publishing are trademarks of Amazon.com, Inc., or its affiliates.

ISBN-13: 9781542031998
ISBN-10: 1542031990

Cover design by Sarah Whittaker

Printed in the United States of America

In memory of Mum,
our constant sunny spot and my biggest influence.

Prologue

Sunday 8th August
4.15 a.m.

The flames cast shadows on their faces as they watch their beloved forest burn down, a rush of wind bringing with it the acrid smell of scorched branches and singed leaves that only the day before had provided a canopy of shade during the hottest day of the summer.

Many of the residents of Forest Grove are still in their night-clothes, tears running down their cheeks, hair turned orange by the light of the turbulent flames ahead of them. Others, having only just been woken by the sound of people shouting and the hiss of flames, are running towards the forest, hands over their mouths as they take in the horror before them.

A human chain forms, buckets of all shapes and sizes passed from hand to hand, so heavy with water people groan at the weight of them. At the front, two men take it in turns to throw the water at the flames. They know it can't possibly make much of a difference as the angry inferno blazes before them. But this is a community where, even in the face of hopeless adversity, something must be *seen* to be done.

Even the slight hope that comes when sirens sound in the distance is tempered by the horror of what's happening to their forest, the increasing gaps left by fallen and blackened trees a devastating testament to what will remain at the end.

The residents clutch at each other, grief-stricken, and yet still somehow hypnotised by it all. The sound of sirens fills the air, the night lighting up with the flashing blue lights of two fire engines that screech up the road behind them. The residents of Forest Grove continue their human chain, while firefighters jump out of their vehicles and run between the lines of villagers with a hose to direct a huge jet of water at the fire.

Then a cry louder than the rest rings out as a woman shoves through the crowds, face tight with fear. She tries to rush into the flames, but the firemen hold her back.

'Let me get in!' she screams. 'He's in the forest! I have to save him!'

Gasps of horror sound out. But one person watches with a smile, refusing to feel any guilt.

Yes, they struck the match. Yes, they revelled in the hiss it made and enjoyed the scorch from the flame on their fingers. But they tell themselves this fire and the prospect of someone being hurt isn't really *their* fault. It's the fault of the residents witnessing the forest's destruction. If they weren't all so blind to the reality that sits at the heart of Forest Grove like a rotting corpse, then making this fiery stand would not have been necessary. The reality is these people's actions can burn like the spectacle before them; the village as stifling as the smoke clogging the air.

Now that rotting heart will be exposed as the walls built around it burn down until, finally, the truth will be learnt about this vicious village.

PART 1

One month before

Chapter 1

Ellie Mileham walked through the forest, enjoying the way the morning light gave the leaves a soft, hazy glow. It helped her think, being among the trees, as it had all her life. And now more than ever, she needed to *think*.

It had been three months since her husband, Peter, had walked out on her. Three months that had felt like a tornado ripping through her life. But now it was beginning to feel like that tornado had stopped. Finally, she could begin to put the pieces of her life back together in the way *she* wanted.

Her dog, a lanky, loving Boxer called Stanley, stopped to sniff at some leaves. Ellie took the chance to pause for a moment, closing her eyes and leaning her head back, enjoying the warmth of the summer breeze on her face.

Yes, she definitely felt a clarity of purpose now. A sense of peace.

As she thought that, a loud bang echoed through the air, sending birds fleeing in terror from their branches. Stanley let out a panicked bark and Ellie jumped in shock, putting her hand to her thumping heart.

'What on earth was that?' she said.

It had sounded like a gunshot. But surely not here in the forest? Another shot pierced the air.

'Stanley, here! Now!' Stanley darted over to her, pressing close to her legs and trembling slightly as she grabbed his collar. 'It's okay, sweetheart, let's get out of here, shall we?'

She quickly turned on her heel and strode away from the sounds of shots, the twigs and leaves that had just a moment before felt like a soft carpet beneath her feet now more like spikes, making her trip and stumble.

Another shot rang out, closer this time, and voices too. She froze as she recognised one of the voices.

Her ex-husband, Peter.

She rolled her eyes. Since when had Peter taken up shooting?

Her irritation was quickly followed by anger. Didn't he realise how bloody dangerous it was, especially for the forest's deer population, which she'd campaigned so hard to protect?

She ran back towards the sound of voices, calling out, 'Stop shooting, please, another human in the woods!' As she drew closer, she saw a section of the woods had been taped off with notices declaring:

SHOOTING PRACTICE IN PROGRESS. **DO NOT ENTER!**

'Shooting practice for what?' she hissed under her breath. A few weeks back, there had been talk that the forest ranger, Frazer Cronin, wanted to apply for a deer-control licence. But Ellie had managed to get that shouted down via the village's Facebook community group. She presumed Frazer had changed his mind after the obvious opposition from many of the villagers who, like her, loved catching sight of the beautiful creatures during early-morning walks.

As she drew closer to the voices, she spotted Peter among the trees with his father, Tommy, the forest ranger Frazer and another villager, a man in his late sixties called Graham Cane. Graham ran the local shooting club, which Peter had been a member of in the months before he and Ellie separated. Graham had once run a farm before moving to Forest Grove and took great pride in owning a shooting licence. When Ellie had lived with her parents, their house had backed on to his house, and he was always complaining about one thing or another. The lifetime of negativity and venom seemed to show on his wizened, old face, his watery, blue eyes filled with spite.

The four men were aiming rifles at targets which had been set up.

Peter turned and looked at Ellie in surprise before lowering his gun. He looked ridiculous in a tweed flat cap pulled over his short, auburn hair and a tweed jacket wrapped around his tall, slim body.

Stanley got out of her grip and darted under the tape, racing over to Peter as Peter laughed, stroking him.

Traitor.

'What on earth are you doing?' Ellie asked. 'Do you realise how dangerous this is?'

'Calm down, love,' Peter said, raising an eyebrow at the other men. 'We cordoned the area off, put up notices.'

Love. How patronising.

Unable to deal with her ex's smug face, she turned towards Frazer. He was much shorter than Peter, his red cheeks the only thing ensuring he didn't blend into the trees with his green forest ranger get-up. 'Are you even allowed to be doing this, Frazer?'

He regarded her nervously. 'It's all above board, Ellie.'

'Yep,' Graham said. 'Just need to get some practice in for the deer-control licence we're applying for, right, Frazer?'

Frazer sighed and Ellie's mouth dropped open. 'But that's going against the villagers' wishes!' she said.

'A post on a Facebook group isn't exactly an official democratic act, Ellie,' her ex-father-in-law, Tommy, said. He was an imposing figure, a big bear of a man who carried his many years as a police detective in the air around him.

Peter nodded in agreement. 'Not to mention that behind closed doors, the same people saying in public they love the deer are complaining in private to Frazer about all the damage they do.'

'Like trampling through my rose bushes!' Tommy said.

Ellie resisted the urge to shake her head. Tommy was always going on about his rose bushes; no surprise he was happy to see wildlife sacrificed to save them.

'And they risk car accidents as they dart across the roads here,' Graham added.

'A small number of incidents,' Ellie said, 'nothing compared to the joy the deer bring.' She turned to the forest ranger. 'You can't just go charging ahead, Frazer. We villagers need to be officially consulted.'

As she said that, a figure approached from the trees behind the men and she realised with horror that it was her and Peter's seventeen-year-old son, Tyler. He looked completely out of place with his skinny, grey jeans, piercings and black hair shaved short at the back, long and dyed blue at the front.

She yanked the tape up, ducking beneath it and walking towards her son. '*What* are you doing here?'

'Just here with Dad and Grandad,' he mumbled as he greeted an exuberant Stanley.

'Not shooting, I hope?' Ellie asked.

'Yep.'

'Jesus, you don't even have a licence!'

'Oh, come on, Ellie, it was just a little practice shot,' Peter said, shaking his head.

Tyler looked down at his trainer-clad feet, avoiding her gaze. 'Kinda regretting it now.'

She felt her heart contract. Tyler and his father had an uneasy relationship, Peter not approving of Tyler's ambitions to be a lead guitarist in a band ('Pipe dreams!' he'd say. 'Be more realistic, get into law like me!' 'Or at least play more sport,' his grandfather would add, 'it's good for mental development, you know!'). She supposed this was Tyler's way of showing his dad and grandfather he could get involved with a sport . . . even if that sport meant doing something that Ellie knew would feel unnatural to him. As she looked at his miserable face, she wished she could just take Tyler back with her now rather than let him go home with his dad. She desperately missed the kids during the days they were with their father. It was one of the many things she'd had to get used to over the past three months.

Ellie turned to her ex, furious. 'I can't believe you allowed this, Peter.'

'Nothing wrong with a bit of informal shooting practice!' Tommy bellowed.

'Dad's right,' Peter said, putting his hand on his son's shoulder. 'It's sport, isn't it?'

'Sport, yeah, right,' Ellie said, shaking her head. 'You should have checked with me first. *Please* don't tell me Zoe is here too?' She looked around for their thirteen-year-old daughter.

Tommy laughed. 'Not a chance! That girl almost faints at the sight of a dead hedgehog. She's with Meghan,' he said, referring to Peter's mother.

'I don't exactly remember Tyler being overjoyed when we found that hedgehog in our garden either,' Ellie said.

'That was two years ago, Mum,' Tyler said, cheeks reddening in embarrassment.

Ellie curled her hands into fists. This was so typical of Peter, just storming ahead to do whatever he wanted, whenever he wanted.

'I'm not happy,' she said, 'and the villagers won't be either,' she added, gesturing towards the rooftops in the distance.

'We're *doing* this for the village, Ellie,' Tommy said in an exasperated voice.

Graham sighed. 'Forget it, Tommy. No point trying to explain, silly women like this just don't get it.'

Tyler glared at him, stepping even closer to his mum. She smiled. For all his teenage sulkiness, he knew when his mum needed his support.

'Silly women?' Ellie said, eyes drilling into Graham's. 'I recall you calling my mother the exact same thing when we lived behind you.'

'Her bloody conifer blocked the sun out!' Graham said.

'It didn't. The council came out to check too and confirmed it didn't.' She tilted her head. 'What is it about you and strong women who speak their mind, Graham? Does it make you feel uncomfortable?'

Graham laughed. 'Strong? Your mother? Hardly. Look at the state of her now.'

Ellie's mouth dropped open in shock.

'Don't say that about my nan,' Tyler said.

'Rein it in, Graham,' Tommy said in a low voice.

'That was below the belt,' Ellie said, trying to keep the tremble from her voice. 'Stanley, come here, time to head home!' Stanley bounced over to her and she attached his lead. She looked at the other men. 'Remember what I said, Frazer,' she said, staring at the forest ranger, 'you must consult the village.'

'Look, Ellie,' Peter said with a sigh, 'I think you need to accept the deer need to be controlled, whether you like it or not.'

'We'll see about that. I'll see you tonight, okay?' she said to Tyler. Then she turned on her heel and walked off, Stanley bounding along with her.

Ellie watched her mother's face that afternoon as she slowly moved the red play piece along a ladder on the colourful board in front of her. Her brow was knitted with concentration and Ellie could see she hadn't rubbed her moisturiser in properly, meaning it was clogging the lines in her face. The old her would have hated that. She'd always been so meticulous about ensuring her skin looked perfect. But now her desire to look as good as she could had gone.

'Nice one, Mum,' Ellie said.

Her mother barely reacted, just continued staring at the board.

Around them, the other residents played board games too. They were sat outside in the Lovat AfterCare Village's gardens, shaded by trees and wooden gazebos. The retirement village had formerly been a large hotel that sat at the north end of the forest near where Ellie used to live with her parents. The building had been there many years before the village grew up around it. After going out of business in the seventies, it had sat abandoned until it was bought by a company specialising in homes for the retired. They had turned it into a retirement village in the early 2000s, a few years before Ellie's mother became a resident. It was a pleasant-looking white-bricked building with vast windows looking out on to the forest. Residents had a variety of needs, from those who could live independently to others who needed around-the-clock care. Her mother was somewhere in between, her lethargy and lack of desire to do much nowadays meaning she sometimes needed a little encouragement. So while she lived in the main building where people got the most care, she was able to do more than the others there.

Ellie had been running games afternoons there for ten years now. She always aimed to visit her mother at least twice a week, sometimes more if she could fit it in. She had come up with the idea of making board games more of a regular fixture in the residents' lives when she noticed how curious they were about the pile of board games Ellie would bring to play with her mother. It was something to connect Ellie with her mother, who seemed to perk up a bit while playing the old games they had enjoyed in Ellie's childhood. Sometimes, if Ellie was lucky, she'd even get a smile out of her mum, taking her back to the good old days . . . before all the light was taken out of her.

She thought again about what Graham had said earlier.

Strong? Your mother? Hardly. Look at the state of her now.

She looked at her mother now, putting her hand over hers. 'This is nice, isn't it?' she asked.

A flicker of a smile.

That was good, that was something.

Several shots suddenly rang out, her mother yelping in shock.

'Don't panic, Helen!' one of the carers shouted out, her mum's favourite, a tall Jamaican woman called Sherry. 'It'll just be Graham Cane doing his shooting practice.'

Ellie clenched her hands into fists. Hadn't he got the message after what happened that morning?

'It's fine, Mum,' Ellie said, squeezing her hand. 'Just that idiot Graham Cane.'

'He *is* an idiot,' her mother replied, her eyes showing an unusual level of emotion.

Ellie looked towards where Graham's house was and sighed. Would men like him *ever* learn? She looked at her watch. She'd already been there two hours. 'I'd better go, Mum, the kids will be back soon.'

She'd told her mum about the separation. Her mother's face had briefly flickered with sadness but that had been her only response.

Ellie gathered everything and stood up. 'Love you, Mum.'

Her mum looked up at her, face expressionless. 'Love you,' she replied. But it just sounded like an echo.

That night, Ellie's sleep was punctured with the same nightmare she often had of her mother. She'd walk into her parents' old room and see her mother sitting with her back to her at her vanity table, a pair of scissors in her hand, strands of her once-beautiful blonde hair – hair like Ellie's – scattered around the floor.

But this time, a new scene quickly emerged of a deer thundering through the forest, stalked by a faceless person with a gun. A shot rang out and suddenly the deer turned into her mother. Her mother collapsed to the ground, blood blooming on her white nightdress as she lay, prone, on the forest floor.

Ellie woke with a start, letting out a small scream.

There was the sound of footsteps in the hallway and Tyler appeared at her door. 'Mum? You okay?'

'Just a nightmare, darling.'

'What was it about?'

She hesitated. 'Your nan.'

'Is it because of what Graham did?'

She'd told him about the gunshots at the care home earlier, invoking an angry shake of the head from Tyler.

'Maybe,' Ellie replied.

'You should post something on the Facebook group.'

'I will, in the morning.'

He walked into the room, the moonlight filtering in through the curtains highlighting his pale face. 'You want me to stay here until you fall back asleep?'

'I'm fine. You're so sweet though.'

'All right, night.'

'Night, darling.'

She watched him walk out then sank her head back into the pillow.

'No more nightmares,' she whispered into the darkness. 'Please, no more nightmares.'

Chapter 2

Sunday 11th July
10.32 a.m.

Ellie Nash

Hi everyone! I thought I'd let you guys know what a nightmare I had yesterday. First, I was walking in the forest and I heard gunshots. Turns out our forest ranger Frazer has decided to ignore us and go ahead with applying for a deer-control licence. Second, I was visiting my mum at the retirement village and the peace was shattered by more gunshots! This time from Graham Cane's house. Scared the residents witless. Can I just ask for a little

consideration, Graham . . . and official consul-
tation about the deer-control plans, Frazer?

Nero Patel

My dad was spooked about the gunshots too,
Ellie. I was about to post about it, you beat
me to it.

Rebecca Feine

Yes, we heard the gunshots all the way from the
pub garden. Frazer, you know how opposed
some of us are to deer control? Didn't we have
this discussion already thanks to Ellie's brilliant post a couple of weeks back? And we all
agreed there's no need for deer control here
in Forest Grove.

Pauline Sharpe

Not ALL of us agreed to it. Many of us think the
little buggers need controlling, they ran out in
the road the other day and nearly caused a car
accident!

Ed Piper

Yes, I was there when it happened. Graham is
within his rights to shoot his rifle in his garden
for practice, Ellie. And before anyone bangs on

about the little 'Bambis', I'll invite you to take a look at pictures of the front of my bumper after one of them ran out on me last year.

Kitty Fletcher

I for one agree with Ellie, the idea of shooting our beloved animals is barbaric!! The therapy they provide, simply watching them on our lawns in the early hours, does wonders for mental health in the village.

Graham Cane

Oh hello, Queen of Snowflakes, Kitty, thought you'd pop along at some point. Didn't realise deer could be therapists now. What next, rocket scientists? The problem with Forest Grove over the past ten years is that too many people have moved here from towns like Ashbridge or even London. No idea what it means to live in a rural setting.

Ellie Nash

I've lived here since the village opened when I was twelve, Graham, and I can honestly say I've never had any issues with the deer.

Tommy Mileham

But others have, Ellie! The rose bushes in our back garden were completely destroyed last summer by a herd of the vermin.

Andrea Simpson

Oh, I remember that, Tommy, such beautiful roses too.

Sheila Leighton

The poor kids will be devastated if deer are shot though!

Graham Cane

Those 'poor kids' need to get used to living in the countryside. Snowflakes, the lot of them. As Pauline pointed out, the animals are becoming a nightmare for residents.

Vanessa Shillingford

Not surprised you're so enthusiastic about it, Graham! Any chance to use your gun. Shooting the poor things is bloody barbaric. We back in the Stone Age or something?

Peter Mileham

'Poor things'. You wouldn't be saying that if they were trampling all over the new bush you planted in your garden at the weekend, Ness.

Vanessa Shillingford

Why are you still a member of this group, dear brother? Go join the Ashbridge Facebook group, won't you?

Meghan Mileham

Now, now, you two!

Andrea Simpson

Okay, I'm going to close comments on this now, this subject was already covered months back.

Ellie Nash

That doesn't usually stop you letting posts through, Andrea! There are countless posts about dog excrement and parking but you still let those go through.

Belinda Bell

Dog poop is a menace to this village!

Vanessa Shillingford

And killing deer isn't?

Ellie Nash

Exactly! I think the deers' lives are more important than dog excrement.

Andrea Simpson

Fine, Ellie, if you think you can do a better job of moderating this page, then feel free! As I told you all in a post last week, my new role as manager at the Forest Centre combined with the roaring success of the 'Tiaras and Tyrannosaurus Parties' I run with Michael means I simply do not have the spare time I once had. Can I take this as an offer to become the new moderator, Ellie?

Rebecca Feine

What a fabulous idea! Ellie would be a wonderful administrator.

Nero Patel

I second that.

Vanessa Shillingford

I third, fourth, fifth and sixth it.

Sheila Leighton

Make that seven!

Meghan Mileham

Eight!

Andrea Simpson

So what do you say, Ellie?

Graham Cane

Oh look, she's gone quiet, all talk and no action.

Ellie Nash

Don't worry, I'm here, Graham. Fine! I'll do it.

Chapter 3

'What have I done?' Ellie said to Vanessa, her dearest friend who also happened to be Peter's sister. They were sitting in the Into the Woods bakery which Vanessa ran with her mother, Meghan. Ellie was a regular there, using it as a base sometimes to do her work. With its forest wallpaper and rustic oak furniture, it gave the feeling of being part of the forest itself. It was right next to the forest, sitting in a courtyard made up of a handy little collection of shops, the doctors' surgery, chemist's and the library, plus the Neck of the Woods pub.

'You're going to make an awesome group moderator!' Vanessa said.

'I barely have enough time fitting in work with everything else on top,' Ellie replied as she looked at all the items laid out on the table. She was working on a crossword book she'd been commissioned to finish within a month by a women's magazine. She'd already come up with the questions and answers for the first puzzle and was now hand-drawing the grid, taking great pleasure in measuring it out. Sure, it was more time-consuming to do it the old-school way. But it was *her* way and she liked it. When she was done, she'd redo it on her computer before beginning on the next puzzle.

'Oh, come on,' Vanessa said. 'You'd only need to check it every now and again.'

'Every now and again? Are you having a laugh? The villagers *love* the Facebook group! It's going to be a nightmare, I can feel it in my bones. I was just so angry at Graham, it was a *completely* impulsive decision. I didn't think it through.'

'Impulsive decisions are the best kind,' Vanessa said. 'I mean, look at me! I decided to co-own a bakery with my mother while absolutely hammered.' She gritted her teeth and waved at her mother, Meghan, who was serving behind the till. Meghan waved back, smiling at Ellie. Even though Ellie and Peter were separated, the three women refused to sacrifice their friendship too. Vanessa and Ellie had, after all, been friends before Peter came on the scene, meeting on their very first day at Forest Grove High school twenty-eight years ago, two twelve-year-olds bonding over the fact they'd both moved into a brand-new 'eco village', as Forest Grove was known. Vanessa was still as tough and vivacious as she had been back then when she was a scrappy little freckled redhead. After Ellie fell for Peter when she turned fifteen, it made the two girls even closer.

'I'd love to have seen Peter's face when he found out you're the group's new moderator,' Vanessa said, lowering her voice so her mother couldn't hear. 'You can ban *all* his posts now he's not officially a Forest Grove resident any more,' she added, blue eyes sparkling. 'Maybe you can ban members like Graham Cane too? Oooh, speaking of which, did you hear about Graham?'

Ellie shook her head. 'What happened?'

'His guns were stolen last night.'

'Really?'

'Yeah. And that's all because you highlighted in the group what an arse he is.'

'I didn't mean for his guns to be stolen though!'

'Not officially stolen, apparently the idiot forgot to lock them away, but still. It's funny, isn't it? No more deer control for him.'

'I'm sure Peter will lend him a gun; he has two of them,' Ellie said with an eye roll.

Vanessa laughed. 'Ergh, Peter is *really* doing my head in at the moment.'

'Doesn't he always?'

Though the siblings looked similar with their height, blue eyes and auburn hair – Vanessa's was long, to her elbows, and curly – that was where the similarities stopped. Peter had always been about status and money, whereas Vanessa saw herself as a bit of an eco-warrior fighting for the underrepresented. It wasn't just about their personalities though. Vanessa had never quite forgiven Peter for putting a stop to the gap year she'd had planned in South Africa while studying sociology at Ashbridge University. Peter had printed out a list of all the dangers and risks for their parents, persuading Tommy to withdraw the money he'd promised Vanessa towards the trip, meaning she couldn't go.

Peter said he'd done it out of pure love for his sister. But Ellie knew deep down it was jealousy: Vanessa had been accepted into a highly coveted placement with the British embassy in South Africa, whereas Peter was struggling to keep up with the demands of law school.

The one silver lining of Vanessa not going away was that Ellie didn't have to endure a year without her best friend, the two of them meeting regularly for lunch or drunken nights out while Ellie worked at the *Ashbridge Gazette* and Vanessa went to university in the town.

But in the year when Vanessa was supposed to be learning about Africa's ecosystems and politics, she fell pregnant by accident and had to leave university. She adored her oldest son, but in moments of reflection, she would yearn after the 'life I should have had', away from Forest Grove, fighting the good fight.

Instead, she'd fallen into working at the Into the Woods bakery for some extra income with her mum, eventually becoming co-owner when Meghan bought the former owner out.

The door to the bakery swung open then and Belinda Bell walked in, looking even more annoyed than usual. She was in her eighties, tall and robust despite her advancing years, with short, curly white hair and a perpetual look of disapproval on her face. Vanessa winked as Ellie smiled.

'Can you believe it,' Belinda said loudly as she walked towards the counter, 'I have just trod in yet more vile dog mess.'

'I hope you haven't brought it inside, Belinda?' Meghan said.

'Of course not!' Belinda insisted. 'I just washed it all off under the outdoor tap. This has *got* to stop. It's becoming the bane of this village's life.'

'Well, I wouldn't go *that* far . . .' Meghan said. Ellie could see she was trying not to smile as Vanessa continued to shake her head behind Belinda's back.

'Two slices of the Victoria sponge, please,' Belinda said as she got out her purse. 'You know Andrea hasn't approved *three* of my posts about the dog-poop problem? Just as well she won't be admin of the group much longer. Never liked the woman – as fake as they come.'

'Belinda! That's not very kind,' Meghan said as she wrapped the slices of cake up.

Belinda dismissed Meghan with a wave of her crêpe-paper hand. 'Give me truth over fake kindness any day.'

'She has a point,' Vanessa whispered.

'You would say that,' Ellie said, 'you hate Andrea.' Vanessa and Andrea Simpson had hated each other at school, getting into multiple arguments. They were so different, Andrea with her perfectly coiffed hair and obsession with all things Disney, compared to Vanessa with her dreadlocks (back then anyway) and obsession with all things political.

'Shame your Peter doesn't live here any more,' Belinda continued as she handed over her money to Meghan, 'otherwise I'd suggest *he* do the admin role over *Ellie*. So *sad* to lose such an asset to the village.'

Ellie sighed. She ought to be used to hearing residents' disappointment over Peter's decision to move to the nearby town, Ashbridge. It felt like she'd heard it non-stop the past three months. Sure, on the surface he might deserve it. He was a regular fixture around the village, volunteering here, there and everywhere. But what villagers didn't know was that his 'charitable' endeavours were entirely selfish: the law company he worked for expected prospective directors to show a commitment to helping the community and Peter was *desperate* to be a director. The things he would say about residents behind their backs after coming home from any voluntary events!

Not to mention the fact that it was actually Ellie who did most of the work, baking cakes to dish out to villagers to sustain them during a village litter-picking event he'd organised (cakes, she learnt later, that Peter claimed he'd made). Or writing and printing out leaflets for a charity event (again, something Peter claimed he'd done). That was just the tip of the iceberg and yet Peter got all the credit!

She was tempted to tell residents all this when they banged on about him, but then she realised how hard she'd worked to get to where she was now: a place of peace, of acceptance. A place where she had the chance to make things *right* again.

Belinda paid for her cake then marched towards the door, pausing when she saw Ellie. 'Oh, I didn't realise you were here.' She looked down at Stanley – who was lying at Ellie's feet, panting – and gave him a look of disgust.

'That's fine, Belinda,' Ellie said, 'I heard every word you said and it's just given me even more reason to be a super-awesome moderator.'

Belinda narrowed her eyes at Ellie then marched out.

'Watch out for dog poop!' Vanessa called after her.

'You two *are* naughty,' Meghan said, the smile betraying how much she enjoyed it really. Meghan had a kind face, short, caramel-coloured hair and pretty brown eyes. 'How's your mum, love?' she asked Ellie.

'She seems fine.'

'I'll try to visit her this week.' Meghan had once been Ellie's mother's best friend, before her mother had lost interest in any friendships.

'Didn't your mum and Belinda have a little disagreement once?' Vanessa asked Ellie.

'Yep,' Ellie said with a smile. 'It was after Mum chose *A Suitable Boy* by Vikram Seth for Forest Grove Reading Club's book choice one month. Belinda came out with some veiled racist comment and Mum went off on one at her.'

'Yeah, I remember thinking how cool your mum was.'

Was.

Ellie's mother had once been so vivacious, so brave. But that had all changed.

The first signs something was wrong had begun three years after they moved to the village, just after Ellie turned fifteen. It hadn't been an overnight thing. It had been gradual, like a tree that loses its leaves in winter. Each week, Ellie could see a change in her mother, a folding inwards. She'd wear less make-up until in

27

the end she wore none. Her clothing style changed, pretty dresses and skirts replaced with baggy jeans and oversized tops. And then one day, Ellie found her cutting her shoulder-length blonde hair off, that scene the subject of Ellie's nightmares.

Ellie's father had been as bewildered and worried as Ellie. He had asked his wife to see a doctor. 'Is it depression, love?' Ellie had overheard him asking one evening in a desperate voice. 'Has something happened? Just *tell* me.'

But her mother had simply shrugged. 'I'm just tired.'

'Get some tests then! Come on,' he'd said, picking up the phone, 'I'll make an appointment with the doctor for you.'

'No!' her mother had shouted. 'No doctors. Just leave me alone.'

Looking back, Ellie knew her mother had been having some kind of nervous breakdown. She was still affectionate with her daughter, cuddling her, cooking for her, doing all the things she ought to on the surface. But something was wrong, very wrong, and Ellie needed to understand *why*.

When it was clear that simply asking her mother what was wrong didn't work (her mother would always reply with something like, 'Just tired, love'), Ellie began hunting for clues, writing down all the little things she noticed and overheard, trying to piece her mother's mysterious condition together like a jigsaw puzzle. But no matter how hard she tried, Ellie just couldn't find the answers she was searching for and it frustrated the hell out of her. She was used to working out clues. But her mother remained a mystery.

So Ellie had given up trying, throwing herself into her relationship with Peter, spending more and more time at the Milehams' house, eventually moving in with them when she turned eighteen.

When her father retired early from his teaching, Ellie was grateful. By then, she had a baby to deal with so it was good to know her dad would always be there for her mum. But then her world was rocked when her father passed away from a sudden heart attack fifteen years ago. He was a smoker, yes, and was known to enjoy his food. But he was still so young, only in his early fifties. Ellie wondered if the stress of dealing with the change in his wife had contributed to his death. A broken heart, in a way, from losing the woman he had once known. There had been talk of her mother moving in with Ellie and Peter. But Peter was clearly not up for that and, truth be told, Ellie wasn't sure she could handle it as well as bringing up two young kids. So her mother eventually moved into the retirement village and had been there ever since.

Another customer walked in, the sound of the bell above the door pulling Ellie from her thoughts.

'Vanessa, new customer,' Meghan called out to her daughter.

'Better go work,' Vanessa said with a sigh.

'Me too,' Ellie replied.

'See you tomorrow night at the pub?'

'Yep.'

She walked off and Ellie tried to focus on the crossword she was creating, but her mind kept travelling back to the deer . . . and her mother. Just as she was about to pack up and leave, the door to the bakery opened . . . and Peter walked in.

He was wearing his 'summer Sunday get-up', as he used to call it: casual, navy-blue cargo shorts and a white T-shirt, his auburn hair combed neatly, his handsome face relaxed.

'Peter, what a pleasant surprise!' Meghan said, eyes lighting up at the sight of her son. But then the look on her face faltered as she glanced between Ellie and Peter.

'Where are the kids?' Ellie asked.

'With my dad.' What a surprise. Peter often liked to palm them off on others when he had them.

'You look . . .' His voice trailed off as he took in Ellie's casual black dress.

'I look . . ?' Ellie said.

'Different. You don't usually wear black.'

'Well, I don't usually do a lot of things I've been doing lately but one has to adapt to difficult circumstances.'

His blue eyes turned cold. 'Actually, it's good you're here. Can we have a quick chat?'

Vanessa watched them, eyes narrowed.

Ellie shrugged. 'Sure. What's up?'

He sat across from her, lowering his voice. 'It's just that Andrea mentioned she saw you crying when she walked past the window the other day.'

Ellie's mouth dropped open. 'What the hell?'

'You need to calm down,' Peter said in a low voice as he noticed his friend Ed Piper and his wife sitting at a table nearby. He gave them a quick wave then turned back to Ellie. 'I'm concerned, that's all. I don't want you having a nervous breakdown, like your mum. Maybe it's best you don't take on the Facebook moderator role, it'll just pile on the pressure.'

Ellie shook her head, not quite believing what she was hearing. 'Number one, I am not having a nervous breakdown,' she hissed. 'Number two, I think it's perfectly normal to have a little cry every now and again when the man you thought you'd be spending the rest of your life with decides to shack up with another woman.' Peter opened his mouth to say something but Ellie put her hand up to stop him. 'And number *three*, Andrea had no right peeking into my window then reporting me, like some kind of spy!'

'Woah,' Peter said, putting his hands up. 'Bit of an overreaction there, Els.'

'No, *you* are overreacting,' she said, standing up and shoving her work into her bag. 'Now tell your little friends to stop spying on me. And it's Ellie, not Els. Oh, and I'll be perfectly fine doing the

Facebook role. I have more time on my hands, after all, considering I don't have you to deal with any more.'

Then she walked out, the sound of Vanessa clapping making her smile.

How dare Andrea report back to Peter?

And how dare he imply she wouldn't handle being Facebook moderator. All her worries about taking the role on dispersed. She'd prove him wrong.

I mean, how difficult could it be?

Chapter 4

Monday 12th July
9 a.m.

Andrea Simpson

Just to make it official: please give Ellie Nash a welcome, the group's new moderator! Ellie is a familiar face in the village, having lived in Forest Grove since its very creation, and you may recognise her from various events around the village which she attended with Peter Mileham (still an honorary member despite abandoning us to move to Ashbridge!). I hope you will give her a very warm welcome . . . and behave yourselves! I'll be keeping a watchful eye . . .

Rebecca Feine

Welcome, Ellie, how fab to have you as a moderator. As I said earlier, you were brilliant with the deer-control posts a few weeks back.

Sheila Leighton

Yay for Ellie!

Meghan Mileham

Perfect match! You'll be great, Ellie.

Vanessa Shillingford

Hurrah, Ellie! Though can I point out, Andrea, people don't know Ellie as her ex's arm candy, she's a woman in her own right.

Pauline Sharpe

Usual feminist BS, Vanessa! Andrea was just pointing out how Peter was such a central part of the community.

Kitty Fletcher

Pauline, is there really a need for that kind of language? Let's remember our promise to 'be kind'.

Graham Cane

'Be kind'. What does that even mean? Another example of the snowflakes gone mad. So nobody's allowed to speak the truth? Sorry, but I'm going to leave this group if it becomes yet another 'be kind' censoring namby-pamby nonsense under Ellie's guidance. All those posts moaning and groaning about gunshots led to my guns being stolen. So much for 'be kind', hey?

Rebecca Feine

To be fair though, Graham, you *do* post about your guns quite a bit on the group, not to mention the fact you keep them in your garden shed. I'm surprised they haven't been taken before now.

Vanessa Shillingford

Very true. And who keeps guns anyway? You're not a farmer any more, Graham. It was surely an accident waiting to happen?

Graham Cane

Are you suggesting this is my fault, Vanessa? Have a word with your daughter, Tommy!

Ellie Nash

Thanks for your warm welcome, everyone! I've been a long-time member of the group, now looking forward to playing a more active role. And yes, Andrea's right, I know many of you, though hopefully in my own right and not just at my ex's side! 😆

Belinda Bell

Sorry to hijack this thread but my new thread about dog poo still hasn't been approved. So may I use this opportunity to bring your attention to it? I posted it last night. As I said in my post, I was in the woods for my daily walk yesterday, and lo and behold, I catch one of our resident Poop Enablers letting their little rug rat of a dog produce a large Mr Whippy-style mess right on the path. Of course dogs poop, that is their right. But I couldn't believe my eyes when its owner just kept on walking! No attempt to scoop the said poop up. Naturally I had to stop him and ask him to PLEASE pick up his dog's disgusting mess, and do you know what he said to me? He said, 'Oh, I never pick poo up in the forest, it helps the ecosystem. I just flick it.' Can you believe the cheek of it? I offered him one of my poo bags. Did he take it? Oh no, he didn't. Instead, he chose to attend to the snivelling baby attached to his chest (yes, you've guessed it, the offender was a young father, *quelle surprise*, who clearly thinks he is too busy with a mess of his own

35

making in the form of a spoilt brat to be bothered about clearing up his dog's mess). So I had to clean it up instead and carry it *all* the way home too!

Andrea Simpson

What a perfect one to start you with, Ellie Nash. I'll leave this to you. Hurrah!

Sheila Leighton

Talk about dropping Ellie in the deep (poo) end.

Vanessa Shillingford

Yawn! Just what we need, another dog-poo post. Ellie, what do you reckon about banning all dog-poo posts?!

Sheila Leighton

And cyclists on footpath posts too.

Pauline Sharpe

Excuse me, Sheila, my posts about cyclists taking over the footpaths are necessary. They pose a real threat!

Rebecca Feine

Vanessa's right, so bored of all the same old posts. And Belinda, come on. No need to get personal about the man's kid. Anyway, I thought it was an unspoken rule, better to flick poop into the undergrowth than bag it and waste plastic.

Vanessa Shillingford

Agreed! And can't we all just accept there are some people in the world who don't pick up their dog's poo? Surely there's a lot worse going on.

Peter Mileham

Now come on, Belinda, surely you know the poo fairy picks it up? In all seriousness, Belinda is right, dog poo has become a major issue in the village. Think of it like this, if the man walks his dog once a day in the forest, that's over 352 dog logs a year which are scattered all over the forest thanks to just *one* owner! And there's no doubt it's got worse and worse over the twenty-eight years the village has been around.

Tommy Mileham

Don't you mean 365 dog logs, Peter – well, 366 if we include a leap year. Unless you're not including national holidays? (And hello, Ellie.)

Ed Piper

😂

Andrew Blake

Dirty buggers! I always pick my dog's poo up. In fact, one time I forgot a poop bag and used my hanky! Had to carry it all the way home, I won't go into detail about how disgusting *that* was.

Sheila Leighton

Wow, that was nice to read during my breakfast, Andrew!

Pauline Sharpe

Next time, get a picture of the person who didn't scoop the poop and post it here, Belinda. Then they won't be so bloody quick!

Ellie Nash

Best not to post photos on here and, as Rebecca said, let's try not to make it too personal, shall we? And while I won't be banning posts on this subject, can I request that people try to keep them to a minimum?

Belinda Bell

This is SERIOUS, Ellie, not one of your board games.

Kitty Fletcher

That's uncalled for, Belinda.

Ellie Nash

I'm not dismissing your worries, Belinda. When the kids used to play in the forest, it was sometimes like playing dodge the dollop. But I'm just asking people to keep in mind there have been many posts on this subject already.

Meghan Mileham

Dodge the dollop! Excellent!

Belinda Bell

This is no laughing matter, Meghan! The tone this thread has taken does not bode well for its direction under the leadership of Ellie.

Vanessa Shillingford

Wasn't this thread about welcoming Ellie to her new role? Cut her some slack, guys. Let's end with a big WELCOME ELLIE and leave the poo posts for another thread.

Ellie Nash

Thanks, Ness.

Chapter 5

'Dodge the dollop?' Ellie's daughter, Zoe, said, wrinkling her nose as she looked at her mother's phone that evening. 'I can't believe you wrote that, Mum!'

'I can! It's brilliant!' Vanessa said. She'd already had a couple of glasses before Ellie and Zoe arrived at the Neck of the Woods pub. Ellie could tell from the mischievous glint in her blue eyes and the flush of her skin.

The pub was set back from the other units in the village court-yard, signposted by several smart-looking wooden benches among the trees, a gravel path leading to a lodge-style building almost within the forest itself. There was more seating behind the pub, benches carefully situated so there was a good mixture of seating for those who wanted to be out in the sun and those who preferred the shade. Ellie and Vanessa had chosen to sit in a shady area, but if Ellie leaned back enough, she could feel the sun on her cheeks as it poked through the branches above.

A new notification popped up on her phone. 'A new thread to approve,' she said, opening it. 'That's the third one this afternoon.'

She frowned slightly, eyes alighting on her Facebook name: *Ellie Nash*. It still felt strange to see her maiden name after years of having Peter's name, but she had been keen to get her name changed in as many ways as she could . . . starting with Facebook.

'Oh, oh, can I press the button?' Zoe asked excitedly. Ellie smiled. She liked seeing her daughter so excited about something her boring old mum was doing.

'Sure,' she said to Zoe. 'Let's read it first though, make sure it's okay.'

This post was from Ed Piper, who lived a few doors down.

> No response from my complaint about my green bin not being collected YET AGAIN last week! Honestly, is it really that hard to miss the largest house on the road? I know the collectors aren't the sharpest tools in the box but, honestly, one would think they'd be able to do a job as simple as this! Let's see how they do tomorrow, hey?

'Largest house on the road,' Vanessa said with a raised eyebrow as she looked at the post too. 'Hardly! *Your* house is the largest one, surely?'

'Not for long,' Ellie said.

Zoe frowned and Ellie felt bad. The kids seemed to be coping so well with the break-up, but the idea of selling the house was getting to Zoe in particular. As for Tyler, Ellie was never quite sure what he was thinking. But Ellie was getting used to the idea. Though losing the family home had been incredibly difficult to begin with, she now saw it as a new start. After all, did she really want to be reminded of that painful part of her life when she woke each morning? She'd already started looking for a smaller property in Firdean, the nearby market town where she'd been born. Despite Zoe's desperation to stay in Forest Grove, Ellie simply wouldn't be able to afford to on her freelance wage. At least Firdean was close enough for the kids to stay at Forest Grove High and be with their dad when it was his turn to have them.

'Can I press the button?' Zoe asked, finger hovering over the 'Decline' button above Ed Piper's post.

'Woah, hold your horses!' Ellie said, laughing. 'I'm the one who makes that decision.'

Vanessa laughed. 'The power's going to your mum's head, Zoe!'

'Why shouldn't it?' Ellie retorted. 'The admin of a community's Facebook group is queen in this new digital world.' She winked at Vanessa to show she was joking.

'Let's do this properly,' Ellie said to Zoe. 'Is Ed promoting any services or goods?' Zoe shook her head. 'Is his post abusive or rude in any way?'

'He *is* mean about the bin collectors.'

'Very true.' Ellie tilted her head, reading the post again. Ed *had* always been like that, looking down his nose at people. She remembered how he would drive around the village in his ugly sports car when she was a teenager and he was in his twenties, sneering at her parents' old estate car. 'While it is tempting to delete Ed's post,' she said, giving Vanessa a look, knowing she felt the same about him, 'freedom of speech *is* important. Though I don't like his tone, I don't think it justifies declining the post, do you?'

Zoe thought about it, then nodded. 'I agree,' she said, looking very serious. Then her blue eyes sparkled with childish excitement again. 'So can I press the button, can I?'

Ellie smiled. 'Go ahead!'

Zoe pressed it, watching as the page refreshed and the post appeared in the group. Then she put her hands in the air. 'I have the powerrrrrr.'

Her cousin, Vanessa's youngest son, Riley, came running over from the park that was at the back of the pub garden. 'What happened?'

'I just approved a Facebook post,' Zoe said proudly, sweeping her blonde hair over her shoulder with pride.

'Okayyyyy,' Riley said, not looking too impressed. 'Did you know Naya's over there?' he said, gesturing to the park.

'Yay!'

Zoe jumped up and followed Riley to the park, leaving the two women alone.

'You're secretly enjoying your new role, aren't you?' Vanessa said, taking a sip of her wine. 'Come on, admit it.'

'Maybe,' Ellie said, laughing.

'Knew it! And you know what, I really think it'll help the village, having someone like you in charge of the group. The power leaned too much towards Andrea and her tribe.'

'Tribe?'

'You know, the nasties? People like Belinda Bell and Graham Cane.'

As they talked, she noticed someone watching from the bench next to them: Adrian Cooper, the local police officer, now off duty and enjoying lunch with some friends. He understood, of course. He'd gone through a divorce from Andrea Simpson, the very person who'd handed over the Facebook admin role to Ellie.

Ellie felt sorry for Adrian. At least Peter had moved out of the village. But Andrea was still there, now sharing the very house she'd once shared with Adrian with her brand-new partner, Michael Garrett, the man who ran the Tiaras and Tyrannosaurus Parties franchise. Though the official line was Andrea had met Michael *after* she and Adrian had split up a year back, there had been rumours she'd hooked up with Michael before, which seemed pretty ironic, considering the image of perfection she tried to exude.

'He's pretty easy on the eye, isn't he?' Vanessa whispered as she looked at Adrian.

Ellie rolled her eyes. 'Honestly, Vanessa!'

'What?' Vanessa said, putting her hands up. 'I mean, you are single. And he probably owns a pair of handcuffs, so . . .'

Ellie threw her napkin at her friend and they both laughed. Vanessa *was* right though, Adrian really wasn't bad-looking, sitting there in the sun in his shorts and a T-shirt. He had a kind face, his light-brown eyes twinkling beneath his baseball cap. Not to mention that Irish accent of his . . .

'What's so funny?' Adrian asked.

The two women burst into laughter again.

'Just an in-joke!' Vanessa said, still laughing. 'More wine?' she asked Ellie. Ellie nodded and Vanessa headed into the pub.

'It's a Boxer, right?' Adrian asked when they were left alone, gesturing to Stanley.

'Yep,' Ellie said. 'Soppy thing.'

'I wish I'd brought mine now.' Stanley started wagging his tail as he looked at Adrian. 'Mind if I stroke?' he asked.

Ellie was pleased Vanessa wasn't in earshot to hear that. 'Of course. He'll be *delighted*.'

Adrian got up and crouched in front of Stanley, stroking his head as Ellie kept his lead tight to stop him from jumping up.

'How are you doing?' Adrian said quietly as he peered up at her. 'Since Peter left, I mean?'

That was the thing with Forest Grove, everybody knew everyone's business, especially when it came to couples splitting up. She wondered if they knew *why* though. Not judging from the way some of them still talked about Peter, like he was some kind of god.

'It's been tough, no denying,' she admitted. 'But I think I'm finally starting to see the light at the end of the tunnel.'

Adrian smiled. 'That's good. How are the kids coping?'

Ellie sighed, looking over at Zoe, who was now in the park at the end of the pub garden with a friend. Nearby, Tyler sat watching a girl with a pink bob serve food to a family. Ellie suspected that girl was the main reason Tyler had started joining them at the pub.

'I think they're okay,' Ellie said. 'Zoe initially had some difficult nights, a few crying fits, but she seems to be over it now. Tyler is . . . well, he's Tyler. Barely says a word, sits in his room most of the time, working on his music stuff. No change there really.'

'I wish Carter had a focus like Tyler does,' Adrian said with a sigh. 'He's been getting into fights at school.'

'I'm sorry to hear that. At least he's getting it out of his system? I worry Tyler is keeping it all bottled up inside.' She sighed. 'It's hard to know what to do. Whenever I try to talk to him, he just tells me to stop fussing.'

'All we can do is be there for them.'

Ellie nodded in agreement.

Stanley had rolled over now and was getting a full-on tummy rub from Adrian.

'He luuuuurves attention,' Ellie said, shaking her head as she smiled.

'I can tell,' Adrian said with a laugh. 'I saw the "For Sale" sign up outside your house.'

'Yep! It'll be good for us, a new start and all that.'

Adrian smiled. 'Great attitude. Will you stay in Forest Grove?'

'I can't really afford to, my freelance work doesn't bring in much.'

'What do you freelance in?'

'I design puzzles, crosswords and word searches for magazines and newspapers. Been doing it for years.'

Adrian stood back up and went back to his table, brown eyes sparking with interest. 'I had *no* idea. That is so cool.'

'Not as cool as being a police officer.'

'Ah, come now.' He tilted his head, the sun shining on his face. 'So what got you into that?'

'My parents loved their games and puzzles. I guess I grew up with it.'

Her dad had been a teacher at Forest Grove Primary School and her mum had worked at the library. They had led a quiet, peaceful life, with Friday-night dinners at the pub, a walk in the forest on Saturdays, followed by a whole day of game-playing on Sundays. Ellie had grown to be obsessed with the puzzle magazines her parents used to collect. It was the 'solving' element she enjoyed. The process of trying to figure something out. Her mother soon noticed it and would set Ellie treasure hunts and draw puzzles for her. Then Ellie started doing it herself, a strange hobby for a teenager but something her mother encouraged by buying her the equipment she needed: rulers, special pencils, drawing boards. Despite her love for her hobby, Ellie never really dreamed it would be her career. After getting her A levels and enjoying the writing side of things, she went for a very badly paid apprenticeship at the local newspaper, the *Ashbridge Gazette*. The idea was to learn the ropes as a journalist, eventually becoming a junior reporter. But when the editor discovered her love of puzzles, she was pulled into the entertainment pages to take over the puzzles on there, eventually becoming assistant entertainment editor, working across other publications too. She picked up other jobs in her spare time, doing crosswords and word searches, as well as the odd sudoku puzzle and quiz as word spread about her talents. It meant that, when it came to having the kids, she was able to leave the newspaper and fit her freelance jobs around family life.

'Wait a minute,' Adrian said, 'are you the Ellie who does the board-game afternoons at the retirement village? My friend Nero told me about them.'

Ellie nodded. 'Been doing it for years now.' She looked down at her wine and frowned. 'My mum's there so it's a good chance to see her too.'

'I didn't realise. How long has she been there?'

'Nearly fifteen years now.'

Ellie didn't mention her mother was only sixty-nine, too young to have been in there for so long. Luckily for her, Tommy knew the manager so had been able to pull some strings to get her mother in early.

'What about your parents?' Ellie asked, forcing herself to smile, not wanting to think about that. 'Are they in Ireland?'

'Yes, Dublin. Have weekly video calls with their foreheads though.'

'Foreheads?' Ellie asked.

'They have no idea where to point the webcam during video chats, no matter how many times I tell them.'

She laughed. 'Bless them. So, I heard on the village grapevine you've bought a house in Cedar Road?'

'Yep,' Adrian said. 'It's small – the room Carter stays in when he's at mine is tiny – but it's not far from the forest, good for walking the dog.'

As he said that, Ellie noticed Belinda Bell marching towards him. A large carrier bag was swinging from her hands and when she got to Adrian's table she slammed the bag on to it.

'Belinda, what on earth are you doing?' Adrian said, holding his nose as he looked at the bag. As he did, a whiff of whatever was in the bag drifted towards Ellie and Vanessa, who had returned with their drinks, both of them curling their noses in disgust too.

'Poop!' Belinda said as she crossed her arms. 'A huge pile of dog poop was shoved through my letterbox!'

Chapter 6

The whole pub garden seemed to go quiet as eyes turned towards Belinda.

'Jesus,' Vanessa whispered. 'Is she being serious? Who would *do* that?'

'When did this happen, Belinda?' Adrian asked, going into police-officer mode as his friends tried not to laugh.

'I just discovered it, I've been out all afternoon,' Belinda snapped. 'I walked in to discover it in my hallway. The smell!' She shook her head, curling her thin upper lip as she did so. 'It was all there, on my new carpet. *All* of it! Look!'

Adrian grimaced then carefully opened the bag, peeking in.

'Christ, that is a lot.' Adrian quickly closed the bag, pushing it away slightly. 'You didn't see who did it then, Belinda?'

'Of course not, I wasn't there when they did it!' Belinda replied. 'I'd have dragged them by their ear to the police station if I had!'

'I don't doubt it,' Vanessa whispered.

'So what are you going to do about it, PC Cooper?' Belinda asked.

'There's not much I can do about it now, Belinda, I'm off duty,' Adrian replied. 'If you call the non-emergency number, they'll log it and I can do some investigations when I'm back in tomorrow.'

'Tomorrow? This is an emergency!'

'I'm sorry, Belinda, my hands are tied.'

She went to walk off, but Adrian called her. 'Belinda! Your – er – your bag?'

She shrugged. 'Keep it, you'll need it for evidence.'

Vanessa pursed her lips, trying not to giggle. Adrian's friends weren't so successful as Belinda gave them sharp looks.

'I'm afraid I can't take it as evidence right now,' Adrian said. 'If you can take it back for me, I'll see what I can do tomorrow.'

Belinda marched back over, grabbing the bag and giving Adrian's friends evils. Then she stalked towards the forest to take a shortcut to her street.

'Remember to keep it in the fridge,' Vanessa shouted out after her.

'Oh, Vanessa, don't be mean!' Ellie said, smiling to herself as she shook her head. She turned to Adrian. 'So, will you have to file a report and everything?'

'Investigating poo being shoved through someone's letterbox isn't going to be the top of my list,' Adrian said with a sigh. 'I'll look into it though.'

'It'll be someone trying to teach Belinda a lesson,' Vanessa said. 'Surprised it hasn't happened before now. Her comment about dog poo this morning was pretty vicious.'

'Comment?' Adrian asked. 'What comment?'

'On the Forest Grove Facebook group,' Ellie said. 'I thought you were a member?'

'I am, but I don't often check it, to be honest,' Adrian replied, grimacing. 'Kind of does my head in.'

'It'll be better now Ellie's taken over as its moderator,' Vanessa said.

Adrian looked at Ellie in surprise. 'Really? Andrea's not doing it any more?' He grimaced at the mention of his ex.

'Nope, too busy with her new "ventures",' Ellie said, using her fingers to make quotation marks.

'Right. So how was Belinda's post vicious?' Adrian asked her. 'Can I see it?'

Ellie got her phone out and showed him the post.

'*Spoilt brat? Snivelling baby?*' he said as he read it. 'Wow. I know Belinda can be . . . well, *very* Belinda. But this is uncalled for. I wonder if what happened to her *was* in response to this post?' he mused.

'It'll make her think twice,' Vanessa said. 'She deserved it, as far as I'm concerned.'

Ellie watched Adrian's face for his reaction. Vanessa *could* be a little blunt sometimes. 'Ness . . .' she said in a low voice.

'What? I'm right,' Vanessa said, drinking more wine. 'Like Graham's guns, that was because of the group too.'

Adrian frowned. 'I heard about that. Did he post something in the group?'

'I posted about villagers shooting in the forest and their gardens,' Ellie explained. 'Graham was one of the villagers.'

'And then his guns were taken,' Adrian said. 'Interesting. Well, let's hope this is the end of it. Thanks for your help, ladies. Better get back to my friends.'

'Let's hope it isn't the end of it,' Vanessa said when he strolled off. 'We need something exciting to happen.'

'I've had my fill of excitement, thanks,' Ellie replied. 'Now, tell me about that book you've been reading.'

As Vanessa chatted away about her book, Ellie looked towards the forest.

Would there be more incidents?

Ellie woke early the next morning, feeling a sense of purpose. She was giving herself the day off so she could properly clean the house ready for viewings then officially begin her search for a new house before heading to her mother's retirement village for a visit. She felt a bubble of excitement in her belly. Yes, the past three months had been truly awful. But she was really beginning to feel like good times were around the corner.

After getting out of the shower, she peered out at the forest. There was no doubt she'd really miss the village. How beautiful it was, how close the woods were, and she'd miss *some* of the people too. But lately she'd learnt just how claustrophobic the place could be. It would be good to get away, even if it was only a few miles away.

She sat at her dressing table. It was a beautiful one, distressed white with gilded legs to go with the vintage French theme of the room. She'd spent ages sourcing it, forking out a fortune getting it renovated too, until it was *just* perfect. It had been worth it though. The daily ritual of getting ready at that table was her way of preparing herself mentally each day, *especially* now that Peter was gone.

Her mother had called it 'putting on her armour', and she was right. From the feel of the base primer being sprayed on her skin, a signal the ritual had begun, to the final appliance of either Chanel's Rose Nocturne lipstick for daytime, or Yves Saint Laurent's Rouge Libre for evening, it was a routine that heralded the beginning of a new day; a routine she'd been undertaking since she was fourteen, when her mother first taught her how to apply make-up. Ellie had always wanted to be like her mother. Her mother had possessed the kind of beauty that had drawn glances as she walked down the street, with her shoulder-length blonde hair, pretty blue eyes and immaculate dress sense. They hadn't been well off as a family, but her mother was an expert at finding the very best designer clothes in the charity shops of Ashbridge, buying her favourite make-up items from her husband for her birthday and at Christmas. Watching her mother at her own dressing table getting ready each morning was as comforting to Ellie as the sight of her parents playing Scrabble on Sundays.

Ellie looked in the mirror now, eyes filling with tears as she thought of her mother, no longer the vibrant woman of Ellie's childhood. She took in a deep breath and continued applying her make-up, using the tips her mother had instilled in her from an early age. Peter had often described her look as 'understated French chic', and he was right, even if he was wrong about many, many, *many* other things. It took money and time to look as 'understated' as she did. She didn't quite have the same knack at finding bargains as her mother had had. Or maybe she didn't have the *need*, thanks to Peter's generous pay. She knew now she wouldn't be able to keep up those purchases, but she didn't mind really. It was all part of the excitement of beginning a new life. She could be more like her mother was, strive hard to find bargains, make it more of a pleasure in a way.

Ellie smoothed Nars foundation over her skin, her fingers pausing as they reached the hint of crow's feet by her eyes. It was hard not to notice the little imperfections, especially with Peter leaving her for another woman. That annoyed her. Her mother had instilled a confidence in her about the way she looked. Not in a vain way, more encouraging *acceptance*. 'When you add up everything you see in the mirror,' her mother would say as she stood behind her, 'the end result is your beautiful self. That includes any imperfections too. Be proud of them.'

But looking in the mirror now, she couldn't help the doubts creeping in.

She shuddered, shaking her head. 'You will *not* let him do this to you.'

And yet the memories from that awful day three months before still came to her, as they did most days, despite how far she'd come.

It had come like a bolt out of the blue; a normal weekday morning, the kids getting ready for school upstairs, Ellie preparing breakfast and packed lunches downstairs while Peter did his daily read of the *Financial Times*. Except this time, he was watching Ellie instead of reading.

She had smiled at him. 'Have I got jam on my face?' she'd joked.

'We need to talk.'

His voice had been serious, the look on his face sombre.

Ellie had sat down across from him, breakfasts and lunches abandoned. The first thought that had come to her was he was ill. Her own father had kept his heart condition from her and her mother, before he eventually had the heart attack that took him from them. 'Peter, what's wrong?'

'I can't do this any more.'

At first, she'd been confused. 'You can't do what? Your job?' As she'd said that, she'd felt a sense of relief. He was so busy all the time! She knew he was chasing that promotion, but the hours he'd been working lately were crazy. Imagine if he just packed it all in! The time he could spend with them. The money didn't matter; it never had.

She had been about to say all this but then he had said the seven words that changed her life.

'I can't do this *marriage* any more.'

The shock of hearing those words had been physical, as if a catapult had shot a projectile into the core of her. She'd even jolted back, the breath coming right out of her.

'No,' she'd said when she eventually found her voice. 'No, Peter, *no*. You can't do this to me. I have done *everything* to save this marriage.'

'I can't help how I feel.'

Tears had started falling down Ellie's face. Above them, she had heard the kids walking around as they got changed. 'You decide to tell me this *now*, twenty minutes before the kids go to school?'

'I couldn't keep it in any more.'

Anger had bloomed within her. 'It's Caitlin, isn't it?'

Caitlin was his first love, a girl he'd lived next door to before he'd moved to Forest Grove with his parents when he was fourteen. She had always been a presence in their marriage, a curvy, red-lipped, dark-haired presence whom Ellie had caught him having an affair with five years before, after finding a perfumed love letter in his suit jacket pocket. When she'd confronted him, he'd sworn it was over, that he wanted to save his marriage. And it had felt like he really did, the past five years seeming better.

But clearly not.

Peter had confirmed her suspicions that he was leaving her for Caitlin by avoiding her gaze and looking down at his splayed hands. 'Yes. I love her.'

'Get out,' Ellie had said in a trembling voice. 'Just go, now.'

'The kids.'

'You'll see them. I just can't look at you right now.'

To her surprise, he'd meekly got up and left. The kids hadn't asked where he was, as he sometimes left early.

Somehow, Ellie had got through the next twenty minutes as the kids ate their breakfast. But the moment Zoe and Tyler had left the house, she'd broken down, falling to the kitchen floor and sobbing until there were no tears left. Since they'd first got together when Ellie was fifteen, she had wrapped so much of herself up in Peter, in their life together, that she had almost been able to feel the walls around her crumbling at the prospect of a life without him.

She took a deep breath now, forcing the memories away, then quickly got changed into the clothes she'd chosen the night before, as she did every night, that were hanging from a silver hanger in her wardrobe. Cropped white trousers with a Chanel belt and a striped navy-and-white top.

When she was changed, her short, blonde hair styled and brushed, she walked downstairs, Stanley bouncing down the steps two at a time after her. It still felt strange walking into an empty kitchen. She had grown used to coming downstairs to Peter drinking his morning coffee after his daily early-morning run, his dark-auburn hair gleaming with sweat. He'd always give her a kiss and she'd always bat him away, telling him not to ruin her make-up, before getting on with making breakfast as the kids stirred upstairs. It had been her favourite part of the day, just the two of them in their beautiful kitchen, views of the forest from the vast window spread out before them.

It felt like a tableau of all she had dreamed of after she'd had the kids.

She sighed and walked down the hallway, past the pastel-blue walls, bare feet cold on the hard, stone tiles she'd had laid the year before. She walked into the large kitchen and went to the expensive coffee machine, pouring the coffee that had automatically been made for that exact time, the same time she aimed to get to the kitchen each morning.

'Kids!' she shouted up the stairs. 'Time to get ready for school!'

No answer.

'Go get 'em!' she commanded Stanley. The dog leapt into action, scrambling upstairs. He could always be relied on to get them up, jumping on each of their beds and licking their faces until all Ellie could hear were fits of laughter, followed by footsteps.

She frowned as she heard a loud commotion outside.

She went to the living-room window, peering out to see Ed Piper in his pyjamas angrily dragging two green bins down the street.

Then she caught sight of what had made him so angry: his usually immaculate lawn was filled with at least fifty green wheelie bins, one from each house on the road.

Chapter 7

Other neighbours came out of their homes to watch as the wheels on the road made a loud clattering sound. Ed yanked one bin up on to the kerb and shoved it towards the drive of the house opposite, then pulled the other one up, rolling it to the house next to that. He then marched back to his house as his wife and kids watched from the front door, looks of confusion and worry on their faces.

Ellie opened the window slightly.

'I don't know whose idea this is, but it isn't funny!' Ed shouted out as people began to retrieve their bins.

Ellie noticed Adrian walking down the road then, in his police uniform. He wasn't as tall as Peter, but he held himself tall, as Ellie's mother used to say. He went to Ed and they had a conversation, Ed wildly gesturing at the bins as Adrian nodded and frowned, getting his notepad out to take notes.

Then she noticed Adrian's ex, Andrea, and her new boyfriend, Michael, both jogging by in matching Lycra, eyes wild with drama. Peter had always described Andrea as a 'poor man's version' of her. Blonde hair and blue eyes like Ellie, but the blonde came from a bottle, the blue eyes heavily caked in make-up, even now when she was out for a run. Although Ellie was hardly Andrea's biggest fan, she hadn't liked it when Peter said that about her neighbour.

As for Michael, he too had bottle-blond hair that he clearly spent time styling to make it as floppy as possible, to match his seemingly ever-present grin. He was slightly overweight but wore tight pastel shirts that accentuated his belly. She'd seen him on his way to various children's parties, dressed up as a prince or a Transformer, and it always struck her as being a bit odd, the way he waved at residents he barely knew and even blew kisses at some.

'Oh, Ellie!' Andrea said with a laugh when she passed her window. 'What a *turn* the group has taken since you took over. I almost feel bad leaving you to deal with it.'

Almost, Ellie thought. Truth be told, she bet Andrea was missing the role. She'd have loved to be at the centre of all the drama.

'What do you mean?' Ellie asked through the gap in the window.

'Isn't it obvious?' Andrea replied in a loud voice. 'First Graham's guns go missing after your gun-control post, then Belinda gets some dog excrement posted through her letterbox after *her* post, then Ed complains about the green bins and now look,' she said, gesturing towards the collection of bins. 'It can't be a coincidence, can it?'

'Maybe,' Ellie murmured.

'I'd be happy to take over again if it feels too much,' Andrea continued. 'Of course, I'm very busy being the co-director of Tiaras and Tyrannosaurus Parties with Michael' – Michael nodded enthusiastically – '*plus* helping run the Forest Centre. But if I must, I will.'

'Andrea's always happy to help those in need,' Michael purred in his faux-posh accent.

'It's fine,' Ellie quickly said. 'I can handle it.'

'Oh *good*,' Andrea said, her eyes telling Ellie she thought otherwise. 'Isn't that your bin? Shouldn't you collect it?' she said, pointing to Ellie's bin with the large number five on it, which sat in the middle of Ed's quickly emptying lawn.

'Yep, just what I was about to do.' Ellie closed the window and walked outside, quickly grabbing her bin, noticing that the wheels of the bins had left tracks in the lawn. As she pulled it towards her house, Adrian joined her. 'Looks like Vanessa got her wish of more incidents,' he said quietly.

Andrea gave him a little wave as they passed. Ellie noticed him grimace slightly.

'Adrian, mate!' Michael called over. 'How are you doing?'

Adrian nodded at him then turned away and pulled his phone out, putting it to his ear.

'It makes life *so* much easier when you can be friends with your ex,' Andrea said as Ellie brought her bin back.

'Such a good bloke,' Michael added.

Ellie resisted the urge to shake her head. It was obvious Adrian didn't feel the same way.

Andrea pouted slightly and put her fingers lightly on Ellie's arm. 'Peter mentioned you're still struggling a bit with keeping things civil. But I'd honestly recommend it, it's the best way when kids are involved.'

Ellie pulled her arm away. 'Peter and I are fine. I'm not exactly sure why he'd say we aren't. When did you talk to him?'

'Oh, it's nothing! Just a quick mention in passing.' Andrea looked at her Fitbit. 'Whoops, we'd better go, darling, I have to be in full Cinderella costume for a party we're running at midday!' She gave Ellie a little wave, then the annoying couple jogged off.

Ellie watched them, shaking her head. How dare Peter talk about her to someone like Andrea? And why would he give the impression Ellie was struggling with being amicable? Sure, she wasn't exactly a ray of sunshine when she saw him, but considering he had left her for someone else, she thought she was handling it pretty damn well!

'You have the same look on your face that I get after I've spoken to Andrea,' Adrian said as he strolled back to Ellie.

'She was just telling me what *wonderful* friends you are.'

Adrian laughed bitterly. 'Yeah, she likes to tell people that. I even overheard her referring to our divorce as a "conscious uncoupling" once, like we're Forest Grove's answer to Gwyneth Paltrow and Chris Martin. I can tell you now, that couldn't be farther from the truth.'

Ellie smiled. 'I suspected as much. So, how's the investigation going?'

He looked towards Ed's house. 'Ed's expecting me to find the culprit asap, as he put it. But he doesn't have a security camera and I was just told many of the street's cameras only point to their own gardens,' Adrian said.

'Yep,' Ellie said with a sigh. 'That'll be because my ex-father-in-law went around telling people to turn their cameras away from other people's property.'

Adrian sighed. 'Tommy, hey. Why did he do that?'

'There was a heated discussion on the Facebook group a few months back about how outdoor cameras can be an invasion of privacy. Not everyone did what he asked, but many did.'

'Doesn't make my job very easy,' Adrian said. 'I thought Tommy would be more sympathetic about the need for security cameras, as an ex-copper.' He leaned towards Ellie, a twinkle in his brown eyes. 'You have to admit, the way the bins are arranged is almost artistic.'

Ellie smiled. 'Yes, almost Tracy Emin-esque.'

'No,' Adrian said, shaking his head. 'Too neat.'

They both laughed.

'Anyway,' Adrian said, coughing and going serious, 'I was wondering if we could have a chat, seeing as you're the group's moderator now? It's clear there's a pattern with these incidents and it all points to the group.'

'I'm not sure I'll be of much use,' Ellie said, 'I've only *just* started moderating it.'

'But it really would be useful to get a bit of an insight from someone more savvy than me.' He leaned close again, lowering his voice. 'And I *really* don't want to have to speak to my ex,' he added with a grimace. 'Please?'

'Of course,' she said as she opened her front door. 'Why don't you come in? I'll make you a frothy coffee.'

'A frothy coffee?' Adrian said as he stepped inside. 'Now that's an offer I can't refuse. Wow, this place is something,' he said as they walked down the hallway.

'It should be, for the money and time spent on it.' It *had* seemed slightly extravagant at the time, to be moving into a five-bedroom house at the age of twenty-two. But Peter's wealthy grandfather had just passed away, leaving his parents a substantial inheritance, a portion of which had been passed down to Peter and Vanessa. Already making waves at the law firm he worked at, Peter had high aspirations, as had Ellie for their life together. Why not move into the house they'd spend the rest of their lives in?

Ellie frowned slightly. So much for spending the rest of their lives there.

'Latte? Americano? Cappuccino?' she asked as they walked into the kitchen.

'What's a black coffee with froth?' Adrian asked.

She laughed. 'An Americano. Gosh, you really do need to be educated in the ways of coffee. Take a seat.' She gestured to one of the stools at the island.

As he took his seat, Ellie set about making the coffee. Upstairs, there were signs of movement as the kids began to get ready.

'Are they as difficult to get up in the morning as Carter is?' Adrian asked.

'Nightmare. I end up having to send the dog up to wake them with face licks.'

As she said that, Stanley came thundering down the stairs and headed straight for Adrian, and he laughed, patting him. 'My Labrador Axl's the same with Carter.'

'Axl? Nice name. Is he named after the Guns N' Roses singer?'

'Yep,' Adrian said. 'You like Guns N' Roses?'

'I do an amazing "November Rain" on the karaoke.'

He looked at Ellie in surprise. 'Now that's something I need to see one day.' They both smiled at each other, Adrian's eyes lingering on Ellie's. 'So,' he said, growing serious as he pulled his notepad out, 'better get down to business. Remind me, how many members does the group have?'

'I know it's over a thousand. Let me just double check.' Ellie picked up her phone and navigated to the group. 'One thousand and forty-five.'

Adrian wrote it down in his pad. 'It's a closed group, right? So only members can see the posts?'

Ellie nodded.

'I can't quite remember, as it was a couple of years ago that I joined,' Adrian continued, 'but can people just join or is there a process?'

'People have to request to join. Andrea set up quite a good system where they need to answer two questions.' She noticed Adrian's nose wrinkle at the mention of his ex's name. They really weren't as friendly as Andrea made out, were they? 'One, they need to confirm they're residents of Forest Grove,' Ellie continued, 'and two, they need to agree that they will abide by the rules. It's then up to the moderator, now me, to decide if I let them in.' She poured some milk into the frother. 'If someone doesn't answer both questions, they're not admitted. Same if they're not from Forest Grove or don't agree to the rules.'

'So, in theory, all members should be Forest Grove residents?'

'That's right.' *Apart from precious Peter of course*, she thought to herself.

Adrian paused. 'Though it would be easy enough to lie?'

'I suppose so. But, like Andrea, I know most faces in the village. If I don't recognise someone, I'd give their social-media profile a quick check, just to make sure.'

'Any new members the past twenty-four hours?'

'Nope.'

Adrian jotted down some more notes. 'And all threads are pre-approved by you?'

'Yes.'

'Comments?'

'No, they automatically go up, so I just cast an eye over them,' Ellie said, pouring the frothed-up milk into two cups of coffee. 'That way I can ensure no abusive posts get through or posts trying to sell something.'

'Have you noticed any strange activity on the group since you became moderator?'

Ellie shook her head. 'No, nothing unusual.'

She brought the coffee over, giving Adrian his mug, and sat across from him.

Adrian leaned down, breathing in the smell of the coffee. 'Okay, this smells like expensive coffee.'

She laughed. 'Only the best.'

Adrian took a sip of his coffee, eyes widening. 'Heaven!' he said dramatically. They both burst out laughing.

'Mum?' They both looked up to see Tyler standing in the doorway in his usual skinny jeans and T-shirt get-up for sixth form. It didn't take him long to get ready, compared to his sister.

He eyed Adrian suspiciously. No wonder, Adrian was in full police uniform, after all.

'Nothing to worry about,' Ellie quickly said as she stood up and tried to rub off some shaving foam from Tyler's face while he batted her away. 'PC Cooper just wanted to ask me some questions about the Facebook group after a couple of incidents. Nothing major.'

'Like all those bins that were on Ed Piper's lawn just now?' Tyler asked with a slight smile. 'His post on the Facebook group was a bit of a dick move.' He turned to Adrian, face serious. 'So do you reckon it's related then?'

'It's an avenue I'm exploring,' Adrian confirmed, 'and as I'm useless when it comes to social media, I need your mum's brains.'

'You sound like a zombie,' Tyler said coldly.

Ellie rolled her eyes. 'You've been watching too much *Walking Dead*.'

He didn't smile at her joke but, instead, continued looking deadly serious. 'It's nothing to worry about,' Ellie said, suddenly aware of how unsettling this all might be.

'I'm not worried,' Tyler said, huffing. 'Doesn't bother me really.' He leaned over and grabbed a bagel, shoving it in his mouth. 'Meeting Aaron early for practice,' he mumbled, sending crumbs everywhere as he walked towards the hallway.

'Okay, darling, see you!' Ellie shouted after him.

He put his hand up as a goodbye then headed outside.

'Teenage boys . . .' Ellie said with a sigh.

'Funny things, aren't they? Tyler's gig is soon, isn't it?' Adrian asked.

Every year, the Forest Centre hosted a 'band night' for local teenagers, allowing local bands to showcase their talents. Pyro was the village's most popular band and, though Ellie wasn't into heavy rock, she was still very excited about seeing them perform. Tyler seemed to come alive on stage, the usually shuffling, awkward teenager suddenly a confident, energetic guitarist.

'Yes,' Ellie said. 'In less than a fortnight.'

Adrian sighed. 'I need to get Carter interested in more than just playing on his PlayStation and fights.'

'Teenage boys can be difficult, I get it.'

'Yeah, you do.' They both smiled at each other. It was *so* easy talking to him.

'Helllllllllo!' a voice called out.

They both looked up to see Peter's parents coming in through the front door.

'Guys, there's a bell, you know!' Ellie said with an awkward laugh, doing her best not to sound as irritated as she felt.

Meghan and Tommy had always had a key to the house. It helped when they had to look after the kids and Ellie supposed she liked the fact they were all so close that they could just let themselves in. But now she and Peter were separated, it just seemed so wrong . . . Adrian felt the same, judging from the look on his face!

'We just saw Tyler, he took a cinnamon roll with him to eat on the walk in! I thought I'd bring some leftovers from the bakery before I headed in,' Meghan said. She paused when she saw Adrian, brow furrowing.

'Adrian!' Tommy boomed, marching down the hallway, treading mud over the tiled floors with his wellies as he followed his wife into the kitchen. 'You here about the green-bin incident? I've just been talking to Ed. Any leads on Belinda's case? What's Ellie got to do with it all?'

Tommy was fond of shooting questions at people in his loud, domineering voice.

'Ellie's just helping me with an investigation in her capacity as a moderator for the community group, Tommy,' Adrian said.

Meghan placed a shopping bag she'd been carrying on the worktop. 'Ah, so it is all connected then.' She looked at her husband. 'Looks like you're right, Tommy, a Facebook Vigilante is on the loose.'

'Wow, they already have a name,' Adrian said with a raised eyebrow as he finished off his coffee and stood up.

'Tommy came up with it,' Meghan said proudly.

'My instincts are rarely wrong,' Tommy said, watching Adrian and Ellie from beneath his bushy, auburn eyebrows.

'Let's hold our horses,' Adrian said. 'These incidents may well be unrelated.'

'Oh, come on, it can't be a coincidence though, can it?' Tommy said. 'Maybe you should post something on the group, Ellie, make it official and warn people to be careful?'

'Let's not make a big deal out of it by posting on the group,' Adrian said. 'No need to worry people.'

'Adrian's right, it's probably just kids messing around anyway,' Ellie added. 'They'll get bored soon enough.'

'Forest Grove kids posting dog poop and cluttering bins? Not a chance!' Meghan exclaimed.

Ellie resisted the urge to sigh. Meghan had such a rose-tinted view of the village; of her son too.

'Right,' Adrian said, 'I'd better be off. Thanks for the frothy coffee, Ellie. I'll be in touch if I need any more information. I'll let myself out.'

'I've always liked Adrian,' Meghan said after he left. 'Awful how Andrea rubs his face in their break-up, walking around the village with that awful new man of hers.'

Ellie bit her tongue, resisting the urge to say anything. Meghan was happy to criticise someone else over breaking up their marriage, but not her own son. As far as Meghan and Tommy were concerned, Peter and Ellie's marriage had just come to a natural end. It had been obvious when Meghan had called Ellie after Peter broke the news to them a week after he'd moved out that he hadn't told Meghan the whole story, about Caitlin, about the years of having another woman in the marriage.

'All marriages have their ups and downs,' Meghan had said as she spoke to Ellie on the phone, the distress clear in her voice. 'It's a case of holding on and riding them out. I wish Peter had fought harder!'

Ellie had considered telling her the truth. But something had stopped her. Meghan was suffering enough, she could tell; why pile on the torment? Anyway, she was sure Vanessa would tell them.

'Where's that granddaughter of mine?' Tommy said now, looking up at the ceiling. 'Not still sleeping, surely? Thought I could walk her to school while Meghan heads off to the bakery and I get on with the gardening. Speaking of which,' he said, looking out at Ellie's overgrown lawn, 'shall I bring the mower over later?'

Ellie clenched her jaw. That was a hint if ever she heard one. 'Thanks, but don't worry,' she said tightly, 'our lawnmower still works perfectly fine, I'll do it later. Zoe!' she called up the stairs. 'Your grandparents are here!'

'Yay!' she heard Zoe declare. 'Be down in a minute.'

'Better hurry before I eat all the cakes we brought you!' Tommy shouted up.

'Noooo!' Ellie heard Zoe reply.

'I got a few other bits too,' Meghan said. Ellie frowned as Meghan started getting items out of her shopping bag, placing them in the fridge.

'Meghan, I've been shopping, you know. The fridge is pretty full.'

'Oh, it's just a few bits that the kids like,' Meghan said. 'I went shopping yesterday and thought I'd grab some extra for you.' She tried shoving a yoghurt in between some Tupperware and Ellie sighed. She really felt the need to grab that yoghurt from Meghan's hand and shove it back in the bag, but she knew Meghan was only trying to help.

There was the sound of running down the stairs and Zoe appeared with a beaming smile. 'Nan! Grandad!' They both gave her a hug. Ellie watched them as they chattered away, Zoe happily eating the cinnamon swirls they'd brought for her.

When it was time for them to walk Zoe to school, Meghan waited behind for a moment.

'You know we're always here for you?' she said as she glanced over at the 'For Sale' sign. 'Even now you're not with P— Peter.'

Meghan's voice cracked, tears filling her eyes.

'Oh, Megs.' Ellie pulled her into a hug. She forgot sometimes what a toll this was taking on her too.

As for Tommy, she wasn't so sure. He'd not said a word about the break-up to her; it had all gone through Meghan. It was as though it had never happened.

She looked up at Tommy over Meghan's shoulder, noticing that his face was unreadable. Then he formed his lips into a tight smile and nodded.

Ellie traced her pen up the ruler the next evening, her tongue between her teeth. Four puzzles down, eighteen to go. She just needed to finish this one before Peter came to pick the kids up. They had been meant to go direct to Peter's after school that day but he'd come up with an excuse about some work meeting, so they'd ended up coming back home to wait for him to finish. He always found some excuse or another to drop the kids off earlier or pick them up later, like Ellie didn't have her own work commitments. Truth was, though, even with her deadlines, she loved seeing the kids as much as she could. That had been one of the hardest parts of the separation, not seeing the kids all the time.

She quickly smoothed her hair down as she walked along the hallway, then instantly hated herself for caring so much about how she looked in front of Peter.

Ellie took a deep breath and opened the door to find Peter standing on the step. Zoe leaned against her mum. 'Can't I just stay with you, Mum?' she asked.

'Do I smell or something?' Peter said with a laugh, sniffing at his armpits.

'No, darling, we've had this talk,' Ellie said, her heart breaking in two as she took in Zoe's miserable face. 'Go and get your things and tell your brother your dad's here.'

Zoe pouted and walked slowly upstairs.

'What's her problem?' Peter asked.

'It's not you. I don't *think* so anyway,' Ellie couldn't help but add for good measure. 'I just think she misses her friends.'

'I told her they're welcome to visit. The problem is, you mollycoddle the girl. No wonder she doesn't want to leave you, you still treat her like a baby!'

Ellie closed her eyes, taking a few breaths to calm herself.

Don't rise to the bait.

'You have to remember,' she said as calmly as she could, 'it's only been three months since you left. Zoe will be feeling more vulnerable and, when she does, she wants to be with me. It's always been the way. You can't expect what you did not to have repercussions on the kids' mental health,' she said quietly.

Peter shook his head. 'Mental health? Who are you, Kitty Fletcher? Jesus, Ellie.'

'You really have no idea what you've done to us, do you?'

'It's not a one-way street, Ellie, you were a nightmare to be married to as well, you know.'

Ellie laughed bitterly. 'Worse than a cheating workaholic who forgot birthdays and anniversaries?'

'Try living with a woman who constantly wants to solve me like I'm a puzzle and slot all our lives into place like pieces on a game board.'

'That is ridiculous,' Ellie said, blinking back tears. 'I can't listen to you any more. I'll tell the kids you'll wait for them in the car.'

Then she slammed the door in his face and let out a scream, muffling it with her fist.

'You all right?'

Ellie looked up to see Tyler watching her from the top of the stairs, his backpack slung over his shoulder.

'I'm fine,' she quickly said.

He jogged down the stairs. 'Just Dad being a dick?'

She couldn't help but smile. 'No comment.'

'You should call Aunt Ness,' he said. 'Go to the pub or something.'

Ellie laughed. 'Okay, *Dad*. Since when have you become so grown up?'

His eyes narrowed as he looked out at his dad through the hallway window. 'Someone needs to act like a dad around here.'

Zoe came down the stairs then and Ellie pulled her into her arms. 'Only a few days, then you'll be back here, okay?' she said, trying her best not to cry.

After they both left, she leaned against the wall, finally letting the tears flow. Then she remembered what Tyler had said. She picked up her phone and called Vanessa. 'Fancy a trip to the pub?' she asked.

It was a warm and bright evening, the trees spilling out from the forest providing a green and golden canopy above them. Other residents seemed to have had the same idea as them; all of the beer garden's benches were full to capacity, a buzz in the air.

'God, my brother is a dick!' Vanessa said.

'I thought I was doing so well. Things have felt really good lately,' Ellie said with a sigh. 'Then I go and bloody cry!'

'So what if you have a little cry?' Vanessa continued. 'You're bound to have them when the weight of what has happened suddenly hits you again, even when things are feeling good! You are strong, you will roaaaaar!'

Ellie took a sip of wine, smiling to herself. It always made her feel better when she talked to Vanessa. It was how they'd first started properly talking. She'd not been able to answer a question that had been directed at her by their particularly strict science teacher. Vanessa could tell Ellie was a bit shaken up afterwards and suggested they go and have their packed lunch outside . . . in the rain. Ellie had thought this girl with frizzy, auburn hair and winged eyeliner was mad, but she had followed her anyway and they had ended up huddling under a huge tree as they ate their lunch, talking so much they hadn't even heard the school bell go.

'What a gorgeous evening!' They both looked up to see Meghan approaching.

Meghan didn't often join them for a drink; she was usually more likely to join them over tea and cakes at the Into the Woods bakery. But Vanessa had said her mum was at a loose end with Tommy attending his weekly gardening club with other residents – he was a bit obsessed with gardening, winning the village's annual 'Gardening Gold' award at the village fete for his immaculate rose bushes – so Ellie had suggested inviting Meghan out.

'Don't say anything about Peter,' Ellie whispered.

'I won't.' Vanessa turned to her mother, smiling. 'Hi, Mum. Wine?'

'Yes, please.'

'So,' Vanessa said after pouring Meghan some wine from the bottle she'd bought, peering around her, eyes intrigued. 'I wonder who's going to be the next victim of the Facebook Vigilante? It's all rather exciting, don't you think?'

'Come on, Vanessa,' Meghan said. 'It can't be very nice having dog excrement shoved through your letterbox and your lawn ruined, like Ed's.'

'Oh, come on, Mum, they're fine. In fact,' Vanessa added, lifting her chin in defiance, 'I actually admire this Facebook Vigilante. I'm not afraid to say it either. Others have said it too.'

'Really?' Ellie asked quietly. 'Like who?'

'People in my yoga class. We were all chatting about it during the downward-facing dog.'

'You were having a gossip *while* doing poses?' Meghan asked. 'Isn't yoga supposed to be meditative and focused?'

'Not the way we do it! Anyway,' Vanessa continued, pouring herself more wine, 'they all agreed that whoever is doing this is a kind of hero.'

Ellie spluttered on her drink. '*Hero?*'

'Think about it,' Vanessa said, leaning even closer to Ellie and her mother as she lowered her voice to just above a whisper. 'All the people targeted so far are douche bags. Ed Piper,' she said, peering over at Ed, who was sitting at a nearby table with another villager, Andrew Blake. 'One of the rudest men I've ever met, always looks down his nose at people. His comment about recycling collectors is a *typical* example of this. Then Graham Cane. Well, we all know how poisonous he is. And Belinda Bell is the *worst*! Moaning and judging people is her hobby. Her *life*! She's been like it for ever, even when we were kids and she'd shout at us from her window for laughing too loudly in the street.'

'God, yeah, I remember that,' Ellie said, laughing.

'But do they deserve all this?' Meghan asked.

'For years of whinging and nastiness? Yes, yes they do.' Vanessa curled her hand into a fist and hammered it on the table's surface. People turned to look and Ellie and Meghan exchanged a smile. Vanessa always got a bit strident after a few drinks. 'I wish I'd bloody thought of doing it myself,' she said with a huff.

Meghan looked at her in shock. 'You don't mean that!'

'I do!' Vanessa said. 'Good on them. Honestly, among the people who count, they're a bloody hero.'

'Who's a hero?' They all looked up to see Adrian walking nearby with his dog, a large brown Labrador that exuberantly stuck its nose in Ellie's lap as she laughed.

'Sorry,' Adrian said with a lopsided smile as he pulled her away, 'Axl likes pretty ladies.'

'Oh, I'm insulted!' Vanessa said, putting her hand to her chest. 'I insist you come over here, Axl, otherwise I won't think I'm a pretty lady!'

The dog bounced over to her and did the same as they all laughed.

'Join us!' Vanessa said. 'We have wine with more to come *and* I've ordered cheesy nachos.'

'You sure?' Adrian asked. 'I don't want to interrupt a girls' night.'

'It's fine,' Ellie said. 'All genders are welcome on our nights out.'

Adrian smiled and sat next to Ellie, tying his dog to the bench leg.

'So,' Vanessa said, 'I was just saying to Ellie that I think this Facebook Vigilante is a hero.'

'Vanessa, you can't say that to a police officer!' Meghan said.

Adrian nodded, face serious. 'I'm afraid your mother is right, Vanessa, hero-worshipping a vigilante is an arrestable offence.'

'Arrest does *not* scare me,' Vanessa said, crossing her arms.

'Vanessa,' her mother said in a warning voice.

'She's not lying though,' Ellie said. 'Vanessa *has* been arrested.'

Adrian gave Vanessa a surprised look. 'Really?'

Meghan put her head in her hands and moaned. 'Do we have to relive the worst years of my life?'

Vanessa laughed. 'Mum, you are such a drama queen.' She turned to Adrian. 'I got arrested when I was fifteen for throwing a placard at a shopkeeper during a climate-change march in Ashbridge . . . the same shopkeeper who punched my friend. But as nobody witnessed it, *I'm* the one who gets punished.'

'Ah, the days before smartphones,' Adrian said. 'So you were a bit of an environmental activist then?'

'How can you not know that Vanessa founded the FKAPS?' Ellie said in mock horror as Meghan smiled.

'The what?' Adrian asked.

'Forest Grove Kids Against Pollution Society,' Vanessa said proudly.

'Shouldn't that be FGKAPS?' Adrian asked.

Meghan nodded. 'That's what I always said!'

'FKAPS sounded better!' Vanessa insisted. 'It's all about brand awareness, guys!'

'She even had T-shirts and mugs made with the logo and the campaign motto,' Ellie said.

'And teddy bears! I still have some!' Meghan added.

'Creating a bridge across the world,' the three women said in unison before bursting into giggles.

'What's a bridge got to do with it?' Adrian asked, his brown eyes sparkling as he looked at each of them in turn.

Vanessa rolled her eyes. 'It was about connecting Forest Grove environmentalists with other environmentalists around the world. We had pen pals and everything.'

'And protests where you got arrested?' Adrian asked.

Vanessa shrugged. 'Just the one.'

Adrian turned to Ellie. 'What about you, Ellie? Did you go to this protest?'

'No, I didn't,' Ellie said quietly.

'Why *was* that?' Vanessa asked.

Meghan smiled sadly. 'Her mum.'

'Ah, yes. Sorry, hon.' Vanessa put her hand over Ellie's and squeezed it. Adrian frowned. Of course, as someone who'd only moved to the village a few years back, he wouldn't know what had happened to Ellie's mum.

Over the next couple of hours, after Meghan went home, Ellie, Vanessa and Adrian sat together and drank. Other residents came to join them after a while, tables being pulled together until there were ten of them around two benches, a mixture of Adrian's friends and old schoolfriends of Vanessa and Ellie, eventually joined by Ellie's neighbour Sheila – a tall, grey-haired woman in her sixties who was always jolly – and the pub's landlady, Rebecca. As the sun set, turning the clouds above pink, Ellie leaned back in her chair and smiled in contentment. It was times like this, when the great and the good were gathered around her, that she felt sad to be moving out of Forest Grove.

'So I hear this one was a rebel as a teenager?' Adrian said, gesturing to Vanessa, who was so drunk she was wearing one of Adrian's friend's ties as a head band. Ellie smiled to herself. At least the kids were with Peter, so Ellie could stumble around an empty house later. No such luck for Vanessa, who'd already had a heated phone call with an annoyed husband.

'She was brilliant,' Sheila said. 'I remember when you used to come over to see my Caroline,' she said, referring to her daughter, 'she says she always remembers you two.'

'Two?' Adrian asked.

'Of course, Vanessa *and* Ellie,' Sheila said.

'It was like Beauty and the Beast,' said another one of Adrian's friends, who had gone to school with Vanessa and Ellie. 'Ellie was the beauty and Vanessa was the beast.'

'How *rude*!' Vanessa said, untying the tie around her head and throwing it at him. 'You can have this back now.'

'I mean *beast* as a compliment,' he replied. 'Like, a rebellious, *passionate* beast.'

Vanessa gave him a scowl, smiling beneath it.

'Speaking of beasts,' one of Adrian's friends said, 'any leads on the Facebook Vigilante?'

'Nothing yet, mate,' Adrian said with a sigh.

'Do you really think the Facebook Vigilante is a beast?' Vanessa asked. 'Don't you admire what they're trying to do?'

'Admire?' Rebecca said. 'I'm not sure there's much to admire about someone having the audacity to shove dog poo through an old woman's letterbox.' She leaned towards the group, voice lowered. 'Even if that old woman is a wicked old witch.'

They all laughed.

'Seriously though,' Ellie said, 'what does everyone else think about this Facebook Vigilante? Don't be scared to express your admiration – we're among friends, after all. And don't worry,' she said, turning to Adrian, 'you don't need to answer, PC Cooper.'

'I think they're ace,' Sheila said as others around them nodded. 'About time someone told the moaning minnies of Forest Grove what's what.'

Vanessa nodded enthusiastically. 'That's what I said! The way that—'

'How *dare* you!'

They all went silent as another resident, Pauline Sharpe, marched over to them. She was a large lady in her fifties who'd recently dyed her hair an unflattering shade of synthetic red. She'd moved to the village the same time as Ellie's and Vanessa's families, her family running the Neck of the Woods pubs before Rebecca took over. Ellie had had to turn down a post she'd made earlier trying to sell some awful-looking beauty products.

She came to a stop at the two tables and loomed over them all, an angry expression on her stodgy face. 'We all heard what you just said. You're all a disgrace, making a hero out of this criminal.' She turned to Adrian, shaking her head. 'And even worse, our local police officer joining in.'

Adrian put his hands up. 'I said *nothing*.'

'Exactly! *Nothing*,' Pauline said. 'You should be telling these people off.'

'There *is* such a thing as freedom of speech, you know,' Vanessa said, as she took a sip of her now-warm wine.

'I know what freedom of speech is, unlike *some*,' Pauline countered, giving Ellie daggers. 'I bet you take great joy in turning down perfectly innocent posts like mine?'

Vanessa stood up, putting her hands palm down on the table and leaning towards Pauline. 'Ellie can—'

Ellie put her hand gently on Vanessa's arm. 'I can handle this,' Ellie said quietly. She turned to Pauline. 'We don't allow posts which advertise products for sale. It's very clear in the rules.'

Everyone around the table nodded in agreement.

'And while you're at it,' Vanessa slurred, 'can you stop posting about bikes on the pathways? We really don't *care*!'

More nods.

'Well, you *would* all agree, wouldn't you?' Pauline said. 'Bunch of snowflakes.'

Vanessa did an exaggerated yawn. 'Not that old phrase. Very predictable from you, Pauline.'

'You snowflakes are the predictable ones!' Pauline said.

Ellie suddenly felt a storm of anger. She was *so* sick of people using that word!

'Okay, let me get this straight,' she said. 'First, you accuse me of being too hard by "censoring" the group,' she said, making quote marks with her fingers. 'Now I'm too soft?'

Pauline looked uncomfortable, her face flushing.

'Come on,' Vanessa said, 'do let Ellie know, she's waiting.'

Pauline crunched her mouth up then let out a frustrated grunt as she glared at Ellie. 'You're just like your bloody mother!'

Ellie froze. 'Excuse me?'

'Looking down at her nose at everyone! Thinking she's the queen bloody bee!'

'How *dare* you say that about Ellie's mum!' Vanessa shouted.

'No point arguing with you lot,' Pauline said, walking off. 'You'll never see any sense!' she shouted over her shoulder.

Ellie watched her, still shook up from her mentioning her mum.

'Ignore her,' Adrian whispered.

'Who's for more wine?' Vanessa said.

Ellie smiled, lifting her glass up, forcing herself not to be rattled by Pauline's outburst. 'Me, please!'

Ellie sat up in bed the next morning, wincing at how sore her head was. She slipped out from beneath the covers, holding on to the bedpost to steady herself as she swayed slightly, the effects of the wine she'd consumed still pulsing through her veins. She took a moment for the dizziness to go, then walked into the bathroom, staring at her face in the mirror.

She looked awful, mascara smeared around her eyes, foundation congealed around her nose, remnants of the lipstick she had been too drunk to wipe off splodged around her face.

She groaned. She hadn't been that drunk in years! She could barely remember how she got home! Thank God the kids were at their dad's. She had a long shower, hoping to clean away the blossoming ache throbbing at her temples, but without success. Quickly getting changed into the most comfortable outfit she could find – some navy leggings and a long, white T-shirt – she didn't even bother applying make-up.

She needed coffee!

As she walked downstairs, she saw the drunken trail of destruction she'd left: a golden sandal on one of the stairs, as though she'd kicked it off. Her tan leather bag teetering on the edge of the kitchen island, some of its contents on the floor. The remains of a midnight feast she'd prepared – tinned ravioli from what she could see, the empty tin upside down in the sink. More wine as well.

She froze as she went to the coffee machine.

A black, leather wallet was there . . . and it wasn't hers.

She picked it up and looked inside, seeing Adrian's handsome face smiling out from his warrant card.

'Oh no,' she said, feeling panic flutter inside. Now she thought about it, he *had* come over, hadn't he? They'd ended up talking alone for a while after Vanessa had ventured into the pub to play a slot machine with one of his friends. They'd all walked back together and then . . .

It was a blank! What had happened between them?

She checked her phone, opening the messages, and let out another groan. One from her to Adrian at 11 p.m.:

Hey, you asleep yet?

A quick answer from Adrian:

Nope. Why?

Fancy a frothy coffee? I can't sleep. Buzzing.

Buzzing from what?

Just had such a great night. Feel FREE.

I'll be over in 10! Have a frothy coffee waiting for me.

I can do one better than that: you can share some of my tinned ravioli.

Ellie put her head in her hands, cringing. Then she looked around her at the two empty wine glasses, the remains of a frothy coffee spilt on the wooden worktop. Her eyes rested on Zoe's Nintendo Switch, which lay in the conservatory, an open case from a karaoke game, two microphones strewn on the sofas.

'Oh no,' she whispered as a memory started to come to her of standing on the conservatory sofa singing 'November Rain' as Adrian whooped and clapped.

She put her fingers to her lips. Had something happened between them . . . had they kissed?

Or even worse?

No, he hadn't been in her bed when she awoke.

A small thought occurred to her.

Would it have been so bad to have woken up beside Adrian?

She couldn't deny that, lately, as she began to look towards the future in a happy, hopeful way, the thought *had* occurred to her about any future man in her life.

The thing was, Peter had been Ellie's first and only love, her first hurried, awkward lover too. It was just how she'd planned it when she first spotted the handsome boy in class. And yet he had hardly seemed to notice her. She was just his younger sister's chatty best friend. Ellie wasn't used to not being noticed. Even at that young age, boys had paid attention to her, with her long, blonde hair and pretty face. But Peter had barely looked at her. He became an enigma to her; a puzzle she needed to solve. She would write down anything she noticed about him each day in her journal, little clues of how she could make him sit up and take notice of her.

Slowly, it had begun to work. Little things, like mentioning loudly that she'd watched the cricket with her dad at the weekend, a sport she had learnt from Vanessa that Peter enjoyed. Or walking by him carrying a book about the world wars, a subject he seemed fascinated with when she observed him in class. He had started to pay her more attention when she came over to see his sister until, one day, he had asked her on a date, much to Vanessa's horror.

Ellie had finally cracked the enigma that was Peter.

Or so she had thought. Throughout their relationship and then marriage, he had often felt like a closed book to her, no matter how much she had tried to probe and draw him out. It had been a constant frustration . . . but also why she continued to love him. He was a challenge, and Ellie loved a challenge.

But now that challenge was gone and maybe, one day, a new man would come along, a prospect that made her feel nervous.

Maybe if she'd slept with Adrian, it wouldn't have been such a bad thing. Like ripping off a plaster.

A very handsome, lovely plaster.

'Oh, stop it, Ellie!' she hissed at herself.

Her coffee machine pinged and she grabbed her mug, sitting at the table and blowing on it before taking a sip.

Then she remembered. How long had it been since she'd checked the Facebook group? She *was* the moderator, after all.

She quickly got out her phone, seeing she had a number of notifications.

'Shit,' she whispered. She opened them up. There were three for the group. She clicked on the first one she'd missed. Andrea had sent it just after 10 p.m. Ellie felt a stab of anger as she read it, remembering how Andrea had told Peter she had seen Ellie crying.

> What on earth is going on at the Neck of the Woods tonight? Sounds like a party of some kind. I'm trying to get to sleep after a busy day but all Michael and I can hear is chatter and laughter from the pub!

There was another message not long afterwards from Graham Cane:

> To the group of people thinking it's funny to sing 'November Rain' at the top of their voices as they walked past my house just now, thank you, you have cracked all of my mirrors.

Ellie put her hand over her mouth, suppressing a giggle. It really *had* been a good night. Her doorbell went and Ellie jumped. She put her hand to her chest and took in deep breaths before walking down the hallway, hesitating when she saw a familiar outline in the frosted glass of her front door.

It was Adrian.

She smoothed her hair, then remembered she had no make-up on. Maybe she could run to her make-up bag quickly and apply some? But then the doorbell went again.

Well, he'd just have to see her as she was!

She opened the door, hoping the morning light that flooded in would be forgiving on her hung-over skin.

'Hey,' Adrian said, smiling at her softly. He looked as tired and as hung over as she did, his brown hair messy, his brown eyes bloodshot. 'Last night was fun.'

'It sure was,' Ellie said awkwardly. 'Oh, I have your wallet here.'

'Yep, that's why I came by. Need it for work later.' He looked embarrassed, avoiding her gaze.

'Come in,' she said, leading him down the hallway, catching sight of her face in the mirror.

God, she really did look awful.

'Here,' she said, grabbing his wallet and handing it over, their fingers touching. She paused, peering up at his face. He held her gaze.

'About last night . . .' she started. 'My memory goes to pieces after too much wine.'

'Don't worry,' he quickly replied, 'nothing happened. Unless you count a really bad rendition of "Cotton Eye Joe" as something happening.'

'I didn't sing *that*, did I?'

He laughed. 'No, that was me.'

Ellie smiled in relief. It didn't feel so awkward now. 'Phew.'

In her hand, her phone buzzed. She looked down at it to see it was a Facebook post submission from Tommy Mileham.

'A group notification?' Adrian asked.

'Yep, Tommy's done a post.'

Then she let out a gasp as she took in the photo Tommy had submitted.

It was of Pauline Sharpe sitting in a hospital bed, her arm in a cast, her face battered and bruised. With the photo, Tommy had written:

> This is getting out of control now. A man in
> a balaclava riding a bike purposely mowed

Pauline down as she walked home last night.
Whoever's doing this can't get away with it.
Police called and they're on the scene now.

Ellie and Adrian looked at each other.

'Tommy's right,' Adrian said, face deadly serious. 'This has gone too far.'

Chapter 8

'I ought to go down there,' Adrian said, pacing Ellie's kitchen. 'See what I can do.'

'There?' Ellie asked.

'Where it happened. Tommy said the police are there now.' He grabbed his keys. 'It's my patch, I should be dealing with it. The others don't know the community like I do.'

Ellie frowned. This really *was* getting serious.

'The path Pauline would take to get to her house, it goes through the west side of the forest, right?' Adrian asked her. 'The one near that huge house in the woods?'

Ellie shook her head. 'No, that one leads to Cedar Street. Pauline lives on Maple Lane so it'll be the path near my mum's retirement village, the new one Frazer got made.'

'Not sure I know that one. Can you show me?'

'On a map?'

'No, come with me.'

Ellie hesitated. 'Really? It's police business, I—'

'It's fine, honestly. Maybe a walk will help us shake off our hangovers?' he added with a grimace.

Ellie sighed. 'Okay, sure.'

A few minutes later, they headed out of the house, strolling down the road. The sky was overcast, but it was hot, the air electric as a storm threatened. They walked past Ed Piper's house and towards the forest, which stood at the end of the road like a dark fortress.

Adrian was deep in thought as they walked, Ellie casting him glances every now and again.

He really did seem worried, and who could blame him?

Pauline was in hospital!

'Pauline was still at the pub when we left, wasn't she?' Adrian asked.

'I really can't remember,' Ellie replied.

Adrian peered at her. 'You were *that* drunk?'

'Yep,' Ellie admitted, face flushing.

'I'm pretty sure she *was* there.'

'Maybe.' Ellie paused as she spotted the small path in the distance, twisting away from the main one they were on and marked out by the new chipped wood that had been lain on it. 'There it is,' Ellie said. 'I can't see any sign of police officers though,' she added, peering through the trees and feeling relieved.

Adrian shook his head in frustration. 'Great. I guarantee they would have given it a cursory glance then walked off.'

They both walked over and Ellie flinched as she noticed a nearby leaf with congealed blood on it. She visualised Pauline walking with that fast, determined pace of hers, then suddenly a yelp of pain after a bike came storming at her.

Adrian crouched down, examining some tracks in the mud beside the path. 'Tyre tracks. Looks like whoever it was came from within the forest,' he said, looking towards the trees. 'This wasn't just a man cycling home. This looks deliberate.'

Ellie's stomach dropped.

Adrian stood and walked over to the narrow ditch that ran along the path. 'Looks like she stumbled, fell down here,' he said, gesturing to an indent in the mud. 'Might be how she got her injuries.'

'So she fell rather than being deliberately attacked?'

'Maybe. Either way, it's not nice.' He frowned. 'I was having a look at the group yesterday. Pauline *is* fond of posting complaints about cyclists on paths. I think it's pretty clear now that someone is targeting members of the group.' He shook his head in anger. 'That's four cases if you include Graham's gun theft. And now we have someone who's been *injured*.' He looked at Ellie. 'I'm reluctant to say this, but maybe we need to temporarily close the Facebook group?'

Ellie was quiet for a few moments, running through it all in her mind. Her eyes strayed towards the trace of blood on the leaf before her.

'I'm sorry, Ellie,' Adrian said in a contrite voice. 'It must be a proper stress for you.'

'No, it's fine, I just didn't expect to have to deal with this within the first few days of being the group's moderator!'

'Even more reason to close it down.'

'I just feel it's a bit drastic. Members will be in uproar. Some people's only daily excitement is that group.'

'We can't risk any more incidents, though, Ellie. Close the group and you take away the source.'

'How about I archive the group?'

Adrian frowned. 'Archive? What's involved with that?'

'It just means members can no longer post, comment or react to posts, but they *can* see old posts. At least this way, I can restore it later when things calm down.'

'*If* they calm down,' Adrian said with a sigh.

'I can think of some members of the group who won't calm down when they learn I've archived it.' Ellie rubbed at her temples. '*Why* did I volunteer for this?'

'Then don't do it any more,' Adrian said, shrugging his shoulders. 'You're perfectly within your rights to give it up, see if someone else wants to take over. I'm sure Andrea would relish the attention.'

'Even more reason not to give up. No, it's fine, I'll sort it.' She felt tears flood her eyes. What a mess.

'Hey,' Adrian said, putting his hand on her shoulder. 'You okay?'

'Oh. I'm just hung over and emotional,' she said, smiling to show she was fine.

'You really care about this village, don't you?'

Ellie looked down at the woodchipped path, nodding silently.

Adrian's thumb brushed against her cheek, a gesture of comfort.

She looked up at him, felt her tummy stir.

'Mum?'

They both pulled away from each other and looked up the path ahead to see Tyler walking towards them. He was with his best friend, Aaron, Sheila's grandson and the lead singer of Pyro, the band Tyler was lead guitarist in.

Ellie quickly stepped away from Adrian, face flushing.

'What are you doing here?' she asked her son. 'You should be at school!'

Tyler kept quiet, looking between his mother and Adrian, brow creased.

'Awkward,' Aaron said under his breath.

'Ellie's right, you shouldn't be here, boys,' Adrian said in his police-officer voice.

'We wanted to see the scene of the crime,' Aaron said, his black eyes excited. 'Didn't we, mate?'

But Tyler didn't reply, his eyes still on his mother.

Ellie walked towards him. 'Tyler, seriously, why aren't you at school?'

'Why are *you* here?' he countered, his eyes drilling into Adrian now. 'With *him*?'

'Your mum runs the Facebook group, remember, dude?' Aaron said. 'It'll be connected to the Facebook Vigilante,' he added dramatically.

'Before you arrest us,' Tyler said, looking at Adrian, 'it's our break.'

Adrian looked at his watch. It was ten thirty. 'You're not supposed to leave school grounds during school hours though. And anyway, what time did your break start? Don't you just get ten minutes or something?'

'Fifteen,' Tyler said. 'It started at ten fifteen.'

'So you're late back, great,' Ellie hissed. 'I'm not impressed, Tyler. We'll talk properly about this later. Your nan won't be happy either, Aaron,' she said, looking at Tyler's friend.

'Please don't tell her,' Aaron pleaded.

'Maybe. But you're both coming back to school with me right now.' She went to put her hand on her son's back then noticed a woman and a man approaching down the path. Ellie was sure they weren't villagers and yet she recognised the woman.

Then it hit her: it was Karin Hawkins, a journalist from the *Ashbridge Gazette*. Ellie remembered her from years ago when she had worked at the paper. Karin had always been the newspaper's best reporter, with a great nose for a story and an uncanny ability to extract information out of even the most discreet of people. There had been rumours that national newspapers had tried to recruit her, but she hadn't wanted to leave the area. She hadn't seemed to age . . . but then she'd always looked older than her years. with tightly permed blonde hair to her shoulders and a lined face which spoke of years of smoking and stress.

Ellie sighed. Of *course* Karin would be there to investigate the 'Facebook Vigilante' of Forest Grove. She was surprised she hadn't arrived sooner.

'Great,' Adrian said under his breath, noticing the journalist too.

'PC Cooper!' Karin called out.

Karin gestured to the bloody leaf Ellie had noticed and the man with Karin went to it, pulling out a camera from the bag he was holding. Aaron tried to get in on the picture but Tyler pulled him away, shaking his head.

'So Forest Grove has a Facebook Vigilante,' Karin said, grabbing a notepad and pen from her bag. 'I believe this is the fourth incident now, clearly an escalation with poor Pauline Sharpe being in hospital with a broken arm. What are your thoughts on all this, PC Cooper?'

'Absolutely a hundred per cent *no comment*,' Adrian said.

'Oh, come on, Adrian,' Karin said. 'Just one tiny comment.'

'Nope,' Adrian said firmly. He looked at Ellie. 'I'll head back now.'

Karin turned her attention to Ellie. 'Are you a resident?'

'She runs the Facebook group!' Aaron said excitedly. 'I'm her son's best friend.'

Karin's light grey eyes sparkled. 'How interesting. So you must be Ellie Nash, formerly Mileham. This all started with the Facebook group, of course. How did you feel when—'

'I won't be commenting either,' Ellie quickly said as she grabbed the sleeve of Tyler's T-shirt and led him down the path.

'Shouldn't you two be at school?' Karin called after them. 'I wonder what the head teacher would say?'

Ellie paused and turned to the journalist. Was she threatening to tell the head teacher if Ellie didn't give her a quote?

Karin saw her chance and jogged up to Ellie. 'It wouldn't look right if the group's moderator didn't offer some words of reassurance and concern,' she said. 'I know when Andrea was the moderator, she was *so* cooperative, always happy to offer her views on any Forest Grove incidents.'

'I bet she was,' Adrian said quietly.

'Do you even *want* the culprit caught?' Karin continued.

'Of course I do!' Ellie said.

'Leave her alone, Karin,' Adrian said.

'I'll quote you on that then!' Karin called after Ellie. 'What do you propose to do about the group? Will you close it down? That won't go down well, will it?'

As Ellie walked away along the path with the boys, the journalist's words echoed in her mind.

Ellie might not be closing the group for good, but archiving it wasn't exactly going to go down well.

And yet what choice did she have? She had to do something before things escalated.

Chapter 9

WELCOME TO THE FOREST GROVE FACEBOOK
CHIT-CHAT GROUP

Ellie Nash

ANNOUNCEMENT

Hi, everyone. As many of you may know, there was an incident last night involving a member of this group which we suspect might be related to posts on this group. As a result, I have no choice but to archive this group at the advice of the police. By doing so, once everything is resolved, the group can be reinstated with all posts still there. I really hope you all understand. Take care, Ellie.

Ed Piper

By 'police', do you mean your 'friend' Adrian Cooper? This is ridiculous, you're censoring us! We can't let the scum who did this to Pauline control us.

Ellie Nash

Ed, it is *not* true I'm censoring you. It's a temporary measure to protect people. All your posts are still floating around in cyberspace.

Tommy Mileham

I understand why you might have thought this was the right step, Ellie, but the truth is, it sends out the wrong message to the person who hurt Pauline. As Ed says, it sends the message out that we're *weak*.

Vanessa Shillingford

Come on, Dad! That's ridiculous.

Tommy Mileham

Is it, Vanessa? I know the psychology of these idiots from my years in the police. They want attention and that's exactly what Ellie's giving them by closing the group.

Ellie Nash

I think we've done the exact opposite, actually. No group, no attention. And remember, I'm archiving it, NOT closing it!

Ed Piper

But you won't stop the villagers *talking* about the Facebook Vigilante, it's all anyone can talk about.

Andrew Blake

Yeah! Makes us look like pussies. Andrea wouldn't have done this.

Kitty Fletcher

Honestly, Andrew, I do worry about the language used in here to describe people.

Ellie Nash

That's unfair, Andrew. I think I've been rather lenient.

Meghan Mileham

I agree, quite unfair! Ellie's doing the best she can in very difficult circumstances.

Ed Piper

If PC Plod did his very best, the little scrote would have been caught by now.

Ellie Nash

That's unfair, Ed, Adrian is doing a great job.

Adrian Cooper

Thank you, Ellie. I don't often post on here, but I want to say Ellie is right and this is something we discussed. In fact, I wanted far more stringent measures but Ellie convinced me to do this instead. As Ellie said, this is a temporary measure and hopefully whoever is doing this will be caught soon. Regards, PC Plod.

Vanessa Shillingford

Nice one, Adrian 😊

Andrea Simpson

I'm sorry to say this, Ellie, I've really tried to stay impartial as a former admin, but I have to agree with Tommy. Surely closing the group just adds to the drama of it all and means that whoever is doing this has won?

Rebecca Feine

Haven't any of you heard of the saying, *don't feed the trolls?* By archiving the group, we take the air out of the balloon. Hopefully it'll now all calm down. I think it's the right move, Ellie, well done.

Belinda Bell

Air out of the balloon? I very much doubt that! Poor Pauline, you should have seen her like I did this morning, all bandaged up and in pain from this vicious attack.

Vanessa Shillingford

Attack? Yes, I agree what happened to her wasn't nice, but are we sure it was an attack? Just a kid playing a silly prank on their bike that got out of hand, surely?

Tommy Mileham

It's clear there was intent there, Vanessa. Intent to hurt.

Pauline Sharpe

Tommy is right! I was deliberately targeted and deliberately hurt! The cyclist appeared out of nowhere and headed right for me! Didn't even pause when I fell into the ditch. As a victim of this vigilante, I request we NOT be snowflakes and don't give in by closing this group.

Myra Young

I hope you're okay, Pauline!

Andrea Simpson

Lots of hugs to you, Pauline.

Meghan Mileham

So sorry to hear what happened, Pauline.

Andrew Blake

Will kill the scum who did this to you, Pauline!

Adrian Cooper

Okay, Andrew, calm down. And Pauline, best wishes to you, we are doing all we can to track down who did this.

Ellie Nash

Hi, Pauline, I hope you're doing okay. I wish I could keep the group open, I really do, but having taken advice from Adrian, this is the best course of action.

Andrew Blake

Well, it looks like someone's going to have to set up an alternative group then . . .

Ellie Nash

PLEASE don't! This has already got out of hand. Don't add fuel to the fire.

Vanessa Shillingford

Yes! We need to trust in Ellie to do the right thing AND our local police officer, Adrian.

Andrea Simpson

Gosh, it's like being at school again with Ness and Ellie bossing everyone about.

Vanessa Shillingford

What on earth are you talking about?

Andrew Blake

Wasn't it you three I saw last night drunk and singing at the top of their lungs with a few others (sorry to dob you in, Adrian, mate).

Andrea Simpson

Interesting . . .

Myra Young

Ah, NOW I know who woke my baby up!

Vanessa Shillingford

Okay, calm down, Fun Police, you moan about everyone else being snowflakes and look at you lot! We are allowed to have a little fun, you know. Anyway, we weren't the only ones down the pub last night, half the village was! Maybe if you guys got out more and had some fun, you wouldn't be so bloody miserable.

Rebecca Feine

Oh, Vanessa, you are naughty, but very funny!

Tommy Mileham

You summed my daughter up perfectly, Rebecca!

Ellie Nash

I think that's enough discussion, so I'm going to archive the group now. Please don't set up a new group, Andrew. I promise this group will be up and running as soon as the police deem it safe. For now, please take care and report any suspicions and incidents to the police.

Chapter 10

Ellie snapped her laptop shut. There, it was done. The group was archived. It was the best thing to do, isn't that what Adrian had said? She flinched as she thought of what Pauline had posted about the cyclist appearing out of nowhere and heading right for her. The doorbell went and Ellie strolled down the hallway, surprised to see Peter standing there with Zoe.

'What are you doing here?' she asked. 'Not that I'm not delighted to see you,' she added, pulling Zoe into a tight hug.

'Zoe forgot her iPad,' Peter said. 'I was at Mum and Dad's so thought I'd swing by to get it. God, you look rough,' he said as he examined Ellie's face.

'Gee, thanks, Peter.'

'Mum looks pretty,' Zoe said. 'She always does.'

'You say all the right things,' Ellie said.

'Mum! You're squeezing so tight!' Zoe squirmed away from her, but the smile on her pretty face showed she didn't mind. She thundered upstairs to find her iPad.

Peter leaned against the wall, crossing his arms. 'So Dad told me Adrian Cooper's been paying visits.'

Ellie gave him a confused look. 'Visits? You mean a visit in his capacity as a police officer to ask some questions about the Facebook group I'm moderating?'

'And getting drunk with him down the pub last night. Ed said you looked pretty cosy.'

This village! Ellie thought to herself.

'How *kind* of Ed, keeping tabs on me, just like Andrea did,' Ellie said, rolling her eyes. 'What does it matter to you, anyway, Peter?'

'You're the mother of my children!'

'And that means I'm not allowed to be friends with our local police officer?'

He looked her up and down. '*Are* you just friends?'

'Yes! And anyway, even if we were more than that, it would have nothing to do with you. So please tell your friends, *and* your dad, to stop reporting back on my life.'

They both went quiet as Zoe appeared back at the top of the stairs, looking down at her father. 'What's wrong?' she asked.

'Nothing to do with you, nosey,' Peter said.

Zoe sighed and skipped down the stairs, her iPad under her arm.

'By the way, I told the kids I'll be picking them up from school,' he said. 'I don't want them walking through the forest after the recent incidents.'

'Now who's the one mollycoddling them?' Ellie couldn't help saying. 'It's perfectly safe out there.'

'I'm serious,' Peter said. 'Whoever's carrying out these attacks is a twisted individual. Who knows what they'll do next?'

'I've archived the Facebook group,' Ellie said curtly. 'It's over.'

'You really think that's enough to deter them? They've got the taste of blood now,' Peter said. 'This won't end.'

'That's a bit dramatic,' Ellie said as Zoe frowned. 'It'll be fine,' she said to Zoe. 'Don't let Dad scare you.'

Peter stepped out of the house with Zoe, straightening his collar. 'Come on then, let's get you home.'

Ellie gave Zoe a quick hug then watched them walk down the path, noticing as Peter stared at his reflection in the car window.

She shook her head. How had she ever loved him?

As she thought that, something occurred to her. She *had* loved him . . . but not now. Finally, she had fallen out of love with him.

The next day was uneventful, which was just as well, because Ellie was busy on the puzzle book she was working on.

But then Saturday morning arrived and, with it, the *Ashbridge Gazette* through the letterbox. Ellie was horrified to see a small photo of herself on the front page, standing with Adrian as they surveyed the scene where Pauline had fallen. It sat alongside a larger photo of Pauline, sitting in her hospital bed, her arm in a sling as she grimaced into the camera.

Ellie shook her head in anger as she read the article.

FACEBOOK VIGILANTE TARGETS FOREST GROVE RESIDENTS

by Karin Hawkins

Forest Grove resident Pauline Sharpe, 53, was mowed down by what residents are now referring to as the 'Facebook Vigilante'.

The incident is the fourth in a recent spate of criminal acts all linked to the village's Facebook community group.

The group's former moderator, Andrea Simpson, expressed the village's worry over the incidents. 'It all began when I left the role,' she told us. 'First, a man's guns were stolen after a post about deer control, then a woman in her eighties was targeted with dog excrement being pushed through her letterbox after she had commented on the issue in the group. Then a resident's front lawn was destroyed after they had complained about the delay in green bins being collected.'

The new moderator of the group, local puzzle creator Ellie Mileham, said she wanted whoever was behind the acts to be caught as soon as possible.

Ellie shoved the newspaper away, not wanting to read any more. This was the *last* thing she wanted, being included in an article about it all. Thank God the group was archived now.

The next morning, she headed to the Into the Woods bakery. Her work on the puzzle book had been slow that week and she reasoned that maybe what she needed was some time at her usual spot.

But as she walked through the busy courtyard towards the bakery, she was sure people were watching her, judging her. Take Ed Piper, for example, who was sitting on a bench with Andrew Blake nearby and casting occasional glances at her. A couple of the school mums whispered in low voices too; even the members of the local knitting group, who were sitting at one table as she walked into the bakery, were watching her strangely.

As she headed to her table, she noticed Adrian was at the till, being served by Meghan. The bakery's young assistant was wiping down tables.

'Oh, hey,' Adrian said, smiling slightly awkwardly at Ellie as she sat down. 'I see we're both famous?'

'It's so embarrassing!' she said in a low voice. 'We didn't give permission for our photo to be included, *and* she used my married name.'

'Yeah, I've made a complaint on our behalf.'

'Thank you. How's the investigation going?' Ellie asked as she laid her stuff out on the table. 'Are you getting more pressure now it's in the press?'

'Nah, we have bigger fish to fry after some break-ins in Ashbridge.'

Tommy strolled into the bakery then, pausing when he spotted Ellie and Adrian chatting. She thought of what Peter had said about Tommy mentioning Adrian going to the house. She was hoping he'd just go straight to the till, but instead he walked over to Ellie's table.

'Hello, Ellie, Adrian,' he said curtly. 'It's good I've got you both in one place, actually.'

Ellie recognised the tone he was adopting. Peter and Vanessa called it the 'police dad' tone, low and serious – the sort of voice Ellie imagined Tommy had used with criminals back in the day, working for the police force. 'I wanted to talk about the closure of the Facebook group.'

'It hasn't been closed, remember, Tommy,' Ellie explained. 'I've just archived it.'

'Yep, as soon as we catch whoever's doing this,' Adrian added, 'Ellie can reinstate it. It's difficult for people who don't get social media to understand.'

Tommy's face tightened. 'I *do* get social media, Adrian. Don't let my age fool you. In fact, I've managed to set up a new group.'

Ellie's mouth dropped open and Adrian shook his head.

'Come on, Tommy,' he said. 'Are you serious?'

'I am serious, Adrian. I just wanted to give you both the courtesy of knowing before making it live.'

'I'm surprised you're doing this, Tommy,' Ellie said.

Adrian crossed his arms. 'Me too. As an ex-copper, I thought you'd know better. I strongly advise against it.' Ellie liked this side of him: tough, direct.

Tommy clearly didn't though, because his chest puffed up and the tops of his cheeks reddened. 'I'm surprised the idiot behind all this hasn't been caught yet, to be honest, Adrian. Back in my day, we'd have banged him to rights already.' He shook his head, looking over at Meghan, who was now taking her apron off. 'Honestly, policing nowadays, far too soft.'

Adrian blinked. Ellie could tell he wanted to say something back but was weighing up how to say it in a way that wouldn't seem unprofessional.

'Too soft?' Ellie said, jumping in. 'What does *hard* mean to you then, Tommy? What exactly would you be doing in Adrian's position?'

'Setting up patrols,' Tommy said. 'Actual boots on the ground.'

'Like we have the resources to do that,' Adrian countered. 'Police work has changed now. It's more intelligence-led.'

Tommy laughed out loud. 'Intelligence-led. What does that make the police now, professors?'

He looked at his wife and laughed again. Meghan didn't laugh back, her eyes betraying how embarrassed she was. But she didn't disagree with him. It had always been that way with Meghan: just let Tommy run his mouth off, then have a quiet word with him later if he took it too far. Maybe Ellie had been like that with Peter, too, like when he would be casually racist during a dinner party. She'd bite her tongue, then bring it up later, annoyed with herself that she didn't have the strength to do it in front of others.

Well, that Ellie was gone.

'Tommy, I think you're taking this too far,' Ellie said firmly. 'I understand your concerns, but there's no need to use this case to criticise the entire police force. It's not fair on your successors in the force. It's not fair on Adrian. Imagine how you'd have felt twenty years back if someone was saying all this to you?'

Now it was Tommy's turn to blink in shock. He wasn't used to Ellie being like this. Adrian gave Ellie a thankful smile.

Tommy looked at them in turn, his face going even redder. 'And how would Peter feel if he saw the two of you like this?' he suddenly blustered back in a voice so loud other villagers passing by outside stopped to take notice. 'Just months after your marriage breaks up, and you're hooking up with another man, rubbing it in all our faces.'

A couple at a nearby table raised their eyebrows, whispering to each other. A man who'd entered the bakery with a newspaper under his arm, his little Jack Russell wagging its tail beside him, stopped too, not even making an attempt to hide the fact he was enjoying the show Tommy was putting on.

Ellie felt the heat rising in her cheeks, aware of everyone's eyes on her.

Now she knew how her mother had once felt.

All her newfound courage deflated and she wrapped her arms around herself, blinking back tears.

'That's low, Tommy,' Adrian said in his calm, firm voice. 'We both know it's *your* son who walked out on Ellie.'

Tommy puffed his chest out, clearly about to say something.

But then Meghan strolled over, gently touching her husband's arm. 'This is silly, Tommy. There's no need for all this. Isn't this what the Facebook Vigilante is trying to do? Create division. And Ellie, of all people, is the last person you ought to be attacking. Come on, let's get home.' She turned to Ellie and mouthed a *sorry*, then marched Tommy out of the courtyard.

'You okay?' Adrian said gently as people turned back to their food, casting Ellie sideways glances.

'Yes,' Ellie said, her voice shaky. 'Thank you for backing me up. I don't know why Tommy's being like this.'

'Maybe it's his way of coping. Denial. Anger. Deflection. Anything other than admitting his own son is a douche bag.'

Ellie smiled. 'You're a regular Sigmund Freud, aren't you?'

Adrian laughed, then his face grew serious. 'You're okay though, right? He was bang out of order to you.'

'Not just to me, you too.'

Adrian shrugged. 'I'm used to it. I appreciated you sticking up for me, too, though. We make a good team.'

Ellie smiled. 'Yeah, we do. My mum always said you need allies in a village like Forest Grove. It's like going to war sometimes.'

Adrian saluted her. 'Agreed, Officer Nash. So,' he added with a sigh, 'looks like our next battlefront might be a brand-new Forest Grove Facebook group. Unless our little chat with Tommy just now put him off the idea and he closes it?'

Ellie shook her head. 'No way. This'll just make him even more determined. And you know what? Let him open his group. If there are more vigilante acts as a result, he'll soon learn his lesson.'

Adrian nodded, then he leaned close to her, light-brown eyes sparkling mischievously. 'Don't tell anyone, but I'm almost hoping there will be one.'

Ellie wagged her finger at him. 'Now, now, PC Cooper!'

That evening the door burst open, the sound of the kids' voices ringing out.

'We're back!' Zoe shouted.

Ellie smiled and walked down the hallway, pleased to see Peter had just dropped them off again without coming in. She gave Zoe a big hug then high-fived Tyler as he smiled slightly, before walking upstairs. She knew she needed to talk to him about seeing him in the forest, but first she'd let him settle in.

While dinner was cooking, she jogged upstairs, knocking on Tyler's door.

'I'm doing it!' came the answer as he turned the music he'd been playing down.

'It's not about the music though it *was* too loud. Can I come in?'

'Yeah.'

Ellie let herself in, resisting the urge to roll her eyes when she saw Tyler had already 'Tylerfied' his room after she'd done her weekly clean of it, clothes from his backpack strewn all over the carpet, a pile of dirty washing in the corner.

'Doesn't your dad do any laundry?' Ellie said as she gathered it all up, shoving it into a wash basket in the hallway.

'Dad's useless, you know that, Mum.'

Ellie smiled to herself as she walked back into his room and sat on his bed, watching as he tapped away on his keyboard.

'Darling, look at me.'

Another sigh. It was his favourite way to communicate sometimes, sigh after sigh. She'd even begun to distinguish between the different types of sighs. This one was a 'Do we really have to talk, Mum?' kind of sigh.

He slowly turned around and slumped in his chair, folding his arms. She noticed he'd changed into a new top featuring some band, no doubt bought for him by Peter – ironic, considering Peter accused her of spoiling them. That was how Peter focused his parenting: *presents*. Each week, the kids would come back with something new. It frustrated Ellie, not only because she couldn't afford to do the same, but also because very often Peter would buy them things she had considered giving them as birthday presents, so she ended up feeling totally undermined . . . *and* out of present ideas. She'd tried to talk to Peter about it, but he carried on regardless in true Peter fashion.

'Right, about Thursday morning,' Ellie said. 'It really is unacceptable to go out of school grounds, Tyler.'

'Everyone does it,' he mumbled.

'Ah, I see. So that makes it all right, does it? I mean, if everyone else decides to jump off a cliff, then what the hell, you might as well do it too.'

'Mum, you are *always* saying that. Don't lump me in with all the sheeple out there.'

'Sheeple?' Ellie asked, confused.

'You know, people who are like sheep, just mindlessly doing what they're told.'

Ellie suppressed a smile. She'd not heard that one before. 'Well, I'm sorry, but in life sometimes you *do* need to do what you're told, especially when it comes to school. The fact that I've not had a phone call suggests nobody noticed you left school grounds . . .

apart from me and the local policeman, of course, who, by the way, has turned a blind eye, which you have *me* to thank for.'

'Why? Because he's your boyfriend?' Tyler asked.

'He is not my boyfriend, Tyler, and even if he was, is it such a big deal?'

'Whatever,' Tyler said with a shrug. 'Don't care, really.'

'Well, he's not my boyfriend, okay? And this is distracting from the main issue here: you were wrong to leave school premises. Promise me you won't do it again?'

'Yeah, sure,' he mumbled.

'You don't sound so sure.'

He peered up at her. 'Yeah, Mum!' he said in a faux-happy voice.

Ellie smiled. 'I love you, darling. You know that, don't you? You and Zoe are everything to me. *Everything.*'

'Bit dramatic, Mum.'

'Come on,' she said, 'you've lived with me and your sister long enough to know dramatic is in our genes. Right,' Ellie said, standing up, 'I'm doing burger and chips, I'll call you when it's done.'

She went to walk out.

'Mum?'

She turned back. 'Yep?'

'I saw your post about archiving the group.'

'You did?'

He nodded. 'I'm not sure that was the right thing to do, to be honest. People online are well funny about censorship and stuff. Sometimes better to just keep things running.'

'Let me guess, you're now going to tell me I'm the censorship police?'

Tyler gave her half a smile under his dark fringe. 'I'll leave that to your *boyfriend.*'

'Oi!' she said, picking up a dirty T-shirt she'd just spotted and throwing it at him. He batted it away, laughing. 'Well, thanks for the advice, Tyler Zuckerberg. I'll be sure to keep it in mind.'

She walked out, smiling to herself. Tyler could be a grumpy nightmare sometimes, but when he came out of his shell with her, it made it all worth it.

'Oh no, Mum,' Tyler called out.

She went back into the room. 'What's up?'

'Grandad set up a new group,' he said, showing her his screen to reveal a new Facebook group.

'Oh, Tommy,' Ellie said with a sigh. 'What have you done?'

Chapter 11

Sunday 17th July
7 p.m.

Tommy Mileham

I won't ramble on much, all that's left to say is welcome to a group where you don't have to fear being censored or closed. Oh, and if the little 'vigilante' scumbag is reading this right now, watch your back . . .

Ed Piper

Loving the description, Tommy. It feels very warm in here, definitely not a place for snowflakes.

Graham Cane

Good idea, Tommy!

Peter Mileham

Yes, very sensible, Dad.

Andrew Blake

Does this mean I can post all those memes that never got approved in the other group?

Tommy Mileham

Go ahead, pal.

Andrea Simpson

Ed Piper

Well well well, controversial! The former admin of the *old* group is here.

Myra Young

Lovely to see you again, Andrea, we missed you!

Andrea Simpson

Thank you, my love. I can be honest here and say I had to turn notifications off for the 'other group'. I'm so grateful to Ellie for taking over . . . but it all seemed to go a bit wrong when she did. I have a feeling this group's membership numbers are soon going to catch up with the other group!

Lucy Cronin

Agreed.

Meghan Mileham

Now, now. None of that was Ellie's fault.

Andrea Simpson

Oh, I know, I'm just saying . . . oh, it doesn't matter. All that matters is we have a brand-new group now!

Pauline Sharpe

My heroes, setting up this group! So, what's the first thing we should complain about?

Pauline Sharpe

Anybody?

Ed Piper

Don't tell me people are too scared. We will not let this scumbag vigilante take our voices away. Right, Tommy?

Tommy Mileham

Right, Ed. And how about I start with this: to the person playing godawful house music until 3 a.m. last night – next time it happens, when I find out who it is I'll be setting my grandfather's gramophone up on your front lawn and blaring it for all to hear. Maybe that will improve your taste in music.

Myra Young

Well said, Tommy. I'd just got the little one to sleep when that racket started. It's not the first time either.

Andrea Simpson

Quite! It annoys me that one person has to sub-ject the rest of us to awful blaring music like this, so selfish.

Andrew Blake

Anyone know what house the music's coming from? Maybe we should pay them a little visit . . .

Tommy Mileham

Andrew, none of that here. What I will be doing is tracking down the music culprit's phone number and phoning them non-stop from 3 a.m.

Andrew Blake

Lucy Cronin

Shouldn't we be careful with that vigilante around?

Tommy Mileham

Maybe that's exactly why I'm posting this . . .

Chapter 12

Ellie tossed and turned in her sleep. She was aware of wakefulness, felt it in her periphery. But the fog of sleep kept dragging her back; back to an image of her mother, sat before her large, ornate mirror, scissors in her hand.

It was the same dream she had most nights, but this time letters were scattered around her bare feet alongside the strands of hair. Ellie couldn't discern what was written on them, just saw the writing, jagged and cruel-looking, ripped envelopes among them.

Her mother began to turn her head, slowly, slowly, and as she revealed more of herself, Ellie moaned in her sleep at the sight of the jagged cuts, the blood mingling with leaking mascara and smeared lipstick on her mother's usually perfect face.

Ellie woke with a gasp caught in her chest, her fingers clawing at her nightdress. She gulped in large breaths, rocking back and forth to calm herself; to drive away the images. As wakefulness returned, the usual peace of the house was disturbed by a distant rumble of sound.

More specifically, *music*. Very loud music.

She looked at the time. Three in the morning.

Who on earth would be playing music at this time? Ellie got out of bed and went to the open window, the summer nights too warm now to sleep with it shut.

Yes, it was definitely music coming from within the village.

In the other rooms, she heard the kids stir.

The music really must be loud if it's waking those two, Ellie thought to herself. They usually slept through everything. She heard the floorboards creaking and Zoe appeared at her door in her purple short pyjamas, rubbing at her eyes.

'What *is* that?' she said.

'I'm not sure, darling. Maybe someone's having a party,' Ellie said, walking over to her daughter and steering her back to her bedroom. 'It's not so bad if you close your window, see?' Ellie said as she did just that.

Zoe yawned and got back into bed, curling on her side and leaning her cheek on her hand. Ellie watched her for a while. She acted so grown up lately, but like this, it felt as if Zoe was her little girl again.

She stepped out of Zoe's room and went to Tyler's door, putting her ear to it. On the other side, she could hear the tap of her son's fingers on his keyboard.

So much for the music waking *him* up. Hadn't he gone to bed yet?

She gently knocked on the door, then let herself in. Tyler was at his computer, the screen lit up. He quickly turned his monitor away from Ellie's view and gave her an angry look. 'Mum! You can't just *walk* in!'

'It's three in the morning, you shouldn't even be awake!' she exclaimed.

'Neither should you.'

'The music woke me,' she said, gesturing towards his open window. 'Can't you hear it?'

'Oh that,' he said, shrugging. 'No biggie.'

Ellie frowned. 'Can you turn your computer off, please? This is a ridiculous time to be up. You'll be exhausted tomorrow.'

'I'm used to it, I'm *always* awake at this time,' he replied, rolling his eyes. 'You're just not awake to know.'

'Jesus, Tyler, no wonder you take an age to get up in the morning.'

'I don't need much sleep, Mum.'

'*Everyone* needs sleep. It's not good for your brain development to have so little.'

'Yeah, sure it isn't, Mum,' he said sarcastically, turning back to his computer. 'I just need to put some finishing touches to the stuff I'm doing for the gig on Saturday. Shut the door on your way out.'

Ellie put her hand on her hip. 'I'm serious, Tyler,' she said in a stern voice, while trying to keep it low enough to avoid waking Zoe again. 'Get to bed now. The finishing touches can wait until tomorrow.'

Her son's jaw clenched and he closed his eyes, taking a deep breath. He *so* reminded Ellie of Peter when he did that. 'Fine,' he said. He quickly typed something then shut his monitor down, standing up and stretching.

'You're still dressed?' Ellie asked, shaking her head in amazement as she took in his tight grey jeans and black skull hoodie, hidden before by his desk and chair.

'Well, I can't get into my PJs with you standing there, can I?'

Ellie sighed. 'Fine. But you *are* going to sleep, okay, or there's no gig at all on Saturday.'

'Mum, you can't do that,' Tyler said. 'We've sold tickets and everything.'

'Then get to bed.'

She examined his face. How had he grown so quickly into this sullen young man? He used to be so cuddly and silly. She missed that little Tyler; she missed their cuddles. For a moment, she thought about giving him a hug. But then she came to her senses and instead gave him a smile. 'Love you, darling.'

Tyler gave her an embarrassed grimace. 'Okay then, night, Mum!'

She stepped out of the room and stood in the darkness of the hallway for a few minutes, listening until she heard the springs of his mattress.

'Happy now?' he called through the door to her. 'I'm in bed now, like a good little boy.'

She couldn't help but smile as she walked back to her room, where the music seemed even louder. There was no way she could sleep now. What *must* the other residents of Forest Grove be thinking? She grabbed her phone and settled into the chair by the window, scrolling through Facebook as she yawned.

Then she paused. There was a new recommendation in her timeline for a group called 'The FG Alternative Community Group'. So Tommy *had* opened a new group. Plus, it was an 'open' group, which meant anyone could view posts in there, even if they weren't members.

She clicked into it. '**Home to Strong Branches and Deep Roots. Not home to totalitarian admins and snowflake censorship**' was its description.

'So childish,' Ellie whispered to herself. It had already attracted 357 members . . . and there were already a few posts, mainly memes posted by Andrew Blake.

But one thread stood out to her: Tommy's introductory thread. As she scrolled down it, she saw he'd made a complaint about a neighbour playing music in the early hours that weekend.

Ellie looked out in the direction of where the music was coming from, heart thumping loudly.

Was the music she could hear now in response to Tommy's post?

But who would be *doing* that?

'For God's sake, Tommy,' she hissed.

She felt a ball of anger inside. The fact was, he was being completely disrespectful to her, as the moderator of the official group. Sure, she and his son were separated, but that wasn't her fault, plus she'd always been good to Tommy . . . not to mention the fact that she was the mother of his grandchildren. Why couldn't he show some restraint and a little bit of respect for her?

She noticed a new post had popped up in the group while she'd been looking at Tommy's post, this time one from Andrea.

> Can anyone else hear that music? Where on earth is it coming from? That doesn't sound like any old music system, it's booming!

'Bloody Andrea,' Ellie whispered to herself.

She scrolled down the comments, seeing posts from the usual suspects, until she got to one from Tommy.

> Who fancies a little night-time walk to track down the music? It only just turned on. The idiot who did it can't be far away . . .

Ellie clenched her hands into fists. 'Tommy, no!' she whispered.

Andrew Blake and Ed Piper replied, agreeing to meet at Tommy's house. Ellie looked at her watch. They'd all be there in ten minutes.

She ought to warn Adrian. He was the right person to deal with any anti-social behaviour, not Tommy and his friends.

She quickly composed a text to him.

Sorry, know it's late! On the off chance you've been woken by the music that's blaring out too, I thought you'd like to know that Tommy and his cronies are planning to meet up soon at his house to track down the vigilante.

He wrote back right away.

Knew something like this would happen after reading Tommy's post in his new group. Am heading down there. Thanks for letting me know.

Ellie bit her lip, peering out over the rooftops towards Tommy and Meghan's large house. Would it be wrong of her to join the 'search' too? Give Tommy a piece of her mind in the process? The kids would be okay without her for half an hour. Tyler was seventeen, after all, definitely old enough to be alone here with his sister.

She quickly pulled on some clothes and scrawled a message for the kids, taping it to her closed bedroom door as she walked out. GOING TO INVESTIGATE MUSIC WITH YOUR GRANDAD. WON'T BE LONG. CALL ME IF YOU NEED ME.

They wouldn't wake up, she told herself, but just in case.

Then she jogged downstairs and let herself out into the darkness. Ellie walked down the road, wrapping her arms around herself. It was colder than she thought it would be. It was so odd being out at this time of night. Even odder having the blaring house music as background to her night-time walk, music that was getting increasingly louder the closer she got to her former in-laws' house.

As she passed by the other houses, she noticed lots of bedroom lights on, people clearly woken by the music. She hoped there weren't too many kids who'd been woken.

She sighed and continued walking, eventually coming to Tommy's house. It was one of the largest in the village, a gorgeous five-bedroom lodge-style house looking out on to the forest. The front garden was a large square bordered with the most beautiful rose bushes, the flowers alternating red and white. You could see the care Tommy put into that garden as soon as you spotted it. It was like a child to him, carefully tended each day.

When Ellie arrived at the house she could see Tommy was already outside with Ed Piper, Andrew Blake and Graham Cane. Andrew was in his fifties and lived with his mother on the outskirts of the forest in a house that looked slightly unkempt, the grass too long, the huge garden behind it filled with bits and pieces. He liked to wear army-style clothes and often hinted at the action he saw on the 'front line', as he called it. But everyone knew the only action he'd seen was a pile-up on the motorway due to his job as a lorry driver. He had his two huge Rottweilers with him – soppy things, really, whenever Ellie bumped into him while out on a walk, but menacing to look at. Beside him, Tommy held a cricket bat in his hands . . . and Graham had a shiny, new gun.

Great.

As Ellie approached them, they all looked at her in surprise . . . especially Tommy.

She felt a puff of pride, and anger too.

Two can play at this game, she thought.

'What are you doing here, Ellie?' Tommy asked. 'What about the kids?'

'I saw your post on the new group,' she said. 'You know, the one which implied I'm a totalitarian dictator and a snowflake all rolled into one?'

'I never said that,' Tommy replied.

'Whatever,' Ellie said, folding her arms. 'You said you needed help – well, here I am. The kids are asleep and, anyway, Tyler's old enough to be there with Zoe.'

'This isn't really an activity for a girl, Ellie,' Graham said.

Ellie's anger shot up to a new level. 'Please tell me you didn't just say that, Graham! You do realise how bloody sexist that sounds?'

'Oh, I think Ellie can handle herself,' a voice said from the darkness. She turned to see Adrian strolling towards them. She gave him a big smile and he did the same to her. He still looked sleepy, making her want to run her fingers through his brown hair to tidy it and adjust the wonky collar on the polo shirt he must have quickly pulled on.

'You two are becoming quite the pair, aren't you?' Tommy said.

'I'm the local PC Plod,' Adrian said. 'Why wouldn't I be here?'

Ed looked embarrassed, no doubt recalling that this was how he'd referred to Adrian in his Facebook comment.

'Can I ask why you have a gun with you?' Adrian asked, eyeing Graham's new gun.

'Protection,' Graham shot back. 'Might be a bunch of the scrotes behind these acts.'

'That gun is to only be used on your property,' Adrian said. 'How about you pop it back in your car? You wouldn't want me confiscating your brand-new toy, would you?'

Graham scowled then went to his car, placing his gun inside and coming back with a cricket bat like Tommy's.

Ellie rolled her eyes. 'You realise you're all looking more vigilante than the actual vigilante?'

'Might just fancy a game of cricket while we're there,' Tommy said, flexing his jaw. 'We're wasting precious time. Let's see where this music is coming from then.'

'I'm pretty sure it's coming from the east side of the forest,' Adrian said. 'Can't say I'm surprised this has happened, considering the comment you made about loud music in your new group, Tommy. A group Ellie and I advised you not to start, may I add.'

'I'm not surprised either, it was my intention to draw the vigilante out,' Tommy said matter-of-factly.

'And now most of the village is awake,' Adrian said, gesturing to a window nearby, where an elderly woman was peeking out.

'You can't make an omelette without smashing a few eggs,' Tommy said as Ed, Graham and Andrew nodded in agreement. 'If we can catch the culprit now, case solved.'

Ellie peered into the darkness of the trees ahead of them, wondering if he was right.

'This isn't *Criminal Minds*, Tommy,' Adrian said.

'It's definitely getting louder,' Graham remarked. 'Probably best to cut through the trees rather than around.'

'Good idea,' Tommy said. 'We can use the lights from our phones.'

Ellie felt a tremor of apprehension as they headed for the forest. With the men all tooled up for battle, the idea of venturing into the woods to find the person behind the music suddenly didn't seem like such a great idea, after all. As though sensing her fear, Adrian drew closer to her as they stepped into the forest, the illumination from the streetlights behind them instantly getting sucked away by the darkness of the trees.

'Who knew we'd be spending the early hours on a forest walk?' Adrian whispered to her as he turned on the torch on his phone, shining it into the darkness as she did the same.

'I hope you don't mind me messaging you,' she whispered back. 'I thought you'd want to know.'

'No, don't apologise,' he said. 'I'm pleased. We have enough vigilantism in this village at the moment without these four causing issues.' He gestured to the men, who were now a few steps ahead of them.

As they drew deeper into the forest, the music took on a distorted, dream-like quality among the trees. The branches of a solid oak nearby creaked and Ellie jumped, her eyes darting from shadow to shadow.

'You okay?' Adrian asked.

'Yep, just never really liked the forest when its dark.'

'I thought you'd be used to it. Andrea told me all the teenagers back then would rampage through the forest at night. That's why the village decided to appoint a forest ranger.'

Ellie laughed. 'I bet she said she wasn't one of those teenagers either?'

'She did, actually. She said she kept out of all that.'

'Rubbish! She was always in the forest, snogging boys. Then, the next day, she'd be shaking her head in disapproval as the head teacher went on a rant about illegal raves.'

Adrian laughed bitterly. 'Doesn't surprise me, to be honest. Andrea's very good at pretending to be something she's not. That's how I got roped into marrying her.'

'Oh, really? So do tell me more about this love story.'

'It was super-romantic. I met her at a friend's wedding. Got crazy drunk. Ended up in her hotel room. Nine months later, Carter comes along.'

'I see,' Ellie said, grimacing.

'Just to add, one-night stands aren't usually my thing,' he quickly said, 'but I'd just come out of a tough break-up from an ex who'd left me for a "more adventurous man", as she enjoyed telling me.' He shrugged. 'So I guess I wanted to prove to myself I could be adventurous too by having a one-night stand. I instantly regretted it the next morning when Andrea treated the waiter like crap when he served us breakfast. We exchanged numbers, but I knew it was unlikely anything would come of it.' He sighed. 'Then she called, telling me she was pregnant. The rest is history.'

'So you married her because it was the right thing to do? Or that's how you felt?'

'Yeah. Realised even more what she's like when we got married, putting on this cutesy Disney princess act when she's more like a Disney villain.'

Ellie couldn't help but laugh. 'That's exactly what Vanessa and I always say about her, more villain than princess.'

'You're not wrong.'

They looked over towards Tommy, who was cutting a swathe through the forest with his cricket bat as Andrew's dogs trotted along, sniffing at the leaves.

'You'd think he'd be embarrassed,' Adrian said as he gestured to Tommy ahead of them. 'It was his post that caused all this, waking the entire village. But he almost seems proud!'

'Like he said, you need to crack a few eggs to make an omelette.'

Adrian shook his head. 'A naive philosophy. Whoever's doing this is determined, clever even. And that's where Tommy will stumble: he thinks whoever's doing this is stupid, like the criminals he was used to dealing with back in the day. But he should give this person more credit.'

Ellie looked at Adrian with interest. 'You really think that?'

'Yep. Watch out, log alert.' Adrian grabbed her hand, making her stop before a large fallen tree in front of her. As he helped her step over the log, her hand still in his, Ellie made the most of the feel of his skin against hers, the cool palm of his hand, the knuckled length of his fingers. He let her hand go, but she was sure he'd held it a little longer than he needed to.

'I actually think whoever's doing this has a bigger plan,' Adrian continued. 'I think they're trying to make a point.'

'What sort of point?'

'I don't know. Maybe they hate this village. The gossip. The pettiness of some of the residents' complaints. Maybe they've had enough, you know?'

'Or maybe they want to prove a point specifically to Tommy in this case?'

'Maybe.'

'So you don't think it's bored teenagers, like others think?' Ellie asked Adrian.

'That's still a possibility. A clever, bored kid. Forest Grove can be pretty claustrophobic and that can have quite an effect on a teenager. I didn't move here until I married Andrea, but I know friends who've lived here since they were teenagers and they all went through a stage of hating the place.'

'Aren't all villages a bit like that?'

'Not as bad as Forest Grove, I'm sure. It's the way people gossip, you know? How quickly news gets around. Like when Andrea and I split up,' he added with a sigh. 'I'd literally told her I was moving out on the Saturday and on Sunday morning I was walking back from my friend's house, where I'd been staying, and Meghan stopped me to say how sad she was to hear about the break-up.'

'That *is* fast.'

'Halt!' Tommy called out at the front. 'Movement, there!' He swivelled his torch around, the light following a shadow in the distance.

Ellie's breath caught in her throat as she searched the darkness.

'Jesus, it's like an army drill,' Adrian whispered, trying to ease the tension.

'It's him!' Andrew shouted, suddenly darting off into the undergrowth as his dogs ran with him, their barks echoing around the trees.

'Great,' Adrian murmured. 'I'd better go after him.'

Ellie watched as Adrian followed Andrew through the bushes, Tommy, Ed and Graham following close behind. She held up her phone, directing its torch after them and trying to follow their path with it.

But the light from her phone suddenly disappeared, plunging her into darkness.

There was a crunch of leaves behind her.

She swivelled around, heart thumping to the rhythm of the music still playing in the distance.

Another branch cracked just a few inches away from her.

She jumped in surprise, letting out a scream.

'Ellie!' Footsteps headed towards her and Adrian appeared in front of her, shining the torch in her face. 'Ellie, are you okay? I heard you scream.'

'I – I think the battery on my phone went. I – I thought I heard something.' She gave him a shaky smile in the semi-darkness. 'I'm being silly.'

'You're trembling.'

'I'm just cold.'

'Come here then.' Adrian drew her close to him, his arm around her shoulders, the heat of his body close to hers giving her warmth. 'It was probably a deer. They're always out here at night.'

'You should go and help the others. I'm just being a wimp.'

'Nah. Anyway, I'd rather be here with you than with that lot.' He paused for a moment and, in the light of the torch, she could see his brow was knitted. 'I'd rather be with you than most people, actually.'

Ellie felt her heart swell. He was telling her he liked her, wasn't he? *Really* liked her. And truth be told, she really liked him too.

It must have shown in her eyes as he drew her even closer and, for a moment, she thought they might kiss.

But then someone coughed.

Ellie and Adrian pulled apart to see Tommy watching them. Behind him, Ed and Andrew were trying to stop themselves from laughing, Graham huffing and puffing in the distance as he tried to catch up with his friends.

Ellie stepped away from Adrian, feeling mortified.

'Well, you really don't waste any time, do you, Ellie?' Tommy said.

'He was just keeping me warm,' Ellie said.

'Heard that one before,' Andrew joked in a low voice to Ed.

'Waste any time?' Adrian said to Tommy. 'Like your son did when he walked out on her?'

Tommy looked at them both in disgust. 'I'm not here to listen to this crap. Come on,' he said to the other men, 'let's find where this music is coming from and leave the lovebirds to it.'

Then he stormed off through the trees, Ed and Graham following him. Andrew stayed behind for a moment, giving Ellie and Adrian a thumbs up, then he jogged to catch up with his friends.

'Well, that was awkward,' Adrian said.

'Yep,' Ellie said, not sure what to say. She'd liked the way Adrian had moved close to her and the look in his eyes, like he really did want to kiss her. But was she ready for all that?

'Come on then!' she heard Tommy shout out.

Adrian smiled at her and they followed the others. As they drew to the east side of the woods, the music was even louder. The forest thinned out and they stepped on to the first street on that side of the woods, residents standing on their lawns in their nightwear.

Ellie felt a sense of relief being out of the shadows of the forest.

'Adrian,' one of the women said when she noticed her local police officer approaching. Ellie recognised her as local therapist Kitty Fletcher. 'What on *earth* is going on?' Kitty asked. 'I think it's coming from the Forest Centre, but who would be having a party at this time of the night?'

'We don't know yet, Kitty,' Adrian said. 'I'm hoping to find out.'

'Is it to do with the Facebook Vigilante?' Kitty asked. 'How intriguing, if it is.'

'I'm afraid I don't know that either,' Adrian said. 'I suggest you get back inside and let me worry about it. Hear that, everyone?' Adrian shouted down the street. 'Back to bed, I'm on the case.'

People did as he asked and Adrian and Ellie continued walking down the road until they got to the large Forest Centre. Kitty was right, the music was clearly coming from there. In fact, Tommy and the other men were already peering through the large windows into the darkness inside.

'That explains why it's so loud,' Adrian said as he walked towards them, having to shout to be heard above the music. 'Someone's managed to get access to the sound system that's been set up for Saturday's gig.'

'Any of you have keys to this place?' Tommy asked, his booming voice just discernible over the music.

'Andrea does,' Adrian said tightly. 'She's the new Forest Centre's manager now. I'll give her a call.'

As he dug out his phone and called his ex-wife, Ellie walked over to Tommy.

'Nothing is happening between Adrian and me, you know,' she said over the music.

'Could have fooled me!' Tommy replied, rolling his eyes at his friends.

Ellie took in a deep breath. 'But even if there was, it would be none of your business.'

'You're the mother of my two grandchildren, Ellie. Of course it's my business.'

'Ah, I see. So you don't want me bringing just any old man home, right?'

'Exactly!' Tommy said.

'Yep, Adrian *is* a bit of a dodgy one, isn't he? What with him being a police officer and all.'

Tommy crossed his arms. 'You get bad apples in the police, you know.'

'Adrian isn't a bad apple, mate!' Andrew said. 'He's one of the good ones.'

Tommy's jaw clenched. 'All I'm saying is surely it's a bit soon for Zoe and Tyler. Haven't they been through enough as it is? It's only been three months!'

'But I am *not* dating Adrian!' Ellie shouted, the music pulsing in her ears. 'And anyway, who's the one who put them through all that? Your bloody son! Did you know that Peter brought Caitlin back to the house a few years back, when the kids were sleeping and I was at my aunt's funeral? Tyler told me the other week. They didn't think he saw her, but he did.'

Tommy looked at her in surprise as his friends exchanged disapproving glances behind him.

'I'm sorry, Tommy,' Ellie said with a sigh, 'but it's what he did. Ask him. You have *no* right to tell me what to do and with whom when *your* son is the one who tore my family apart.'

'She has a point,' Andrew said.

'What was that?' Tommy asked his friend, straining to hear above the music.

'I said, she has a point!' Andrew shouted back.

Tommy threw him a look.

Adrian walked over then. 'So, what did Andrea say?' Tommy asked, clearly pleased to be off the topic of his cheating son.

'She'll be here soon,' Adrian replied.

As they waited for Andrea, Ellie went over to the centre and placed her hand on the glass door, the sound of the music vibrating through her.

Who had done this?

She looked into the trees behind the centre. Was Tommy right? Could they be watching right now, revelling in the excitement?

She shivered at the thought.

Eventually, Andrea approached from the path. Ellie could see in the light from Tommy's torch that she was wearing a full face of make-up. No wonder she'd taken as long as she had.

Then Ellie noticed Michael trailing behind her, his hands over his ears. 'Gosh, it is loud, isn't it?' he shouted.

'What on earth are you doing here, Ellie?' Andrea asked her.

'It doesn't matter, Andrea!' Adrian shouted as the music continued to blare around them. 'We need to get the door open. The music is waking the whole town up.'

Andrea narrowed her eyes at him, then walked to the entrance-way, shoving her keys into the door and pushing it open.

The music boomed even louder now the door was open, so loud it made the ground vibrate.

'I have *no* idea how anyone could get in here,' Andrea shouted as she switched on the light and illuminated the entrance foyer. They all walked through the foyer into the large hall to find that the music system was on the stage. The music was so loud they all had to put their hands over their ears.

Adrian ran up to the plug sockets. He pulled out the plugs and the music instantly stopped. Everyone sighed a breath of relief and Ellie could feel her ears ringing in the silence.

'Timer plugs,' he said, holding up the leads. The normal black plugs had been plugged into white plugs with a digital display on them. 'They were all set to turn on at three in the morning.'

Ellie frowned. So whoever had done this could be back home by now . . . or watching them from the trees outside.

'Isn't that the time your neighbour's music went on till, Tommy?' Ellie asked pointedly. 'The time you posted about in the group?'

'Yep,' he said. 'Looks like my bait worked.'

'Bait? That's irresponsible, Tommy,' Adrian said. 'You've woken the whole town and half deafened us all!'

'I didn't wake them,' Tommy shot back. 'The scumbag who orchestrated this woke them!'

'Who else has keys to this place, Andrea?' Adrian asked her.

'Me, Frazer . . . and whoever might be hiring the hall.' She turned her attention to Ellie and crossed her arms. 'In fact, right now, that'll be Aaron Leighton, Tyler's best friend. He's had the key for the past few days so he can prepare for the gig on Saturday.'

'*Very* interesting . . .' Michael said.

'Aaron wouldn't do something like this,' Ellie insisted. 'He's a good kid.'

'You know, Meghan and I have never liked him,' Tommy said. 'Peter never has either. You shouldn't have encouraged that friendship, Ellie.'

'Why don't you all like him, Tommy?' Ellie shot back. 'Is it because his mum is single and he lives in a smaller house than you? Well, guess what? Tyler and Zoe will be in the exact same position in a few weeks, thanks to your son.'

Tommy's face went red.

'Let's not jump to conclusions,' Adrian said. 'You know from your own police work that's not the best way to approach things, Tommy. Like Ellie said, Aaron's a good kid. I'll talk to him in the morning.'

Tommy took in a deep breath. 'Fine. But you come and see me straight after.'

'I don't have to do that,' Adrian said calmly. Tommy opened his mouth to protest, but Adrian put his hand up. '*But* as a thank you for your help tonight, I will as long as you don't go talking to him yourself.'

Tommy thought about it, then nodded.

Ellie felt a swell of pride as she watched Adrian. He was so good at this policing business. The more she got to know him, the more she realised what a good man he was. Adrian turned and caught her eye, smiling slightly.

Andrea tilted her head as she looked at Ellie and Adrian. 'So why *are* you here, Ellie?'

'I heard the music, I wanted to help these guys out,' Ellie replied, feeling her cheeks flush and kicking herself for it. Clearly Andrea thought something was going on between Ellie and her ex-husband.

Was the connection between them so obvious? Ellie realised she liked that thought.

Andrea turned her gaze to Adrian, but he ignored her.

'Now, let's all go back to bed,' he said, looking at his watch. 'I don't know about you, but I wouldn't mind getting a few more hours' sleep.'

Andrew yawned and nodded and they all headed back out into the darkness.

As they walked, Adrian joined Ellie. 'Well, that was fun.'

'Wasn't it just?'

He was quiet for a few moments then leaned in close, lowering his voice. 'So, I was thinking. Maybe we could go for a drink or something? No pressure!' he quickly added.

Ellie smiled. 'I'd like that.'

Adrian's face lit up. 'Are you free Friday night?'

Ellie nodded, trying to keep her cool. She was being asked out on a date! She couldn't *wait* to tell Vanessa. 'Friday's perfect,' she said. 'I'll have the kids, but Tyler can look after Zoe.'

'Great.' He looked towards Tommy and Graham who were strolling in front of them. 'How about we get out of Forest Grove. I can book somewhere nice in Ashbridge?' he asked hesitantly.

'Sounds fab.'

Adrian looked down at her feet and smiled and they continued walking, Ellie feeling Andrea's eyes drilling into her back every step of the way.

Chapter 13

Monday 19ᵗʰ July
10 a.m.

Pauline Sharpe

So come on then, what was that loud music about? Did the Facebook Vigilante strike again?

Tommy Mileham

Looks like it. And as we speak, Adrian should be talking to the culprit.

Andrew Blake

Suspected culprit, mate, nothing confirmed yet.

Lucy Cronin

Oooooh, do spill. Who is it?

Ed Piper

Best not to say until we know for sure. But what I will say is NICE ONE, Tommy, your plan worked.

Peter Mileham

Yep, good one, Dad. Miss having men like you in the police.

Pauline Sharpe

What plan are you talking about?

Andrew Blake

The oldest of tricks. Set a bait and snare the scum. Tommy's post about loud music playing had the intended outcome.

Rebecca Feine

Was that what you were doing with your post then, Tommy?

Tommy Mileham

Probably best not to say anything. But . . .

Pauline Sharpe

So that's a yes then. Clever, Tommy, very clever.

Myra Young

Is it clever? I'm sure I'll get shouted down for this, but after getting NO sleep most of last night (having already been up until two with the baby) I'm not impressed. Aren't you just winding up the Facebook Vigilante?

Rebecca Feine

I agree.

Kitty Fletcher

Me too.

Ed Piper

But we've caught the vigilante!

Kitty Fletcher

Have we though? I happen to know who you're referring to and he wasn't even in Forest Grove last night. So I'd hold on to your jubilation for now. The Facebook Vigilante is still out there somewhere.

Myra Young

And God knows what they'll do next. I feel like the attacks are getting worse and worse. I'm going to leave this group as I don't want to be a target.

Rebecca Feine

Maybe it's a good thing anyway? This village has always had an issue with people taking their moaning too far. I don't condone what this vigilante has been doing, but maybe I see their point. It's no coincidence they target people who make complaints. Not just any complaint either but, let's be honest, particularly rude ones. I was looking back at some of the posts of those targeted and they all had one thing in common: the authors of said posts took it a step too far. First Graham making that comment about deer. Then Belinda referring to the father who didn't pick up his dog's poo as having a 'snivelling baby' and 'spoilt brat'. Next Ed and his snootiness about recycling collectors. Finally, Tommy, baiting the vigilante and being rude with it. These are just examples of some of the vicious words spread about our very own neighbours. It's wrong, and this Facebook Vigilante has highlighted that.

Vanessa Shillingford

Well said, Rebecca. I *completely* agree (sorry, Dad).

Pauline Sharpe

Good riddance! Snowflakes, all of you!

Chapter 14

Friday 23rd July
6.30 p.m.

The rest of the week passed with no incidents and as Ellie applied her make-up for her date with Adrian on the Friday, whistling to an upbeat Adele track on the radio, she felt happy. She'd spent the day in Ashbridge getting a new outfit. It was difficult. What did people *wear* on dates nowadays? On the rare occasions she and Peter had gone out alone, he had liked her to wear dresses. Well, he had never said it outright: *Wear a dress, woman!* But she knew he liked it when she wore one, so she always got a new one. Things felt more natural with Adrian though. She felt more like *herself*, which meant in the end that she opted for a smart pair of jeans with a gorgeous white silk blouse.

She looked out at the swaying trees, the evening sun above casting them in an orange glow. It really had been a good week. No drama. Just working hard on the puzzle book, *not* seeing Peter (always a blessing) and a good gossip with Vanessa in the bakery and, one evening, the pub.

And now she was going on a date!

'There,' she said as she spritzed primer over her make-up. 'Perfect.'

She went to her wardrobe and pulled out her new outfit, putting it on before examining how she looked in her full-length mirror.

'You look pretty, Mum.' In the reflection, Ellie saw Zoe watching her. She turned to her daughter and smiled. She'd told the kids she was meeting some friends for dinner. She didn't want them to know yet about her and Adrian. She needed to ease them into the idea. Tyler had reluctantly agreed to stay in to watch over his sister.

'Thank you, darling.'

Zoe walked over and wrapped her arms around her mum's waist. Ellie suddenly got a flashback to doing the same with her mother. Her mother had been all dressed up in a lovely red dress, a little shorter than normal, but it suited her perfectly. It was a big night for Forest Grove, three years since the village had been built, and its first pub – the Neck of the Woods – had held a party to celebrate its grand opening. Ellie remembered thinking she had never seen her mother look so beautiful or so happy.

In fact, the more she thought about it, the more she realised that it was around then that her mother had started to change.

'You seem really happy,' Zoe said now.

'Well, that's because I am,' Ellie replied.

'Good,' Zoe said. 'You deserve to be happy.'

'Oh, darling! That is *so* sweet of you.' She put her hands on her daughter's slim shoulders and looked down at her. 'How about you? Are you happy?'

Zoe thought about it, then nodded. 'I think so.'

Ellie frowned. '*Think* so?'

'I was sad about you and Dad splitting up. And sometimes I think about it and get sad again.'

Ellie pouted. 'Oh, sweetie.'

'But it's fine!' Zoe replied, face lighting up. 'I feel better about it now. Plus, we get *double* the presents now.'

Ellie laughed. 'There *are* benefits, I suppose.'

'By the way, Mum,' Zoe added, biting her lip, 'I know you're going on a date.'

Ellie's face flushed.

'I can tell,' Zoe added. 'You went shopping today, I saw the receipt in the kitchen. And you look *super*-pretty, even more than normal. Is it Adrian, the policeman?'

Ellie didn't know what to say. She hadn't *wanted* to tell the kids! But Zoe was just too damn clever.

'It is,' she said softly.

To her surprise, Zoe's face lit up. 'Good. I like Adrian. He's really kind and nice. He'll make you happy, Mum.'

Ellie pursed her lips. She felt like crying! Instead, she gave her daughter a big hug. 'It's just a drink between friends, darling. But thank you.' She paused. 'Does your brother know I'm meeting with Adrian?'

'I think he does,' Zoe said with a shrug. 'He doesn't care though, you know what he's like.'

Ellie wasn't so sure from the way Tyler acted whenever she was with Adrian. She peered towards his shut bedroom door, the sound of keyboard tapping coming from within. Then she looked at her watch. 'Yikes. I'm supposed to be there in ten minutes.'

'Isn't Adrian coming to pick you up?'

Ellie laughed. 'It's not like a school prom, darling. We're past all that now. I'll be back by ten, okay? You can call or message if you need me. There's popcorn and Giant Buttons downstairs.'

'I'll be fine,' Zoe said. 'Just go!'

Ellie grabbed her bag. 'I'm off now, Tyler,' she shouted out, checking her lipstick in the mirror. 'Look after your sister!'

There was an indiscernible mumble from behind Tyler's bedroom door and Zoe rolled her eyes. 'I bet he doesn't even come out of his room all night 'cos he's preparing for the gig,' she said.

'Probably. But you *must* go and get him if you need him.'

'I won't need him. I'm planning a movie fest night, just me and Stanley, right?' she asked, patting the dog's head.

Ellie stroked her cheek, then jogged downstairs, grabbing her car keys and letting herself out. It was a glorious evening, not a cloud in the sky. Adrian had texted her to say he'd booked them a table on the veranda of one of the nicest pubs in Ashbridge. Her tummy tingled in excitement. A night out!

She was about to get into her car when her phone rang.

It was Adrian.

Is he cancelling? she thought, her heart sinking.

She tentatively put the phone to her ear. 'Hello?'

'You want the good news or the bad news?' he asked her.

'Erm, bad news?'

'I just saw on Facebook that the restaurant I booked has had a power cut. So no food.'

'Oh.' Ellie sighed. 'Did you book another? Please tell me that's the good news?'

'Look across the road.'

Ellie frowned and looked across the road to see Adrian watching her from beneath a nearby tree. He was carrying two heavy shopping bags and looked smart in blue jeans and a short-sleeved, patterned shirt.

She put her phone away and walked over. 'The good news is you're stalking me?' she asked.

'Who could blame me if I was,' he replied, looking her up and down. 'You look gorgeous.'

She blushed. 'Thank you. So, what's all this?' She pointed to the bags in his hands.

'This is the good news. I got all the ingredients needed to make my famous pancetta gnocchi. I saw you had beef at the pub the other day so I presume you're not a vegetarian?' Ellie nodded. '*And* I got us some wine, so we can walk to my house for dinner courtesy of *moi.*' He watched her expression. 'If you're okay with that? I'll even walk you back.'

Ellie smiled. She'd been looking forward to a nice night out, but now she was really warming to the idea of dinner at Adrian's. And he was right, she could have a couple of glasses of wine now that she wasn't driving. 'Sounds perfect.'

'Great,' Adrian said, looking relieved.

As they set off down the road, Ellie peered over her shoulder to see Tyler watching them from his bedroom window, a frown on his face. She lifted her hand and waved, but he didn't wave back.

Adrian's new house sat on the outskirts of the village, a small two-bed terrace – one of ten that had been built a few years back as part of an initiative to attract more first-time buyers into the village. They overlooked a park with a small pond. As Adrian let them in, his brown Labrador came running towards them, jumping up at Ellie's new jeans.

'Down, you little bugger!' Adrian said, gently pushing the dog away. 'Sorry, he really seems to like you.'

'I bet you say that to all the girls.'

'Yes, the whole zero girls I've had around here.'

Ellie smiled to herself. So she was the first to be invited back.

'This is nice,' she said, peering into a small living room with a log-burning fire. Yes, it was small, but it was ideal for Adrian and his son on the days he had him. And it was Adrian's. That was what she wished she had, a place to call her own. Maybe soon she would, if she actually found any time to properly look. Every time she did, some drama seemed to happen.

'Needs some updating,' he said, gesturing to some scuffs on the pale green walls. 'But other than that, it's in pretty good nick.'

He led her into a small kitchen-diner, a round, pine table next to French doors that looked out on to a long, narrow garden.

'It's perfect,' she said.

'Take a seat,' Adrian said, as he started pulling ingredients from his bag.

'Can I help?' she asked, sitting at the table.

'Not a chance. Wine?' he asked, producing a bottle of red wine from one of the bags.

'Lovely, thanks.'

He poured her a glass, then set about making their dinner.

'So did you manage to speak to Aaron?' Ellie asked him as she sipped her wine.

'Yep, this morning,' he replied. 'Him and his mum just got back from an overnight stay for a family wedding, so he definitely wouldn't have been responsible for the music.'

'Oh, yes, Sheila told me about that,' Ellie said. 'That's a relief. I like Aaron. He really is a sweet kid. I just can't see him doing this. So you're back to square one?'

'Not necessarily. We just need to figure out who was able to get hold of a key to the Forest Centre.'

'Did you see that comment Rebecca made in Tommy's Facebook group?' Ellie asked.

'Nope, I'm trying to avoid the bloody thing.'

'It's good this time.' She showed him the comment Rebecca had posted.

Adrian smiled. 'I like it. She has a point.'

'She does, doesn't she? I think she summed it up perfectly,' Ellie said, leaning back in her chair, 'how whoever is doing all this has held up a mirror to the community. Maybe people will think twice before spreading gossip and making disparaging comments.'

Adrian looked at her cynically as he chopped up some tomatoes. 'I'm not so sure.'

'Oh, come on, have some faith in our little community. I think we might see a bit of a change now.'

'I admire your optimism.'

'So you wouldn't call yourself an optimist?'

'My philosophy,' he said as he waved the knife in the air, 'is if you don't expect much, then you'll always be pleasantly surprised.'

'Oh,' Ellie said, raising an eyebrow, 'I'm not sure how to take that.'

'I wouldn't take it the wrong way. When it comes to you, I'm breaking my own rules. You're way out of my league.'

'That's nonsense!' Ellie declared. '*You're* out of *my* league! You're such a good person.'

'And you're not?'

She thought about it. 'Not always.'

'I think we can all say that about ourselves. I think it's the people who insist they're good who turn out to be dodgy.'

'You have someone in mind?'

He scraped the tomatoes into a pan with some garlic then went to the shopping bags, getting some pork out.

'Maybe,' he said. 'Take Andrea, for example.'

'Ah, the ex,' Ellie said, smiling as she sipped her drink.

'Sorry, am I talking about her too much?'

'No, no, it's fine, really. Carry on.'

'She is *so* obsessed with appearing like this perfect, do-good member of the village.'

'That sounds familiar,' Ellie said with a sigh.

'Peter?'

'Yep. Everyone here seems to think he's the Messiah, but he's always moaned about the very villagers he pretends to be friends with.'

'Yep, Andrea's the same. I mean, she likes the village itself, but any chance she could get, she'd be slagging people off, the very people she'd just been cooing over.'

Ellie laughed. 'Soooo familiar.'

Adrian popped the pork into a roasting tin, then placed it in the oven before taking a seat across from Ellie.

'You'll find this funny,' he said, taking a sip of his wine. 'You know Andrea put up all those "No Smoking" signs in the forest and people complained as they looked ugly?'

Ellie nodded. 'Oh yeah, it was after Fraser's campaign about the risk of forest fires from disposable barbecues?'

'Yeah, well, get this: Andrea smokes and I'd catch her sneaking into the woods at the back of our garden for a sneaky smoke most days.'

'No way! You know, I remember her smoking at school. I used to go around the side of the bike sheds – cliché or what! – with Vanessa when she smoked and would see Andrea there too. But I had no idea she *still* smoked. *What* a hypocrite. Is that why you split up? You got fed up with it all?'

'Partly.' His jaw clenched. 'Also, partly because Andrea got a little too close to the man she was working for.'

'Michael?'

Adrian nodded. 'She'll deny it, but I swear they were having an affair. I confronted her and she flipped, told me how awful I was to accuse her of such a thing and that, without trust, a marriage is pointless. That argument led to us agreeing to separate. The sad thing is, neither of us were that gutted. Andrea because, I suspect,

152

it freed her to be with her Prince Charming. Me because it freed me from being with her.'

'I wish I could say the same,' Ellie said, brow furrowing.

'You still love Peter?'

'God, no!' Ellie quickly said. 'I mean, I thought I did. When he told me he was leaving me for his old flame, I was devastated. But then it soon dawned on me how he was doing me a favour.'

'Did he admit to the affair?'

'Oh, it's been going on for years. I caught him a few years back and he promised he'd not go near her again. But he just couldn't resist.'

'And you caught them in the act again?'

'No.' Ellie felt tears spring to her eyes at the memory. 'He just told me out of the blue he wanted to be with her . . . for good.'

Adrian's hand slipped across the table, enclosing hers. 'Sorry, Ellie.'

Ellie forced a smile. 'Oh, it's fine. The memory hurts, but the fact he's gone doesn't hurt so much any more. I mean, at least he was honest this time. No denying the affair.'

'Unlike Andrea,' Adrian said, sighing.

'Michael is certainly an, erm, interesting character?'

'That's one word. Did you know . . .' He paused.

'What?' Ellie asked, leaning forward.

'I shouldn't really be saying this, but he was a bit of a troublemaker when he was a kid and was living in Ashbridge.' He grimaced. 'I checked his records in a moment of weakness, which is totally frowned upon.'

'What kind of trouble did he make?'

'Just a bit of vandalism. But it's just the way he makes out he's Mr Perfect, you know? I guess that's why they suit each other, two fakers.'

'Must be difficult living in the same village as them. At least Peter is out of sight most of the time.'

Adrian took another gulp of wine. 'Yep. Initially I was angry, humiliated even,' he said as Ellie nodded in sympathy, 'but now I just find them both annoying. It's a bloody pain bumping into my ex and her new bloke all the time.'

Ellie wrinkled her nose. 'That must be awful. I'd hate it if I bumped into Peter and Caitlin.'

Adrian examined her face. 'Have you met Caitlin?'

'A few times, many years ago. They knew each other when they were little, his first true love,' she added with an eye roll. 'She comes from money; her parents own a huge house outside Ashbridge. She loves her horses and a bit of shooting too. I mean, you couldn't get more different from me, really. She's a brunette, all curvy and sultry and rich.'

'Hey, don't downplay yourself. You're bloody gorgeous.'

She blushed. 'I don't know, I can't help but doubt myself.'

Adrian was quiet for a few moments. 'Can I ask you something?' he said softly.

'Of course.'

'Can I kiss you?'

Ellie's mouth dropped open in surprise.

Adrian blushed. 'Sorry, I—'

'Yes!' she shouted out.

He laughed and leaned across the table, pressing his lips against hers. She instantly responded, wrapping both arms around his neck and moving her lips against his.

Ellie's head swam. She was kissing a man who was *not* Peter! And it felt good. No, not just good, but better, tons better than it had ever been with Peter. It felt like a kiss for a kiss's sake, not something that was only initiated to lead to sex, as it always had been for Peter.

Relief and joy mixed with a deep yearning inside her as she wrapped her arms around his neck, kissing him even more urgently as she felt all the pent-up desire within her let loose, like a tightly wound-up ball of wool being unravelled.

Maybe, just maybe, this was the beginning of something?

The next evening Ellie walked to the Forest Centre with Zoe. Tyler was already there, doing last-minute tweaks for the gig. As they approached the centre, they were joined by other villagers, some of them waving a hello to Ellie. Events like this usually did attract most of the village. Other than the pub and restaurant, it was the only place where you could enjoy a few drinks without the worry of driving into Ashbridge, so most people saw events like this as a chance to have a good Saturday night out. It didn't matter that most of the adults there didn't really like the type of music being played. Enough wine or beer and it soon became just background noise.

As Ellie approached, she wondered if Adrian would be there already. She knew he was planning to go. Her tummy tingled at the thought of seeing him again, memories of their date making her smile. They'd eventually got around to eating dinner after a few more minutes kissing, then they'd resumed their kiss-fest in his living room. Though it had been so tempting to go upstairs too, she knew both of them weren't ready for that . . . especially Adrian, whose relationship with Andrea had started with a one-night stand. He didn't want to have history repeating itself.

'Mum, you can*not* stop smiling,' Zoe said as she looked at her mother.

Ellie's face flushed. She was embarrassed her daughter had caught her thinking about such things only months after Peter had walked out. But at least, finally, she felt as if life was coming together for her.

When they got to the Forest Centre, the entranceway was all lit up. People were handing over their tickets to volunteers standing at the doors into the main hallway. Loud rock music blared out from inside the hall in preparation for the live gig. Ellie could see some dazzling lights illuminating the darkness within and she felt a sense of pride. That was all down to her son too! Tyler had set them all up on his computer. She was so very proud of him – and of Zoe. Considering all they'd been through with their father, they were coping so well.

After handing their tickets over, they walked inside. It was already crowded, at least three hundred people dotted around the hall. It was a large space with glass windows which looked out on to the forest dominating two walls of the room. Forest artwork had been hung on the other walls. On the right, drinks and snacks were being served from a hatch into the kitchen. Ahead of them stood the stage with a set of purple drums at the back, a microphone in the middle, then Tyler's black guitar leaning against a stand next to it. A projector had been set up, the band's distinctive name – Pyro – appearing in purple graffiti scrawl across the wall behind the stage with flames curling out of it, something she knew Tyler had been working on.

Ellie's heart sank as she noticed Peter standing nearby, talking to Ed Piper. She knew he'd be there. The plan was for him to take the kids back with him that night.

She supposed not *everything* could be perfect.

She smiled tightly at Peter and he nodded back.

Zoe ran off to greet some friends and Ellie scoured the crowds for any sign of Adrian as she walked to the bar, joining the growing queue waiting to be served.

'Oh, hello, you,' a voice said.

It was Mr and Mrs Fake, Andrea and Michael. Carter was skulking nearby. It was hard to believe he was Adrian's son. While

Adrian was warm and open, Carter looked perpetually angry. But then Ellie supposed Tyler was much the same, all those teenage hormones raging through them.

'My love,' Michael said as he kissed Andrea on the cheek, 'let me find us a table. You talk to your lovely friend.'

Andrea smiled as he walked off. 'Isn't he just gorgeous?' she said with a sigh.

Ellie didn't say anything, just cringed.

'Strange to think we were all here in the dead of night the other night, isn't it?' Andrea asked.

'Hmmmm,' Ellie said non-committedly. She didn't want to get into a conversation about it.

'Turns out Aaron Leighton is *completely* innocent,' Andrea continued as they shuffled forward in the queue. 'But I'm hearing rumours that all is not lost. There's been a breakthrough in the case, supposedly.'

Ellie looked at Andrea in surprise. Adrian hadn't texted her to mention it. In fact, now she thought of it, he hadn't texted her all afternoon after the initial flurry of texts she'd got in the morning. 'Really?'

'That's what Carter told me,' Andrea said, gesturing to her son. 'She overheard Adrian on the phone.'

'Is Adrian here?' Ellie asked, looking around.

'Somewhere,' Andrea said, waving her hand about. 'So tell me, what's the deal with the two of you?'

'What do you mean?'

'I mean, clearly you have something going on with Adrian.'

Ellie's jaw tensed, her face flushing.

'Oh, come on,' Andrea said. 'Adrian and I are old news. You can tell me.'

'It's not up to me to say,' Ellie said tightly.

'Ah, so there it is, confirmation!'

Ellie didn't say anything, feeling increasingly awkward.

'Honestly,' Andrea continued, 'I'm fine with it. *I* dumped *him*, after all.'

So you could shack up with someone else, Ellie wanted to say.

'I'm sure the two of you will be better suited,' Andrea continued. 'You have the same outlook on life.'

'What outlook is that, then?' Ellie asked as she reached the front of the queue. 'A white wine, please,' she said to the person serving.

'Oh, you know, everything needs to be carefully thought through. I mean, I used to be like that, but then I met Michael,' Andrea said, giving a cheery wave to her new partner, who was watching them from a nearby table. 'He's brought out my true impulsive self! The new me would never have married someone like *Adrian*,' she said, wrinkling her nose.

'You mean a *loyal*, kind, generous man?' Ellie countered, annoyed as she paid for her drink. 'No, I can't see Adrian being suited to you either, Andrea.'

'Wow, defensive much,' Andrea said, looking around her and laughing as the people behind her watched.

Adrian suddenly appeared from the crowds then and Ellie sighed with relief. She went to walk towards him, but then noticed he wasn't smiling. In fact, he looked downright serious. He stopped in front of her, not even looking at his ex-wife.

'Everything okay?' Ellie asked.

'Can we go outside for a quick chat?' Adrian replied, voice solemn.

'Lovers' tiff,' she heard Andrea whisper to someone. But Ellie didn't care.

Something was wrong. Seriously wrong.

'Sure,' she said, her heart beating fast with worry.

She followed him through the hallway, checking to see that Zoe was okay. She was standing with her dad now, showing him something on her phone.

As they stepped outside, Ellie tried to read Adrian's face to figure out what was up.

'What's going on?'

'Aaron called me earlier. Sheila convinced him to tell me the truth after he confessed to her.' He took in a deep breath. 'Turns out *Tyler* got the key to the hall copied. And when I checked some doorbell camera footage from a house across the road from the centre, it shows Tyler walking by just after eleven that night. I think he might be the Facebook Vigilante, Ellie.'

Chapter 15

Ellie looked at Adrian in horror.

'No,' she said. 'No way is Tyler the vigilante.'

Adrian raked his fingers through his brown hair. 'Look, it was definitely him on camera. I've seen him wearing the same hoodie, the one with the skull on the back.'

Ellie's stomach turned as she imagined Tyler sneaking out in the dead of night, heading through the forest all alone with this prank in mind.

'I'd like to speak to him after his performance,' he said, looking towards the stage through the open door. 'I probably ought to do it officially, but I thought it might be better to do it casually? Just get a sense of what he's up to?'

'*I* know my son,' Ellie said vehemently. 'He would *not* do this.'

'We all *think* we know our kids, Ellie, but you said it yourself, boys this age are mysterious creatures. You can't blame me for wondering. Tyler's a clever kid, he knows his way around a computer. Plus . . .'

He hesitated.

'Plus what?' Ellie pushed.

'He's been through a lot lately.'

'What's that supposed to mean?' Ellie said, crossing her arms, feeling her heart beat rapidly against her wrists. 'You're referring to me and Peter breaking up, right? Well, Carter's been through it too. What if it's him? We all know what *he's* like.'

Adrian's eyes hardened.

Ellie realised she'd taken it too far. She closed her eyes, pinching the bridge of her nose.

'I'd better head back inside,' Adrian said. 'But I'll find Tyler after, okay?' He looked into her eyes, his own full of emotion. Then he walked away.

Ellie stayed outside for a few moments, taking deep, low breaths. It felt like she was spiralling, losing a grip on the ties of her life which she'd so carefully put back together lately.

No. She couldn't let herself spiral. She needed to find Tyler before Adrian did!

Ellie darted back inside and walked through the crowds, dashing to the area behind the stage where she knew Tyler would be. She found him with the two other band members – Aaron and Elvin, their drummer.

Tyler's face was lit up with energy and excitement, his eyes sparkling. Ellie felt like crying. He was so buzzed about his gig and now she was about to burst that bubble of happiness. But she needed to talk to him before Adrian did!

Tyler caught Ellie watching him from the door. 'Have you *seen* how busy it is out there, Mum?' he said, caught up in the wonder of it. 'The room is *buzzing*.'

'It's *so* busy, Tyler. You can tell it's sold out!' She peered over at his friends. 'Look, can we have a quiet chat?'

Tyler frowned. 'Now? We're on in twenty minutes, I need to get some stuff sorted.'

'I won't be long. It's important.'

'But—'

'Please? A quick chat.'

'O – okay,' he said hesitantly. He turned to his friends. 'Just need to help the old ma with something, be back in a mo.'

Ellie led Tyler out into the hallway to a side room and shut the door.

'What's up?' he asked, crossing his arms as he leaned against the wall.

Ellie took a deep breath. How was she going to put this? 'Do you have a key to this centre?' she asked.

Tyler's blue eyes blinked rapidly and he looked away. Ellie's stomach sank. He did that when he was nervous.

'That's a yes then,' Ellie said with a sigh. 'Did you have it copied?'

Tyler's jaw flexed. 'Yeah, saved me having to keep going to Aaron's to get it.'

'Were you here the night the music was played and woke the village up?'

Tyler looked down at his trainers.

'Tyler! Were you?' Ellie pushed. 'Did you turn that music on?'

He looked up at her. 'Yeah, I did. What's the big deal?'

Ellie sunk on to a nearby chair, putting her head in her hands. 'Oh, Tyler.'

'It's just music!'

She looked up at him, eyes filled with tears. 'But now Adrian knows. Aaron told him about the key and there's video footage of you.'

His face went white. 'What?'

'He wants to talk to you. He – he thinks you're the Facebook Vigilante.'

Tyler went very still, his eyes on Ellie's eyes. 'I'm not though, Mum, because – because *you're* the Facebook Vigilante.'

PART 2

Chapter 16

Ellie looked at her son, unable to quite process that he'd found out *she* was the Facebook Vigilante.

She hadn't *meant f*or anyone to find out. She'd been so *careful.*

'H–how do you know?' she whispered in a trembling voice.

'I saw you sneak out of the house that first time, after that nightmare you had. I couldn't get back to sleep, then I saw you go out so I followed you. I thought you might be sleepwalking or something. I couldn't believe it when I saw you take Graham's guns.'

Ellie put her hand to her mouth.

'It's okay, Mum!' he said. 'I'm cool with it. That's why I did the music thing. I wanted to help.'

She stood up, pacing the room. 'No, no, no! What have you *done*, Tyler?'

'But what about all the stuff *you* did?' he asked, looking confused.

She turned to him, heart thumping against her chest. 'I regret it all now. It got out of hand, especially after what happened with Pauline—' She took in a sharp breath as she thought of the blood on the leaf again. 'I realised I had to stop.'

'But this village deserves it,' Tyler spat. 'They're all idiots, it's good what you did.'

'Not when it ends up hurting people, Tyler! And I didn't do it all because of that. There was another reason, a—'

'What reason?' a voice asked. Tyler's eyed widened and Ellie turned to see Adrian watching them, his face ashen. He marched in and slammed the door shut. 'What the hell is going on here?' he asked as he looked at them in turn. 'You're saying *you* did all this, Ellie?'

'You heard all of that?' she asked, her voice a tremor.

It was all falling apart around her ears, but the worst part was the thought of Tyler getting into trouble . . . because of *her*!

'Not all of it, so you'd better explain,' he said, arms crossed as he looked at them both. 'So?'

Tyler went to open his mouth, but Ellie jumped in. 'I did it all. I'm the Facebook Vigilante.'

Adrian shook his head. 'No. You're lying to get Tyler off the hook, right?'

'No, I'm not lying. I did it all . . . including the music the other night.'

Tyler went to open his mouth, but Ellie put her hand up. 'Tyler was just confronting me.'

Adrian closed his eyes. 'I can't believe this.'

Tears started falling down Ellie's cheeks. Tyler looked pained, turning away. 'I know it sounds mad,' she said in a trembling voice. 'You *have* to let me explain.'

'What could possibly justify the things you did?' Adrian asked.

'My mum,' Ellie said. 'This place destroyed her. These people did.'

'Nan?' Tyler asked. 'I don't understand.'

Ellie turned to him. 'You know how your nan is.'

He nodded. 'She had a nervous breakdown.'

'Yes, and there was a reason. I never knew what that reason was. I'd been searching for the answer for years, but never found it. Until recently.'

Adrian got his phone out. 'I haven't got time for explanations, I need to report this.'

Ellie hurried up to him and put her hand on his arm. 'Please, Adrian,' she pleaded, 'just listen to me and then you can do what you want. *Please?*'

He thought about it for a few moments, then nodded. 'Fine.'

Ellie felt a sense of relief. At least he was willing to listen. She turned to Tyler. 'You need to go and get ready to head on stage.'

'But Mum!'

Ellie put her hand up. It was clear he was desperate to admit to the music prank, but she simply wouldn't allow him to be drawn into this. She gave him a stern look. 'Tyler, *listen* to me. Go and get ready. I will deal with this. I'll be fine, I promise.'

He hesitated for a moment, then turned to Adrian. 'Don't arrest my mum.'

Ellie's stomach sank. How awful to hear Tyler have to say that.

'I can't promise that, mate,' Adrian said softly.

Tyler's own eyes filled with tears. 'She's been through a lot. Hear her out. Please.'

'Okay,' Adrian said. 'I'll hear her out.'

Tyler nodded, then walked out the door. When he left, Ellie looked at Adrian, seeing the disappointment in his eyes, the shock and sadness. And she felt it all herself! There had been times in the past few days when she'd looked in the mirror and wondered what the hell she was doing. Especially when Pauline Sharpe got injured. She'd never meant to *hurt* people, just give Forest Grove a taste of its own medicine.

'Go on then,' Adrian said stiffly. 'I'm listening.'

Ellie swallowed, taking in a deep breath. 'A couple of weeks back, I was clearing through some boxes in the attic, getting ready for the move. I kept a few of Mum's things up there after she moved from her house to the retirement village. I thought I'd have a look at them, for old times' sake. In one box I found a bundle of letters, fifty of them.' She sighed. 'At first, I thought they were old love letters between Mum and Dad. They wrote hundreds back and forth as teenagers when they first started dating, passing them secretly to each other in class.' Ellie smiled up at Adrian. He didn't smile back.

'But when I read the first one, I knew they were not love letters,' Ellie continued. She got her phone out, finding the photo she'd taken of the first letter she had read. 'Here, see for yourself.'

Adrian took her phone and started reading the letter.

Dear Helen,

I saw you last night at the party in that tacky red dress, simpering around like a whore. All the wives know you're trying to steal their husbands, the way you walk around the village in your slutty dresses. In fact, I overheard some of the school mums this very morning gossiping about you, talking about what a floozy you are.

You think you look so beautiful, but the truth is, you just look like a whore with your red lipstick & clumpy eyelashes. Those dresses do you no favours, you know. Those calves of yours are like a bodybuilder's calves! Not to mention last night, I could see tyres of your flesh through that whoreish dress you wore. Have we been eating a bit too much cherry cake, my dear?

Maybe you should do us all a favour & tone
it down a bit?

Yours thoughtfully, A Concerned Villager

'Jesus,' Adrian whispered as he finished reading it.

'There are dozens more like it,' Ellie said. 'Fifty in all, the first
one from the 5th of March 1996, the last the 27th of August of
the same year. That meant my mum got two of those awful letters
every week for nearly six months.'

Ellie thought about that afternoon in the loft, reading through
those vicious letters that had been sent to her mother. As she'd read
them, one after the other, each worse than the next, she imagined
her poor mother doing the same twenty-five years ago. It all began
to make sense why her mother had changed so much! These letters
had drained the confidence and vivaciousness out of her.

And yet her mum had never told anyone. She had just read
them, then hid them away, each one eating away at her soul, chang-
ing her, day by day.

Adrian handed her phone back, quiet as he let it sink in. 'Okay,
so you find these letters and decide to take revenge on the residents
of Forest Grove on your mother's behalf? You blame an *entire* village
for the actions of *one* person?'

'That makes it sound too simplistic.'

'Isn't it?'

Ellie sighed. 'Whoever wrote those letters represents all the
worst elements of Forest Grove. Its *essence*, something that's been
built up over years. The judgemental, hypercritical, unforgiving
attitude of these people. Whether it's a letter,' she said, gesturing
to her phone, 'or comments in a Facebook group. These people
think it's fine to eat away at someone's soul with their nasty little
complaints.'

'Jesus, Ellie, we're all allowed to complain every now and again without fear or recrimination. And the stuff in the group is nothing like what was sent to your mother.'

'Isn't it?' Ellie asked, leaning forward. 'You'll notice the people I targeted took their comments a step too far and made it personal . . . just like this person did to my mum. Plus, you can't deny, they're the most likely culprits behind the poison pen letters sent to Mum. All vicious, all lived here since the letters were sent.'

'Ah,' Adrian said. 'So you were being a bit of a detective too.'

Ellie looked down at her clenched fists. 'Yes, I suppose.'

Of course, Ellie had tried to puzzle through who might have sent them. There were no clues on the envelopes and the paper used was standard white A5, the letters written in black biro. Though there were some distinguishing marks in the handwriting – like hearts used to dot the 'i's and 'j's, and the use of ampersands instead of 'and' – nothing led to the identity of the writer.

So she began to think about all the people who had lived in the village since 1996. Who had a habit of making people feel like crap? Who disliked her mother?

After seeing Graham Cane the day she caught him shooting with Peter, she couldn't stop wondering: could *he* have been behind the letters? He had argued with her mother all those years ago about the conifer in their garden, after all. Maybe he'd hoped to grind her down into submission by weakening her confidence? And then he'd caused her mother more pain by shooting his gun near the care home, scaring her.

So an idea had begun to formulate in Ellie's mind.

It was just a fun idea at first, not something she would act on. But then it formed into more than that. It was unlikely she would ever be able to track down her mother's faceless tormentor, but maybe there was another way she could avenge her?

172

And at first, it had felt like a game. Creeping to the forest at night, going to Graham's garden all ready with the bolt cutter Peter had left behind in the garage from the time he'd removed a wire fence at the back of their garden. She couldn't believe it when she found the guns propped up by the fence, not even locked away. She hadn't even needed the bolt cutter! She was even giggling to herself as she took them. Her heart was racing, the adrenaline pumping, and yes, a voice inside her had whispered how crazy this was, how *wrong*. But her anger at Graham's nastiness and the possibility that he could have written those poison pen letters to her mum had spurred her on.

'Why not stop with Graham if you thought he was behind the letters?' Adrian asked.

'I told myself I would. One little stunt to sate my desire for revenge. But when I took up the moderator role of the Facebook group, I began to get more of an insight into the community's members . . . and who else might have written those horrible letters. It began to dawn on me how Belinda had never liked Mum either. I remember them having a massive argument over Mum's book-club choice and began to wonder if it might be *her* behind the letters. So when she posted that awful comment about dog excrement, well, you know the rest.'

When Ellie had seen a furious Belinda striding through the pub garden that afternoon, the madness of what she'd done had finally hit her.

What if Belinda was actually heading towards her? What if she knew it was Ellie?

But then Belinda had walked straight to Adrian's table and Ellie could tell that people thought it was just what a woman like Belinda deserved. *Finally*, one of the village's nastiest busybodies had got their comeuppance, just like Graham had when his guns were taken.

'But you didn't stop with Belinda, either?'

Ellie avoided his hard gaze, ashamed. 'Ed's always been so rude and judgemental. When I saw that awful comment he'd posted about the recycling collectors, I suddenly remembered how he'd looked down on my mum and her car as he drove around the village in his flashy car. I began to ask myself, could Ed have been the poison pen writer? I – I thought somebody would stop me when I was rolling the bins to his lawn in the dead of night. Surely somebody would hear the sound of the wheels on the road and catch me in the act?'

'But they didn't.'

'No,' Ellie whispered. She began to think it was fate, not being caught. And then when Adrian called it 'artistic' later, it propelled her on. It *was* artistic! Artistic justice. She was like Banksy, using mild vandalism to make a serious point.

She got carried away. It became *more* than just vengeance for her mother.

'I suppose having Pauline Sharpe be outright rude to your mum was just too much to resist?' Adrian said.

Ellie sighed as she thought of that night at the pub when she'd realised that people she respected were full of praise for the Facebook Vigilante. Drunk on the wine and the respect, and still angry at the way Pauline Sharpe – one of the worst busybodies in Forest Grove – had made a dig at Ellie's mum, Ellie had snuck out again after getting home, using Peter's bike to pursue Pauline down the path. She'd lost control, though, and found herself almost crashing into Pauline, then riding off at top speed. She hadn't realised Pauline had fallen into the ditch.

'I barely remember it,' she admitted now. 'I didn't mean to hurt her, just spook her. I lost control of the bike and had no idea she had fallen into the ditch. I woke the next day with an awful feeling of regret. Honestly, Adrian, when I learnt Pauline was badly hurt, I was devastated.'

'So you decided to take a walk to the scene of the crime with me,' Adrian said, shaking his head. 'I guess Tommy was right, criminals do return to the scene of the crime.'

Ellie flinched at his use of the word 'criminal', but then she supposed he was right. She *was* a criminal.

'You were so insistent,' Ellie said in a quiet voice.

She'd told herself no more after that, but then Tyler decided to copy her. It made her realise she hadn't really taken into account the impact on her own family. She had been living in a dream of revenge and now she'd been jolted awake.

'Wow,' Adrian said, shaking his head. 'I just remembered the newspaper article. You said you wanted whoever was doing this caught . . . and it was you all along! The hypocrisy!'

Ellie felt her face flush with humiliation.

'And then the music?' Adrian asked.

She turned away, hoping her expression wouldn't reveal the truth. 'That was another impulsive move. Tommy wound me up.' She turned back to Adrian. 'Honestly, Adrian, I didn't *mean* this to spiral out of control like it did!'

'Well, it did! This isn't one of your puzzles,' Adrian said. 'This is real life, Ellie, with real consequences.'

'I know that now! I – I even returned Graham's guns!'

'He knows?'

Ellie shook her head. 'I just left them outside his shed.'

They were quiet for a few moments, standing silently in the small room.

'So what happens now?' Ellie asked eventually. 'Do you arrest me?'

Adrian's face flinched with pain. 'I have no choice, do I?'

Thoughts ran through Ellie's mind: what would the kids think? They'd be so ashamed! What would *Peter* say? He'd think she'd gone off the rails.

Maybe she had.

Maybe she was having a nervous breakdown of sorts, like her mum had? A delayed effect of having her husband walk out on her and losing the perfect marriage she'd dreamed of.

Her heart started thumping painfully against her chest, tears stinging her eyes. If Peter found out, would he ask for full custody of the kids?

'Will you wait until after the gig?' Ellie asked. 'I know Tyler will be so worried if he doesn't see me in the crowds he won't be able to focus.'

Adrian sighed heavily. 'Okay.' He looked at his watch. 'We'd better go now then.'

They headed back to the hall in silence. She saw Peter watching the performance from the other side of the room, now joined by Tommy and Meghan, who were chatting to Zoe. They were just in time because the music that had been playing turned off, the lights dimming. The drummer was the first to walk on stage, cheers going out as she raised her arm. As she took her seat behind the drums, Tyler appeared at the side. His eyes searched the audience, a hint of worry on his face. He was wearing a black T-shirt with an eagle made of white smoke on it over skinny purple trousers. His blue eyes, which were circled in black kohl, scanned the room for his mother, filled with anxiety. Then he spotted Ellie. She smiled, gave him a thumbs up, and he seemed visibly relieved. He straightened his shoulders and strode on to the stage, picking up his guitar as more cheers went up. He looked so confident up there. Ellie felt a burst of pride, which was quickly followed by abject horror at how she'd risked his freedom . . . and at the consequences she was about to face.

But right now, she needed to be there for Tyler. She swallowed her torment and focused on the stage.

The lights went even lower and the room fell silent as Tyler began strumming a low, hypnotic beat out on his guitar. The drummer behind him joined in. Slowly, surely, the music got faster and the atmosphere around them turned electric.

'Tyler looks great up there, Ellie,' a voice said. Ellie turned to see it was Sheila.

'He does, doesn't he?' she replied, aware that Sheila knew about Tyler copying the key.

'Oh, is that your son up there?' another person asked, interrupting them. 'He really looks the part.'

Ellie forced a smile. 'He sure does.'

Any other time, Ellie would be buzzing. But all she could think about was what a mess she'd made of everything. The idea of Tyler being arrested filled her with horror. Her darling boy, born two weeks early, so keen to see the world. He'd always been so independent compared to Zoe, running into nursery without a backward glance, while Zoe would cling on to her mother. Ellie had always felt like Tyler didn't really *need* her.

But as she watched him, she knew she'd let him down when he'd needed her the most.

Aaron strutted on stage then and Sheila jumped up and down, clapping, as Ellie smiled at her. 'That's my grandson!' Sheila shouted.

Ellie watched the rest of the gig in silent sorrow. Near the end, she noticed Vanessa approaching, weaving her way through the crowds, looking slightly stressed. Her long red hair was up in a high ponytail, a patterned green headband and gold hoop earrings complementing her colouring. She was wearing a green jumpsuit and black sandals. She spotted Ellie and waved. She leaned down to her kids, pointing in the direction of their cousin and grandparents. The kids ran over and Vanessa walked towards Ellie.

'So bloody late,' Vanessa said when she got to her. She peered at the stage, smiling. 'Look at Tyler. I can't believe he weed in my shoes once when I was looking after him.'

Ellie tried to laugh, but she just couldn't muster it and let out a small sob. Vanessa frowned. 'What's going on? Is it my arsehole of a brother again?' she said, glaring at Peter.

'It's nothing. I'll explain later.' Ellie could see Peter watching her from the other side of the room.

'Mum!' Zoe said as she ran over. 'How cool does Tyler look?'

'He does, doesn't he?' Ellie replied, forcing herself to smile as Vanessa cast her worried glances. She pulled Zoe close, imagining what she would say if – no, when – she found out that her mum was the Facebook Vigilante.

When the gig finished and Zoe was pulled away by some friends, Vanessa grabbed Ellie's arm. 'You and me, outside now.'

Ellie searched the crowds for Adrian, finding him leaning against a wall, nursing a beer and looking miserable. She was supposed to talk to him after the gig. But Vanessa was already pulling her through the crowds and outside towards a quiet area around the side of the Forest Centre where there was a small bench.

'Sit,' Vanessa commanded.

Ellie did as she asked and Vanessa sat next to her, turning to look at her. 'What's going on?' Ellie couldn't help it; she burst into tears. 'Oh my God, it must be bad.' Vanessa silently hugged her friend, knowing she just needed to let it all out.

Finally, Ellie managed to control her tears, gulping in quick bursts of air. Then she took in a deep breath, putting her head on her best friend's shoulder.

'Tell me everything,' Vanessa said.

Should she tell Vanessa everything? They had never kept secrets from each other before. But then she thought of Adrian's disappointment. Would Vanessa feel the same? And then, what? She'd lose her best friend too.

But Vanessa wasn't Adrian. She knew this village and how horrible it could be. She knew Ellie!

So Ellie wiped her tears away and took a deep breath.

'I'm the Facebook Vigilante,' she said.

'Ha-ha, very funny.'

'I'm serious.'

At first, Vanessa looked shocked. Then a huge smile spread across her face. 'That. Is. Amazing.'

'No, Ness, it's bad.'

'Why? Nobody got hurt. It's about time someone shone a light on this rotten place.'

'Pauline got hurt.'

'Boo-hoo, a little arm sprain.' Vanessa grabbed Ellie's hands, eyes shining with excitement. 'I can't believe it! You did it all? The guns? The poo? The bins? The loud music?'

Ellie hesitated for a moment. No, she couldn't tell Vanessa about Tyler. She couldn't tell anyone. 'Everything,' Ellie lied.

'I can't believe you didn't tell me. I would have *gladly* helped!' Vanessa's face grew serious. 'Oh, shit. Have you been caught? Is that why you're crying?'

Ellie nodded. 'I just told Adrian.'

'No way! Why would you do that, you fool?'

'Long story.'

'So, what, is – is he going to *arrest* you?'

'I think so. He – he said we'd talk about it after Tyler's performance.'

Vanessa shook her head vehemently, her ponytail shimmying around her shoulders. 'He won't do it. He's *crazy* about you. I can just tell from the way he looks at you.'

Ellie laughed bitterly. 'Not any more.'

Vanessa was quiet for a few moments. 'Well, I'm sure he won't arrest you. He knows you won't do it again, right?'

'No, Ness, this is serious. I committed a crime. *Crimes.* He's a police officer, he has a duty to arrest me.'

Vanessa stood up. 'I'll talk to him.'

Ellie grabbed her friend's hand. 'No, please, just sit here a bit.'

Vanessa sighed and sat back down. She examined Ellie's face. 'Why did you do it, hon? I mean, I get the reasons. But what triggered it?'

Ellie told Vanessa all about the poison pen letters she'd found in the attic. 'I think that's why Mum had her nervous breakdown in the end. Getting those letters every week just tipped her over the edge.'

'I'm not surprised,' Vanessa said, peering out towards the forest. 'This place can tip anyone over the edge.'

There was the sound of footsteps and they both looked up to see Adrian turning the corner. He took one look at Vanessa and sighed. 'Don't tell me, you've known all along?'

'No!' Ellie said quickly. 'I've only just told her.'

She wiped away her tears and Adrian flinched.

'You can see how sorry she is,' Vanessa said. 'You can't arrest her, for God's sake, Adrian.'

Adrian's hands curled into fists. 'I have no choice. I won't make a big deal of it. We'll just go to the station together in my car, as long as the kids are staying with Peter tonight?' Ellie nodded miserably. 'It's unlikely you'll have to stay overnight or anything. I'll just be questioning you with a colleague, then you can go home.'

'Interrogating her, more like,' Vanessa huffed.

'Ness, don't,' Ellie said.

'Come on, Adrian, you don't seem like the kind of guy who'd lock someone up over a few little pranks.'

'They weren't little pranks, Vanessa,' Adrian said. 'Someone got hurt.'

'You know Pauline sprained her arm, right? She didn't break it, like she tells anyone who'll listen. Ellie didn't actually do it. It was an accident. She never could ride a bicycle.'

Adrian shook his head, standing his ground. 'Pauline was still hurt. There have to be consequences for what Ellie did.'

'It isn't like she – she burnt down the forest or something,' Vanessa said, gesturing to the forest. 'She's made her point now, it's over. Like Rebecca said in Dad's group the other day, she was brave enough to hold up a mirror to Forest Grove. To some, she might be seen as a *hero*!'

Ellie shook her head. 'Vanessa, I know what you're trying to do, but I'm no hero, I'm – I'm a criminal.' She looked up at Adrian. She really was a criminal, as much as it pained her to admit it. It had taken the disappointment in Adrian's eyes to make her see her actions for what they really were: reckless acts of vandalism that had consequences. 'Adrian's right, there needs to be consequences.'

Vanessa was quiet for a few moments. 'What if Ellie agreed to get help? See a therapist?'

Adrian frowned.

'Think about it,' Vanessa said. 'You've been through a marriage break-up, you know how it messes with your head. Ellie's been through the same, and trust me when I say my brother is the king of all arseholes. Ellie is a good person, really good. Better than me, that's for sure!' she added with a bitter laugh. 'This is completely out of character, you know that. You deal with scumbags all the time, Adrian. Is Ellie a scumbag? Does she deserve to be raked over the coals for this? Do Zoe and Tyler deserve to endure their mother being arrested on top of going through the trauma of their parents separating?'

Ellie watched Adrian's face. He wasn't protesting, he was actually listening. Maybe Vanessa had a point? And maybe this was a way out of being arrested . . . a way to ensure nobody else found out.

More importantly, a way to ensure Peter didn't find out and try to take the kids.

'I can book an appointment with Kitty Fletcher,' Ellie quickly said. 'I hear she's pretty good when it comes to the whole therapy thing. What if I tried that first, show willing to change?'

Adrian sighed. 'Ellie, I—'

'I *know* you're risking your neck,' Ellie said, feeling desperate now at the thought of Peter taking the kids from her. 'But just one last chance?'

Adrian went silent and Ellie held her breath. Then he slowly nodded. 'I can't believe I'm doing this. Fine, make an appointment with Kitty Fletcher. But if there is any little hint of another prank, you're coming to the station with me.'

Ellie let out a breath of relief.

'You're doing the right thing,' Vanessa said. 'I'll keep an eye on her, even bloody move in with her if I have to.'

Adrian kept his eyes on Ellie. 'Do you realise how much I'm risking?'

'She's worth it,' Vanessa said.

'Thank you,' Ellie whispered. 'Thank you *so* much.'

She went to put her hand on his arm, but he stepped away, turning his face from her. Then he walked into the forest, heading home.

Vanessa put her hand on Ellie's shoulder. 'He needs time. What he just did for you shows how much he likes you.'

'No,' Ellie said, shaking her head. She knew any chance she had of a relationship with the kindest, most genuine man she'd ever met was gone.

But at least he wasn't going to arrest her . . . yet.

Ellie climbed into bed when she got back, thinking she felt exhausted enough to sleep. But every time she closed her eyes, she saw Adrian's face and the deep disappointment on it.

Maybe she did catch an hour or so, but when she rose the next day, she felt as though she'd been run over by a tank. After getting dressed, she sat in the kitchen, looking out at the forest, coffee in her hands.

'What now?' she asked the empty room.

One thing she knew was that she needed to book an appointment with Kitty Fletcher. So she picked up the phone, managing to get one for the end of the week.

Over the next couple of days, while the kids were with Peter, Ellie took the chance to hide away. She had lots of work on anyway with the puzzle book, so she threw herself into it, burying her troubles in clues, letters and lines. In the evenings, she continued her search for a house, requesting viewings for two small but lovely cottages in Firdean.

Each time her mind wandered to the whys of what she had done she pushed them away. She could explore all of that with Kitty. For now, she just needed to rest her mind and get herself into the right headspace to be with the kids from Wednesday evening.

On Wednesday morning, she made herself go through her usual routine of applying make-up, carefully choosing her outfit. When she heard the kids' voices as they let themselves into the house after school, she felt a sense of relief. As awful as she felt, she *had* saved Tyler from being arrested. She'd managed to talk briefly to Tyler before she left the Forest Centre and his relief when he heard Adrian wasn't going to arrest her was palpable. Adrian had given her a golden opportunity to truly get on with her life – *their* lives – away from Forest Grove.

Ellie made her promise to herself: no more drama.

Chapter 17

*Wednesday 28th July
5 p.m.*

Andrea Simpson

Why oh why can't people keep their firework parties to 5th November? My poor darling cats were terrified by the fireworks last night. Why is every single little opportunity an excuse to let off those godawful things?

Rebecca Feine

It was for Nero's fiftieth birthday. We could see them from the bedroom window, I bet the kids loved it.

Meghan Mileham

Yes, it was, and a lovely party it was too!
Kitty Fletcher

Yes, fabulous party for a lovely couple (though I do worry about the carbon footprint of fireworks).

Graham Cane

Andrea is right. The things should be bloody banned!

Nero Patel

Says the man who shoots his guns off at every opportunity! And yes, I did post about it, warning people, a few weeks back.

Andrew Blake

You don't have to apologise, mate. My hounds are fine with fireworks. Your dogs can probably sense your paranoia, Andrea.

Lucy Cronin

It was just a couple of fireworks, turn your TV up!

Pauline Sharpe

It's not a case of simply turning the telly up, Lucy! It sounded like WW3 had begun last night, our cats were hiding under the sofa and trembling. They need to ban the sale of fireworks at any time other than the first week of November.

Andrea Simpson

Completely agree! Actually, why not ban them all together? A simple bonfire will suffice on bonfire night . . . I mean, isn't that why it's called that?

Rebecca Feine

Oh, so kids miss out on seeing fireworks? Don't be silly, Andrea. You do know it's perfectly fine to let them off during legal hours, which was when last night's display was.

Myra Young

Uh-oh. Be careful, you guys, the Facebook Vigilante might be reading this . . .

Andrea Simpson

I don't care about the Facebook Vigilante. I have a right to express my views!

Andrew Blake

Famous last words . . .

Chapter 18

Ellie was having the same dream she had been having most nights ever since she found the poison pen letters addressed to her mother, of her mother at her dressing table, the letters scattered around her, her hair shorn off. This time was different though. There was the sound of sirens in the distance.

Then Ellie realised the sirens were actually real, piercing the usually silent night.

She sat up in bed, heart thumping.

'Mum?'

Ellie looked towards her door. Tyler was standing there, his pale face lit up in the dark by the phone he was holding. She looked at her clock. Just past 2 a.m.

'What's up? Is everything okay?' she asked.

'Carter's mum's house is on fire! I can see it from my room.'

Andrea! She thought of Andrea's post in the Facebook group the day before.

No, surely not . . .

She jumped out of bed, her heart thumping as she went to the window. She opened the curtains and saw orange flames leaping into the night sky in the distance.

Ellie felt panic flutter inside. What if it was an act of arson? People would surely think this was the Facebook Vigilante at work.

'They'll think it's the Facebook Vigilante,' Tyler said quietly, as though reading her thoughts.

'It wasn't me,' she whispered back.

'Not me either.'

Ellie sighed. What a situation she'd dragged him into. 'I know you'd never do something like that. Get back to bed, okay, darling?' she said. 'I'm sure Carter will be okay, the fire engines are there. Can't you hear them?'

Tyler nodded and walked out, his eyes on his phone. Ellie grabbed her own phone and sat at the end of her bed, hesitating for a moment before quickly typing a message to Adrian: *I can see flames from Andrea's house. I hope they're okay.*

She waited for a reply, but there was none.

She walked to the window again, seeing an arc of water appear over Andrea's house. It didn't look like such a big fire; it seemed to be at the front of the house. The flames jumped and danced at first, but were eventually beaten back until all that remained of the blaze were small, orange sparks rising up into the coal-black night sky.

The smell of smoke seeped through her window and Ellie banged it shut, leaning against the wall as panic began to overwhelm her. If it was anything but an easily explained accident, this could be really bad for her.

She went on to Facebook and found Tommy's group. There were no posts about the fire . . . but Andrea *had* made a post about fireworks. Panic rose inside Ellie. If there was any evidence this fire was related to Andrea's post, Adrian would naturally assume Ellie had done it, wouldn't he?

And also . . . if it *was* connected to Andrea's Facebook post, who on earth *was* responsible if it wasn't her or Tyler?

She sat on her bed for an hour, thoughts whirring through her mind. When her phone buzzed, she jumped in surprise. It was Adrian calling. She put her phone to her ear. 'Adrian, I—'

'I'm outside your house.'

She frowned, looking at the time. Three in the morning!

She got up and put her dressing gown on, quietly going downstairs and opening the front door to find Adrian standing beneath the lamp light. His face was grey with ash, his hair thick with cinders.

'Is everyone okay?' she asked quickly.

'How could you do this?' he asked, his brown eyes wild with anger.

'Adrian, I swear to you, I did *not* do it!'

'Carter was in there. You could have killed my son!'

'Oh God, is he hurt?'

'No, but Michael has been taken to hospital for smoke inhalation.'

'W–what happened? How did the fire start?'

Adrian took in a breath, eyes closing. When he opened them again, they were cold and hard. 'It started because you put a firework through the letterbox, Ellie. And all because Andrea posted a complaint about fireworks in the Facebook group,' Adrian continued. 'You could have killed my son!' he said again.

Ellie took a breath. She was crying now, tears running down her face; confused and terrified about what this might mean for her . . . for the kids.

She needed to be careful how she handled this. 'I completely get why you'd think it was me,' she said as calmly as she could. 'It was my first thought – that you would think that. But I swear to you, on my children's lives, I had nothing – *nothing* – to do with this! Look at the stuff I did before,' she said, lowering her voice. 'This is in a totally different league!'

He didn't look convinced.

She raked her fingers through her hair, wracking her brains about how she could prove it. 'I've been here all night, with the kids. I haven't left the house. You have to believe me.'

'I'm finding that very, very difficult, considering you're my only suspect.'

'But I'm not responsible for this!' Ellie cried, not caring now if the neighbours heard. 'You have to catch who's doing this.'

'You did this, Ellie. I know you did. Why lie to me?' He put his phone to his ear. 'I'm sorry, Ellie, I really am. You clearly need help. I have to report this.'

Ellie leaned against the wall, her face in her hands. She couldn't blame him. And anyway, maybe this *was* all her fault in some way. She'd started this, after all.

Then something occurred to her. She grabbed his arm, making him almost drop his phone.

'You *mustn't* get involved,' she said quickly. 'I'll go to the station first thing in the morning.'

He paused.

'Think about it, Adrian, you didn't report me to the police, did you? That would get you in trouble, right? If I go to the station in the morning and just tell them everything – minus the bit about telling you – then it's all laid out on the table.'

He blinked, obviously torn. 'I can't lie.'

'You don't have to. It's not like anyone's going to ask if you knew. You *know* it makes sense,' she pushed. 'You can't risk your career for this.'

He considered it for a moment then nodded. 'If I don't hear you've gone in by ten, then I'll report you myself.'

Ellie let out a breath of relief. She really didn't want him to get into trouble. She watched as he walked away, then looked in the direction of Ashbridge, where the police station was.

It was time to confess . . . officially.

Chapter 19

Ellie sat in Ashbridge Police Station, trying her best to hold herself together. She had passed the large concrete building hundreds of times, whenever she drove into town for shopping or to pick the kids up from some club or another, but she had never been inside before.

She folded her hands into her lap, clenching them to stop them from shaking. She felt cold, despite the heat outside, the hairs on her arms standing up. She'd thought carefully about what to wear that morning and had eventually decided on jeans with a blouse and blazer, all navy. There was nothing to be done about her skin, which had taken on an ashen appearance.

'Fear,' she'd said to herself as she applied her make-up. 'That colour is your fear.'

And she *was* scared. Terrified, to be more accurate, of talking to the police and the consequences. But she knew she had to do it. It had all finally caught up with her. How foolish she'd been to think she'd get away with it. The irony was that it was someone else's actions that had brought her here . . . and put a man in hospital.

'Mrs Mileham?' a voice said. Ellie looked up to see a young, slim, dark woman watching her with a stern expression.

'Yes, that's me,' Ellie said in a shaky voice as she stood up. 'Well, I'm actually Miss Nash now, if that's okay? My husband and I are no longer together.'

'Fine. I'm Detective Powell,' the woman said in clipped tones. 'Come through.'

Ellie followed her down a long corridor until they got to a small room with a table and several chairs around it.

'Please sit,' the detective said, gesturing to a chair.

Ellie sat down as the detective took the seat across from her.

'So you have some information about the fire in Forest Grove?' the detective said, looking down at her notepad.

'Not specifically the fire itself. But I have . . . I have some background.' She paused for a moment to compose herself. 'You see, I've made some mistakes lately and I think they might have led to what happened last night.'

The detective peered up, dark eyes intrigued. 'Okay. Tell me more.'

Ellie took a deep breath, tears filling her eyes.

Hold it together, Ellie, she told herself.

'I guess you could call them pranks,' she said, repeating what she'd practised in front of the mirror that morning. She didn't want to refer to them as 'vigilante acts' or 'vandalism', as that made them sound illegal. 'Pranks' felt more . . . innocent. Even ridiculous.

'What kind of pranks?' the detective asked.

'A local man scared people in the retirement village by shooting his guns in his garden so I – I found the guns in his garden and hid them in the forest.'

'What is this man's name?'

'Graham Cane. I put the guns back though!' Ellie said, leaning forward and watching as the detective wrote his name in her book. 'Then I put dog poo in a bag through the letterbox of a resident called Belinda Bell who complained about someone not picking up their dog's mess on the local Facebook group.'

Ellie felt so embarrassed as she said it.

The detective sighed. 'I see.'

'And then a neighbour of mine moaned about the green bins not being collected and criticised the recycling collectors too. So I lined up all the green bins from our street on his lawn.'

'That must have taken some doing?'

'I suppose. And then a woman complained about cyclists on paths so I cycled along her path to annoy her. That went wrong and – and after I saw her I rode off so I wasn't aware she fell over and hurt herself.'

The detective raised an eyebrow. 'And what did you hope to achieve by doing all this?'

'My mum received some awful letters. I recently found them. They led to her having a nervous breakdown.'

'How does this relate to the criminal acts you committed?'

Ellie flinched at her use of that phrase. 'The people who were the targets of these pranks were exactly the kind of people who might have targeted my mum.'

'So, what, this was some kind of revenge act? Why so many suspects?'

'I suppose it all got a bit out of control. It became more about Forest Grove as a whole, I guess.' She examined the detective's face. 'I don't know whether you know Forest Grove very well.'

'Unfortunately, I do,' the detective said with a sigh. 'I was involved with the Patrick Byatt case.'

'Oh. Wow, that was . . . well, this is completely different, of course,' Ellie said with a nervous laugh.

The detective didn't even raise a smile. 'I didn't say it was the same.'

'Right, of course. So,' Ellie continued, 'in many ways, it's a wonderful place to live. But it can be very claustrophobic too. People like to poke their noses into everyone else's business. Not just that, they like to judge and gossip. This is amplified in the community Facebook group. So it began to be about teaching certain villagers a lesson. Holding a mirror up to their true selves. But they were all harmless pranks really.'

'A sprained arm isn't so harmless though, is it, Miss Nash? Stealing someone's guns isn't, either.'

'I didn't intend for Pauline to get hurt,' Ellie replied in a small voice. 'And I didn't steal Graham's guns, they were in an unlocked shed and I did return them after hiding them in my garage!'

The detective sighed, leaning back in her chair as she examined Ellie's face. Ellie wondered what she saw: a respectable, middle-class woman with a life so pathetic she had resorted to pulling pranks on her neighbours?

Ellie suddenly very much didn't want this young, stern-looking detective to think that of her.

'I'm a good person, honestly,' she said. 'I went through a horrible divorce and—'

'That's irrelevant,' the detective said quickly. 'Now, on to the more recent event where Andrea Simpson had a lit firework shoved through her letterbox. Did you want to teach her a lesson too?' the detective asked, eyes drilling into Ellie's.

Ellie swallowed uncomfortably. 'That wasn't me, I *swear* to you.'

'But surely you see there is an escalating pattern of behaviour here, from the more trivial to the more serious?'

'Of course, I understand how it must look. But there is absolutely no way, no way at all, that I would do *anything* as dangerous as posting a firework through a letterbox.'

The detective tilted her head to the side, eyes narrowing. 'Maybe you didn't think it through properly, like when you caused Pauline Sharpe to fall over when you cycled into her?' she suggested.

'But I didn't know she had!' Ellie objected.

The detective ignored her. 'Maybe you didn't expect the front porch to catch on fire and a man to end up in hospital with smoke inhalation?'

Ellie felt panic tremor through her. The detective clearly thought Ellie was responsible for the firework incident.

She could be arrested for arson! For actual bodily harm, even attempted murder!

'I didn't do that. Is – is Michael okay?'

'He was released this morning, he'll be fine.'

Ellie let out a sigh of relief.

'Can you prove where you were last night?' the detective asked her.

'I was in bed, sleeping. I have two kids, but they were sleeping too. Can't you track my phone?'

'That's difficult in a rural area like Forest Grove. There are two masts, but if you live in the same mast area as where the fire was . . .'

'I probably do,' Ellie said with a sigh. 'I don't know what to suggest then, other than my word. I *didn't* do it.'

The detective thought about it, then stood up. 'Wait here a moment.'

Then she left the room.

Ellie sat in the empty room for several minutes, the four walls seeming to press into her.

She was going to be arrested for the fire, she just knew it.

'The kids,' she whispered. 'Oh God, the kids.'

Peter would definitely try to get full custody of them. She'd lose them!

Finally, the door opened again and the detective walked in with a file in her hands. 'Stand up for a second,' she said.

Ellie stood on trembling legs. Was this it? Was she about to be arrested?

Detective Powell looked her up and down, then opened the file, staring at whatever was in there, before looking at Ellie again.

'You're too slim, a little too short too,' she said.

'Excuse me?'

'We have footage from a doorbell camera across the road from Andrea Simpson's of the person who put the firework through the letterbox. It's clearly not you.'

Ellie sunk to the chair, putting her head in her hands as she let out a sigh of relief. The detective sat back down across from her, gesturing to the photo that was now between them. 'Any thoughts of who it might be?'

Ellie looked at the photo. It was blurry, a fleeting glance of a figure dressed all in black. 'I have no idea.'

'Fine. Well, on this occasion, I'm going to give you a caution. No more pranks, okay? Or, as we tend to refer to them, acts of *vandalism and theft*.'

Ellie quickly nodded her head. Was she really being let off?

'Any little hint of anything else like this from you,' the detective continued, 'and you *will* be arrested, which will, frankly, annoy me, as we are way too busy at the moment for yet more drama in Forest Grove.'

'Understood.' Ellie paused. 'You *will* be investigating this, though? You said you're busy. But we need to find out who did that with the firework.'

'*I* need to find out.' Detective Powell sighed. 'I'll confess, it won't be top of the pile, but it's *on* the pile and that's what matters.'

She stood and opened the door. Ellie got up and walked towards it.

'You were good to come forward,' the detective said. 'You'll feel better now you've got that weight off your chest. And I do understand about the divorce thing.'

Her dark eyes softened and Ellie almost noticed a hint of sympathy in her eyes. Then the stern look returned to her face and Detective Powell led Ellie out of the station.

The next morning, Ellie decided to visit her mother before going for her first therapy session with Kitty. As she waited for the receptionist to return from a toilet break and let her into the retirement village, she checked her messages. She'd texted Adrian the day before to tell him she'd gone to the police and they'd ruled her out of being behind the firework. She'd also asked how Carter was after what he'd endured, Andrea and Michael too. Plus, she mentioned she was seeing Kitty that day.

But she hadn't got a response. She shouldn't be surprised really.

The receptionist came out and buzzed Ellie through. When she got to her mother's room, her mother was watching something on TV. It was more like an open-plan suite than a room, with its own small kitchen and living room with a separate bathroom. It even had a balcony overlooking the gardens.

'Mum, we need to talk about the horrible letters you got all those years back.'

Her mother frowned slightly. 'You know?'

'Yes, I found them.'

Her mother turned her face away, pursing her lips. 'It was years ago. It wasn't just me anyway.'

Ellie frowned. 'Other people got letters?'

'Lots did. Don't you worry about it, though. It doesn't matter. They opened my eyes, helped me.'

'*Helped* you? Mum, don't be silly. They're utter rubbish. The person who wrote those letters was a spiteful, pathetic person desperate for attention. It was a misplaced attempt to—'

Ellie paused.

A misplaced attempt to hold a mirror up.

Just like she had done.

She looked at her mother, who was chewing her lip anxiously, and suddenly she felt a huge wave of guilt. Ellie had thought she was getting her revenge on the poison pen writer but, in the end, how was she any different? Her actions had created an atmosphere of fear, just like the poison pen letters had. Ellie had convinced herself that her mother would approve – that she'd want revenge on Forest Grove – when, in reality, she would have been appalled.

'You're crying,' her mum whispered, putting her fingers to Ellie's face.

Ellie hadn't even realised she'd been crying. She quickly went to wipe her tears away, but her mother opened her arms. 'Come here.'

Ellie sank into her mother's arms. It had been so long since her mother had embraced her. Over the years, her mother had withdrawn so much into herself she rarely showed affection. But now here she was, somehow sensing Ellie needed her more than she ever had.

She peered up at the clock. 'Oh, Mum,' she said, wiping the tears from her face. 'I really need to go, I have an appointment.'

'You go, love,' her mum said, turning back to the TV.

Ellie gave her a quick kiss, then headed out. As she stepped outside, she saw Meghan approaching with a basket full of muffins, something she brought in for the staff whenever she visited Ellie's mum. They gave each other a hug. 'How is she?' Meghan asked.

'Quite talkative today, actually.'

'That's good.' She bit her lip. 'Remember it's Tommy's birthday today.'

'Yes, I'll drop a card off.'

'You know how much I'd love you to come to the dinner . . .'

Each year for his birthday, Tommy invited up to fifty family and friends to join him for a grand, fun-filled dinner. They'd pull two long tables together out in the back garden if it was dry, and the night would be all about great food, drink, music and gossip. It always felt like a bit of a privilege to get an invite . . . and a snub not to. Her parents had been invited the first three years after moving to the village, but then casually left off the list when Ellie's mother had begun to decline. Ellie had always been present though . . . until this year, of course.

'I wouldn't expect an invite,' Ellie said. 'It's fine, honestly.'

'We'll really miss you. Peter too.'

Ellie laughed. 'I doubt it!'

'It's been difficult for Peter too, you know.'

'Come on, Meghan. Really? Peter left me. Left *us*. He really did a number on us.'

Meghan looked down at her basket. 'I don't condone what he did. But it can't all be on Peter's shoulders.'

'Oh, Meghan, I know you think the sun shines out of your son's backside, but he's really not all you think he's cracked up to be. He was, frankly, a bloody awful husband.' Meghan frowned. 'You know he forgot my birthday last year? Not to mention the fact he isn't exactly the most hands-on dad. So much overtime, always looking at the phone. You see it yourself, Meghan!'

'He's a good father!'

'The kids deserve better than *good*, Meghan,' Ellie said gently. Part of her felt bad, but Meghan needed to know what an arse her son could be. 'He gives this impression of being the perfect man, but he isn't.'

Meghan blinked, clearly surprised by what Ellie was saying. Ellie clamped her mouth shut. Maybe she'd taken it too far? 'I'm sorry, Meghan,' she said gently. 'I shouldn't have said all that.'

'No, no, it's fine.' Meghan took in a deep breath. 'You have every right to say what you think. Tommy always says I'm a bit naive.'

Ellie gave her a quick hug. 'You're lovely. Never change.'

Meghan smiled, stroking Ellie's cheek. 'Peter didn't just break your heart when he left you, he broke mine too.' She paused. 'And Vanessa's.'

'Ness?'

'She doesn't show it, but it hit her hard. She's always felt like a bit of an outsider, even with us, her family. But having you there at family events has always given her a boost. Her little comrade in arms. Now that's gone.'

'It's not gone! Just because I don't go to the odd family event now, we still see each other all the time. We're best friends, always will be! Why has she never said?'

'Vanessa likes to pretend she's strong, love. Especially for you.' She peered inside. 'I'd better go. But you take care, okay?'

They waved goodbye. As Ellie jogged to Kitty's place, she thought of what Meghan had said about Vanessa. It had never even occurred to her that her friend had been hit hard by her and Peter's separation. In fact, Ellie had thought she was happy about it. She'd always said Ellie was too good for her brother.

Maybe Meghan had a point?

But she couldn't dwell on all that. She had other things to think about.

As she walked to Kitty's, she mulled over what her mother had said. So her letters hadn't been an isolated incident. There had been a poison pen letter campaign in Forest Grove? Something rang a bell for Ellie, but then she had been so wrapped up in her blossoming romance with Peter, she wouldn't have taken much notice of something like that. There was always some drama going on with Forest Grove residents 'bitching' about each other, as Vanessa would call it.

She looked at her watch and quickened her step. She couldn't be late!

Kitty ran her practice from her large house on Birch Road, her office in an extended room with a vast window which looked out over the forest. Kitty was a bit of a celebrity in Forest Grove, thanks to her occasional appearances on national TV promoting her books about bringing children up 'the natural way'. Ellie hadn't properly met her before, but Peter had volunteered to help build a play park that Kitty had masterminded a few years back and he had enjoyed telling Ellie what a 'new age, vegan, lame woman' she was.

But the sixty-odd-year-old woman who answered the door to Ellie seemed anything but lame. There was an energy about her – Ellie couldn't decide if it was the good kind of energy or the draining kind. She was an explosion of colour with bright pink lipstick, purple-framed glasses and a long, patterned kaftan dress. She certainly seemed to enjoy her 'fame', judging from her office when Ellie got up there, which contained a large bookcase filled with Kitty's own books and various framed photos of her TV appearances.

'Choose your seat,' Kitty said with a smile.

Ellie looked around her. The room had several different seating options from beanbags to a patchwork chaise longue. Ellie opted for the chaise longue as Kitty took a large, purple armchair across from her.

'So tell me,' Kitty asked, probing Ellie with her sharp, green eyes. 'Why are you here today, Ellie?'

'I – I'm going through some stuff.'

Kitty nodded. 'Okay. Why don't you tell me about that stuff?'

'I guess it started with my husband Peter walking out on us.'

'I see. When did this happen?'

'Three months ago.'

'And how did that make you feel?'

Ellie felt tears spring to her eyes. Vanessa had told her that therapists always made their clients cry, but Ellie had promised herself she wouldn't do that. She took a deep breath to calm herself. 'Awful, obviously. I thought we had our lives mapped out together.'

'And what did that *map* look like, Ellie?'

'When the kids went to uni – they've both said they want to – Peter and I had talked about going travelling more. Maybe even buying a holiday home.' Ellie sighed, looking down at her hands. It was strange saying all this out loud. 'I imagined us growing old together, having the kids around with their partners for Sunday roast. I'd help out with childcare when they had their own kids. And then – then Peter would retire from his busy job, I'd wind down my work and we'd just potter, like retired people do.'

Kitty leaned towards the low oval coffee table between them, pulling a tissue from a gold-coloured cube and handing it to Ellie. Ellie put her hand to her cheeks, realising they were wet.

Damn you, Vanessa, you were right, she thought.

'So those dreams you had were ripped away?' Kitty asked.

Ellie nodded, patting her wet cheeks with the tissue. 'Yes. I thought I had it all figured out. But the past three months, I've had to figure something new out.'

'All figured out,' Kitty repeated, tapping her forefinger on her chin. 'That's an interesting phrase. What is it you do for a living, Ellie?'

'I design puzzles. So crosswords, word searches, that kind of thing.'

'The kinds of puzzles that people need to figure out?'

Ellie smiled. 'I see where you're going.'

Kitty smiled back at her. 'Yes, but it is interesting, isn't it? How when I asked what the separation did to you, you started with how the life you had mapped out fell down around you? Rather than the fact you lost the man you . . . loved?'

Ellie frowned. 'Yes, I suppose you're right. I hadn't thought of it like that.'

'Plus, who's to say your husband would have done all those things you'd planned? The travelling, the holiday home . . . the retirement? You mentioned he has a busy job. Who's to say that busy job would have allowed all of that?'

Ellie nodded. 'You're right.'

'And how do you feel now, three months later? Have you solved the puzzle of a life post-divorce?'

Ellie laughed. She liked Kitty, and, truth be told, she had thought she wouldn't after all she'd heard about her. She'd just always seemed a bit too holier than thou. But as a therapist, she was making all kinds of sense. 'I think so,' she said. 'I'm selling the house, hoping to move to Firdean.'

'Lovely village.'

'Yes. There's a job going for an entertainment editor at the *Ashbridge Gazette* too. I was thinking about applying, have some stability. I used to be the assistant entertainment editor there, after all.'

'Very good.'

Ellie frowned as she looked down at the scrunched-up tissue in her hands. Would she even have a chance of getting the job if it came out that she was the Facebook Vigilante? She thought of the journalist Karin Hawkins and how good she was at uncovering the truth. How long before she unmasked Ellie? Not getting the job would be the least of her problems if that happened. Ellie shuddered as she thought about how the villagers would react if they found out what she did.

'I sense a fly in the ointment,' Kitty said. 'Or maybe a missed letter in the word puzzle of Ellie?'

Ellie looked up at the therapist. Now was the time to tell Kitty the real reason she was there. That she was the Facebook Vigilante. There was nothing to lose, really; the police knew about what Ellie had done now. So she wasn't risking anything and Kitty wouldn't be able to tell anyone what they discussed; it would be against the code of conduct, surely?

Ellie took a deep breath. 'Yes. There is a rather large fly in the ointment. I presume you know all about the Facebook Vigilante?'

Kitty nodded, eyes curious. 'I do.'

'Well . . . that's me.'

Kitty's face registered her shock in the widening of her eyes, but she quickly recovered herself. 'Interesting.'

'The police are aware,' Ellie quickly added. 'And I was *not* behind the firework incident the other night.' Obviously, Ellie wouldn't tell Kitty about Tyler's role in the music prank, as much as she trusted her. She just couldn't risk that ever getting out.

Kitty leaned forward, green eyes sparkling. It occurred to Ellie that this was probably the most exciting revelation she'd heard in a while. But then the villagers of Forest Grove did seem to have an abundance of lies and secrets.

'What made you carry those acts out, Ellie?' Kitty said.

'It started when I discovered my mother started receiving poison pen letters three years after she moved here,' Ellie replied. 'I thought it was just her, but I recently learnt that other people also received them.'

'Yes, I remember those,' Kitty said with a knitted brow. Ellie wondered if she may have received some herself. 'You only just learnt that your mother received some?'

'Yes, Mum never said. I found them recently in the attic.' Ellie realised she was crying again and pressed her tissues against her face. 'She had a – a nervous breakdown when I was young. She hasn't been the same since. And I'm convinced now that the letters triggered her nervous breakdown.'

'Ah. So this has all been very personal for you?'

Ellie nodded.

'So you decided to . . . avenge your mother by targeting the more – how shall I put this? – vocal members of the community?'

Ellie nodded again. 'Also, part of me wondered whether the people I targeted could have been behind sending the poison pen letters to my mum.'

'Interesting. Another puzzle you've been trying to solve.'

Ellie smiled slightly. 'I guess you're right.'

'And did you get anywhere with that?'

'Not really. Just a whole load of regret.'

'So you regret carrying out those acts?'

She looked up at the therapist. 'Absolutely.'

'And you say you *weren't* behind the firework incident?'

'No, I would *never* go that far. The police have proof, too. They caught someone on camera who looks nothing like me.'

'Interesting,' Kitty said as she swirled her pen between her fingers.

'I played my part though,' Ellie admitted. 'I mean, it can't be a coincidence someone targeted Andrea after her Facebook post, just as I targeted others.'

'So you understand the similarities between the poison pen letters and your pranks, that is part of your regret?'

Ellie nodded. 'My pranks probably caused a similar sense of fear in the community, like the poison pen letters must have. Though that was never my intention.'

Kitty smiled. 'That's the "disinhibition effect" for you.'

'The dis-what?'

'It's where anonymity means people lack the restraint they would usually have. Take the incident with Belinda Bell. If she had been watching you as you carried out the act, of course you would never have dreamt of posting dog excrement through her letterbox.'

Ellie nodded, feeling humiliated.

'The anonymity gives you a misplaced courage,' Kitty said. 'But this is also about *anger*. Seeing those letters directed at your mother made you angry. Of course, we all get angry, but when combined with other issues – in your case, your husband leaving – it can explode in unexpected outbursts. This is particularly prevalent with poison pen writers. I compare it to an incident of road rage. There is always more going on beneath the surface.'

'That's very true,' Ellie said, taking a sip of the water Kitty had got her. 'I guess, before now, I saw the person who wrote those letters to my mum as some angry, faceless person.' Ellie sighed. 'But maybe, like me, there was so much more going on.'

Kitty nodded. 'The key is ensuring it doesn't escalate. In your case, you went to the police, admitted what happened. Though things *did* escalate a little, you stopped before that rage could really take hold. That's a positive to hold on to.'

Ellie let out a breath of relief. It was so good talking it all through like this. 'Yes, you're right. But now someone else is letting their own issues spiral. Putting a lit firework through Andrea Simpson's letterbox. That's a different league.'

'And interesting that it's fire,' Kitty mused.

'Exactly, it's so different from what I did . . . from the poison pen letters too.'

'Not necessarily.'

'How do you mean?'

'There have been instances where poison pen writers have moved on to arson attacks, like a case I read about a few years ago where a man targeted his neighbours in a Cotswolds village with poison pen letters.'

Ellie's heart thumped loudly against her chest. 'Wow.'

'Of course,' Kitty quickly added, 'the person behind the firework incident could just be someone who dislikes Andrea for some reason and they see the "Facebook Vigilante" as a way to target her without being caught.'

'Yes, that's true. I mean, Andrea *does* have a few enemies.'

Kitty didn't say anything, but Ellie could tell she agreed.

'Or,' Kitty eventually said, 'you have an admirer.'

Ellie frowned. 'What do you mean?'

'A copycat.'

Ellie thought of Tyler. He'd copied her, hadn't he? But there was no way he'd risk someone's life. He'd seemed genuinely worried about Andrea's son being hurt.

'So you think there's a possibility somebody might be out there who wants to emulate what I did?' Ellie asked as she looked out at the forest.

'Maybe.'

'What if they do something else? The police are bound to suspect me, even after knowing I wasn't behind the firework incident. Oh God,' Ellie whispered.

Kitty leaned forward, her hands on the table. 'You mustn't let it worry you. It's unlikely. My best bet is this is someone who has a particular vendetta against Andrea.'

But Ellie couldn't help it. If there was a copycat out there and they did something else, what would that mean for Ellie?

Even worse, if their behaviour escalated, what would that mean for the next target?

Chapter 20

WELCOME TO THE FG ALTERNATIVE COMMUNITY GROUP

Friday 30ᵗʰ July
6 p.m.

Tommy Mileham

A message for the Facebook Vigilante

I am posting this on behalf of the residents of Forest Grove following the fire at Andrea's house.

WE WILL NOT BE SILENCED BY YOU.

After this post, any members of this group who have a complaint and want it aired can do so anonymously. Simply message me and I will make a post under my name. The vigilante will have no way of knowing who posted it and no victim to target.

It's no coincidence this village's motto is Home to Strong Branches and Deep Roots. A community as strong as ours will never be weakened.

Regards, the community of Forest Grove

Ed Piper

Yes! This reminds me of that scene in *Spartacus* where Kirk Douglas stands up to admit he is the leader of the slaves, then the slaves also say they're Spartacus so the Romans can't tell which one to execute.

Rebecca Feine

Execution seems apt, Ed. I think you may have signed your own execution papers with that post, Tommy.

Lucy Cronin

I for one think it's a very good idea, Tommy, though I'm sure the 'sheeple' of this town won't!

Belinda Bell

Very clever, Tommy. Let's see what the Facebook Vigilante does now.

Andrew Blake

He'll just target Tommy, surely? Be careful, mate.

Tommy Mileham

No he won't. The whole point is he targets those who complain. It would go against his whole *raison d'être*.

Andrew Blake

Look at you with your posh language!

Tommy Mileham

Well, now I'm sixty-five years old (yes, it's my birthday today!), I'll have you know I'm the height of sophistication and yes, all the spelling and grammar will be corrected before I post any anonymous posts!

Rebecca Feine

Happy birthday, Tommy! But please be careful though, I have a bad feeling about this . . .

Chapter 21

That night, while the kids were at Tommy and Meghan's for his birthday dinner, Ellie treated herself, curling up on the sofa with Stanley, a film and a pizza she'd ordered from the pub. It felt strange not being involved in Tommy's birthday celebrations. Ellie wondered if Caitlin would be there with Peter. Surely it would be too soon?

She tried to push the thoughts away, focusing on the film she was watching instead. Just as the ending of her film was nearing, the doorbell went. Stanley peered up, letting out a solitary high-pitched bark.

She felt the sense of trepidation, the added worry that came when the kids were away from home. What if someone was coming to tell her something bad had happened to Tyler or Zoe?

She walked down the dark hallway as Stanley loped after her, peering through the frosted glass of the door to see if she recognised the late-night visitor. Whoever it was, they were tall, broad-shouldered.

'Who is it?' she shouted through the glass.

'Adrian,' came the reply.

What was *he* doing here at this time of night? Her stomach sank. Had something else happened . . . and was he here to blame her again?

She fumbled with the lock and quickly opened the door.

Relief flooded through her when she saw he was smiling. 'Hey,' he said, a slight slur in his voice as Stanley jumped up at him.

She laughed. 'You're drunk.'

'Yeah, maybe,' he said, shrugging in embarrassment as he fussed over the dog.

She leaned against the wall, wrapping her long cardigan around her and hoping the light above was flattering enough to hide the fact she was wearing no make-up. 'How's Carter?' she asked.

Adrian frowned. 'Okay.'

'And Michael, has he recovered fully?'

'Voice a bit strained . . . which is probably a good thing,' Adrian added. 'Ooops, naughty me.'

'You got my text yesterday, right? About the police ruling me out.'

'Yep.'

'Is – is that why you're here?'

'Just wanted to check how the session went with Kitty Hoohah. Concerned citizen and all that.'

He leaned against the doorframe, his face inches from hers.

'It was good, actually,' she said. 'We worked through some of my issues. She's not a bad therapist, after all.'

'Wow, wonders will never cease.'

He stumbled slightly and Ellie grabbed his arm.

'You really are drunk,' she said, laughing. 'Maybe a frothy coffee will help?'

Adrian went serious, mulling it over in his mind. Then he shrugged. 'Sure, why not?'

Ellie led him down the hallway, feeling nervous. He was quite obviously drunk and would no doubt regret this tomorrow. And yet he was here, wasn't he, drunk or not? That was a good thing; it meant he didn't *hate* her.

'So I take it you've been to the pub then?' she asked casually.

'Yup. Had myself a little argument with Graham Cane.'

'Really?'

'Yup. He was banging on about snowflakes, so I told him where he can shove his snowflake theory.'

Ellie burst out laughing. 'What did he say to that?'

'He said I was Detective Snowflake.'

'I *like* that title for you,' Ellie said as she poured their coffee.

'Me too. Detective Snowflake!' he said, pulling a Superman pose. 'It's like some kind of ice-powered superhero.'

She smiled as she brought his coffee over and placed it on the coaster in front of him. Before she moved her hand away, he softly grasped it.

'Ellie,' he whispered. 'Why did you have to mess things up? I thought we had something.'

Ellie flinched.

He put his head in his hands. 'Man, I really need to stop drinking. Thing is,' he said, peering up at her with sad eyes, 'after being married to someone like Andrea, I promised myself, no more drama. I meet you, think, *Wow, this woman is a class act* and then you turn out to be the Facebook Vigilante!' He put his fist to his chest and pretended to make an explosion. 'Heart broken.'

'Heart?' she asked.

'Yeah. Couldn't you tell? I was falling for you.'

He held her gaze and Ellie felt like her own heart was exploding. 'Oh, Adrian, I was falling for you too. I really have messed up, big time.'

They both jumped at the sound of frantic knocking at the door, Stanley barking.

'*What* is going on tonight?' Ellie said.

She ran to the door, opening it to find Sheila on the doorstep in her dressing gown. 'I tried to call,' she said, peering behind Ellie at Adrian.

'What's going on?'

'I know your kids are there, I thought you'd want to know. There's a fire at Tommy's!'

Chapter 22

'Jesus,' Ellie said, peering in the direction of the Milehams' house. She could see a brief hint of orange flickering in the distance. 'I'll head over.'

'What's going on?' Adrian asked as she closed the door.

'There's a fire at Tommy's. The kids are there!'

'Shit. I'd better go.'

'Me too.' She pulled her shoes on, grabbing her jacket and letting herself out. As they walked down the road towards the Milehams' street, more people were heading that way too. The smell of ash clung to the air, but she could no longer make out the hint of flames she'd seen a few moments before.

They arrived at Tommy and Meghan's house to find a crowd had already gathered outside. The fire seemed to be under control now, but Tommy's beautifully maintained lawn and rose bushes were charred black.

Familiar faces were dotted around, some clearly having been to Tommy's birthday celebrations, including Andrea and Michael, Graham, Ed and Andrew – the usual suspects.

Ellie frantically searched the crowd for Zoe and Tyler and was relieved to find them standing on the next-door neighbour's lawn with their cousins. She ran up to them, pulling Zoe into a hug.

'It's so horrible, Mum,' Zoe said. 'Grandad loves his rose bushes.'

'What happened?' she asked.

'We don't know,' Tyler replied. 'We were inside, listening to Aunt Vanessa do karaoke,' he said with an eye roll, 'then Grandad noticed the flames.'

Ellie looked at what remained of Tommy's pride and joy, not quite believing her eyes. So whoever had targeted Andrea was at it again . . . and Ellie might be a suspect. But then, she had been with Adrian, surely the best kind of alibi?

She peered towards Tommy and Meghan. Peter was with them, both of them talking in low tones while Vanessa comforted her mum. Ellie watched Vanessa, remembering what Meghan had said about how hard the separation had hit her.

Peter caught sight of Adrian and jogged over. 'PC Cooper,' he said.

'Peter,' Adrian replied. He was doing a good job of appearing sober, the sips of coffee he'd taken helping. 'What happened?'

'Someone set fire to Dad's rose bush, then it spread to the lawn.' Peter's nostrils flared. 'No coincidence it happened after Dad did his post on the group.'

'What post?' Adrian asked.

Ellie got her phone out with trembling hands and showed Adrian.

'Great,' Adrian hissed, shaking his head.

'Why would Tommy do that?' Ellie said. 'It's just provoking things!'

'He's right though!' Peter countered. 'We shouldn't be silenced by this bloody vigilante! I mean, honestly, what sort of loser does stuff like this?'

Ellie looked down at her shoes, face flushing.

'I'll go and chat to Tommy,' Adrian said, casting Ellie a quick look before heading over to Tommy and Meghan.

Peter was about to join him, then paused, turning back to Ellie. 'You came here together.'

'And?' she asked, jutting her chin out.

Peter gave her a hard look, then walked over to join Adrian, his parents and Vanessa. Ellie noticed a dark-haired woman was now with them.

Her stomach sank as she realised that woman was Caitlin.

So she *had* attended the party.

Caitlin peered over at Ellie, looking just as uncomfortable as Ellie felt. The last time they'd seen each other was six years ago, for Peter's thirty-fifth-birthday party. It was at that very party that Ellie had first had her suspicions about them, watching the way they had danced closely. A year later, she had found the love letter in his pocket.

Caitlin looked the same as she had then: curvy, tall, her dark hair up. She was wearing a red V-neck checked dress and stilettos. Ellie wished she could say she looked awful, but she looked nice. The dress wasn't too tight, the heels not too high.

Damn her.

Tyler caught his mum's eye, then looked over at Caitlin. He leaned down and said something to his sister and they both walked over to Ellie, Zoe slipping her hand into her mother's.

Ellie felt her heart soar. How lucky she was to have her beautiful, supportive kids.

Vanessa jogged over to Ellie, a grimace on her face as she peered behind her at Caitlin. 'She *refused* to do karaoke with me,' she whispered.

'We can't all be karaoke queens,' Ellie said. But she didn't feel like joking as she stared at the charred remains of the lawn she was so familiar with. 'I can't believe this.'

'I know,' Vanessa said, suddenly deadly serious. 'It's not good.'

'I can't believe all Grandad's rose bushes have been ruined,' Zoe said as they took in the black stumps the fire had left behind.

'Don't worry,' Tyler said, putting his arm around his sister's shoulders. 'We can get him other ones.'

'Nice idea,' Ellie said, smiling at him. What a good brother he was.

'Well, at least their house wasn't burnt, unlike *mine*,' a voice said from behind them. They turned to see it was Andrea, her eyes sparkling with drama as she talked to Michael. She was wearing a short, sparkly silver dress with silver high heels. Michael wore a matching silver shirt with black, too-tight trousers, his hair even more quiffy than ever.

'Quite, darling, quite,' Michael said. 'A lawn is easily replaced, but a porch and a perfect voice box isn't,' he said, stroking his throat. 'It could have been a lot worse for us, too, I suppose. Imagine if it had spread farther into the house?'

'I shudder to think,' Andrea said, putting her hand to her chest.

'Excuse me,' Vanessa said, crossing her arms as she turned to them. 'This isn't a "Who Had the Worst Fire?" competition!'

'Here we go, Vanessa spouting her opinions all over the place again. Not the time and place, Vanessa!' said Andrea.

'Spouting opinions?' Ellie said. 'That's rich, coming from you.'

'What's that supposed to mean?' Andrea jutted her chin out.

People in the crowd began to look over, intrigued.

'Forget it,' Ellie said, aware of the kids being so close . . . though Tyler *was* smiling.

'Come on, Ellie, you clearly have something to say,' Andrea said, raising her voice so more people paid attention.

'I just think it's a bit rich you saying Vanessa's opinionated when you're probably one of the most opinionated people in Forest Grove,' Ellie replied with a shrug as Vanessa smiled.

People raised their eyebrows. Peter and Adrian now looking over too.

'Who's to say there's anything wrong with being opinionated?' Andrea asked, crossing her arms.

'I quite agree,' Michael said in a croaky voice. 'Hasn't *opinionated* been used instead of *strong* when it comes to women for centuries now?'

'Yes, darling, you're so right,' Andrea said, giving his hand a squeeze. 'If *I'd* still been in charge of the Facebook group, I have no doubt all this vigilante stuff would never have happened,' she added, gesturing towards the burnt lawn. 'If you hadn't silenced the community's voice, we may have tracked down this vigilante already.'

'That's ridiculous,' Vanessa said.

'Look at the two of them,' Andrea said to Michael. 'Bullies, just like they were at school, like two witches brewing a new potion.'

Zoe scowled at Andrea.

Vanessa laughed. 'Us, bullies? You were the one who gave the other kids hell at school, Andrea. Gossiping, judging. You haven't changed!'

'Come on, guys, calm down. This isn't the school playground,' Ed Piper called over.

'Isn't Forest Grove a permanent school playground?' Tyler said.

'What a ridiculous thing to say!' Andrea said. 'What have you been letting him watch, Ellie?'

Ellie felt anger build up inside. 'He's right though! Maybe if people here weren't so judgemental, things like this wouldn't happen,' she said, gesturing to the smouldering grass.

'So you think Tommy and Meghan deserve this, do you?' Andrea asked. 'Your children's grandparents? *Your* parents?' She turned on Vanessa.

'Well, I'll be honest, I did warn Dad not to post any more on Facebook,' Vanessa said, shrugging.

'Wow. Cold,' Andrea said.

'No, just the truth,' Vanessa said. 'Ellie's right, this village is a bloody nightmare.'

'Then leave!' Andrea said. 'That's what I don't get about you, Vanessa. Ever since you were a teenager, you have banged on about escaping Forest Grove, and yet here you still are!' She looked Vanessa up and down. 'If you hate it so much, then why don't you just go with Ellie when she moves out? It will be very welcome to see the back of you both, let me tell you.'

A murmur went through the crowd, even a few nods of agreement from people like Belinda and Graham. Other people, like Rebecca and Sheila, shook their heads though.

'Uh-oh,' Vanessa whispered. 'Here comes trouble.'

Ellie followed her gaze to see Karin Hawkins watching them all with interest.

'Okay, that's enough,' a strong voice called out. Adrian was walking through the crowd, suddenly looking very sober. 'Let's not turn this into a spectator sport. Everyone, go home, please.'

'PC Cooper, can I have a quick word?' Karin said, running up to him.

'No, I'm afraid not,' Adrian replied. 'You'll need to go through the force's press office.'

'Like *they're* any use,' Karin said. 'What about you?' she called over to Ellie. 'As the Facebook group's moderator?'

Everyone turned to look at Ellie.

'No,' Ellie said, shaking her head.

'I'll talk to you!' Ed shouted over.

'Fab,' Karin said, going up to him with her notepad and pen.

'At your house, please, Ed,' Adrian instructed.

The residents of Forest Grove began to reluctantly leave, including Andrea and Michael, who shot daggers at Ellie and Vanessa as they walked away.

'I'd better go and help the folks,' Vanessa said. She gave Ellie a quick hug then jogged over to her parents. Ellie stayed where she was with Adrian and the kids, Andrea's words still stinging.

'So the Facebook Vigilante strikes again,' Tyler said pointedly. Of course, he knew very well it wasn't the Facebook Vigilante, as Ellie had stopped her pranks.

'This isn't good,' Adrian said. 'We're seeing an escalation here.'

Ellie examined his face. Thank God he'd come over when he did. Otherwise he might have suspected her.

'Oh no, what will they do next?' Zoe asked.

Ellie hugged her close. 'Don't worry, darling. Adrian's on the case.'

Adrian gave Zoe a salute. 'PC Cooper at your service.'

She giggled, relaxing against Ellie.

As she did, Peter strolled over . . . with Caitlin. Up close, Ellie could see she had aged since she saw her all those years ago after all. Or maybe that had happened in the last three months living with Peter.

'I thought this might be an opportune time to introduce our new partners,' Peter said, his voice slightly slurred.

Ellie's face flushed. 'Adrian isn't my partner, Peter. And I wouldn't say this is an *opportune* time,' she added, gesturing to the burnt lawn.

Caitlin looked at Adrian and Ellie. 'Oh, we thought—'

'You thought wrong,' Adrian said. 'Ellie and I are just friends. Speaking of which, shall I walk you home?' he asked, looking at Ellie.

Ellie smiled at him, grateful. He could easily just walk off, leave her alone with her ex and his bit on the side. But instead, he was standing by her. Sure, it stung to have it spelled out – *just friends* – but she'd take being friends with Adrian over nothing.

'Can we come home tonight, Mum?' Zoe asked, clinging to Ellie's arm.

'You're supposed to be staying at your grandparents' tonight,' Peter said. 'We all are.'

Ellie clenched her jaw, trying not to imagine Peter and Caitlin sleeping in one of the spare rooms together.

'I want to go home with Mummy,' Zoe said.

'Mummy!' Peter mimicked, shaking his head. 'Come on, Zoe, you're not a baby.'

Tyler took in a sharp breath, clearly struggling not to say anything. Ellie noticed Caitlin flinch too. Good, now she could see what Peter was *really* like.

'Nothing wrong with calling me Mummy, darling,' Ellie said as she hugged Zoe. 'I've heard your dad call Nan Mummy when he's had a few drinks.'

Tyler laughed as Adrian smiled. Peter, though, just scowled at Ellie.

'Maybe it's best if they do go back with their mum, Peter,' Caitlin suggested. 'It's been a bit unsettling,' she added, looking towards the scorched garden.

Peter sighed. 'Fine. Go get your bags from my car then,' he said, throwing his car keys at Tyler, who caught them with one hand.

'I won't make this a habit though,' Peter snapped as they went to get their bags and say goodbye to their grandparents. 'Zoe, in particular, needs to get used to this new situation.'

'I'm sure she'll get used to it,' Ellie said. 'I have, and am rather enjoying it.'

His face faltered and she noticed Caitlin smile slightly.

'Right, let's go,' Ellie said when the kids got back. Then she turned on her heel and walked down the road.

'Nicely handled,' Adrian said as they got out of earshot, Tyler and Zoe walking ahead in the darkness.

'It went better than I thought.' Ellie wrapped her arms around herself, looking into the distance. 'Maybe it's because my cheating ex isn't really my biggest issue any more. Who do you think is doing this?' she whispered.

'I don't know. I'll chat to Detective Powell when I'm back at work tomorrow, see where they've got with the investigation into the fire at Andrea's.'

'You do know it's not me, right?' she asked. She just needed to be sure.

'Yeah. The fire was started when I was with you.'

'Thank God for drunken late-night visits,' she joked.

At first, she thought Adrian would joke back. But instead, his face grew serious. 'I shouldn't have done that.'

Ellie tried her best to hide her disappointment.

They approached the house and Adrian stood at the end of the drive. 'Take care, you guys,' he called out as Ellie let them in.

'You too,' she said, watching Adrian.

What would have happened if Sheila hadn't banged on the door? Would she and Adrian have kissed?

'You got a letter, Mum,' Zoe said.

Ellie turned to see Zoe holding a white envelope up. Ellie took it, then froze.

The 'i' in her name was topped with a heart, just like the poison pen letters that had been sent to her mum!

Chapter 23

Ellie tucked the letter into her back pocket. She didn't want to alarm the kids.

'It's late,' she said. 'Get upstairs to bed. I just forgot to tell Adrian something.'

Tyler watched her, brow furrowed.

He knew something was up.

'Bed, now,' Ellie said, smiling.

They both jogged upstairs and she ran out into the darkness, chasing Adrian down the street.

'You okay?' he asked.

'I just found this.' She handed him the envelope and he looked at it under the streetlight above.

'I don't understand.'

'See the way they use a heart instead of a dot?' Adrian nodded. 'Whoever wrote those letters to my mum did the same.'

Adrian's eyes widened. 'You think this might be a poison pen letter?'

'I don't know. I guess I won't know until I open it. Will you come back to the house so I can open it with you?'

'Of course.'

He followed her back to the house and they went to the living room, the kids getting ready for bed upstairs. Stanley jumped on to the sofa and leaned his chin on Adrian's leg.

Ellie opened the letter with trembling hands.

> Dear Ellie,
>
> I have you all figured out. You think nobody knows the real you, but I see you, Facebook Vigilante.
>
> Shame you can't do a proper job of it. That's why I've had to step in with my matches and some fireworks. The problem with you, Ellie, is that you are FAKE. As fake as they come with your layer of expensive make-up (oh, the irony that it costs so much to look 'natural') & your Princess Di copycat hair dye. You're no Princess Di though, oh no. You're just a pretender, playing a role you think is perfect when you're anything but. I've seen you without make-up, the reality of your uneven skin & blue-veined legs.
>
> You're just like your mother! You're both the same: two fake sluts who aren't worthy.
>
> The sooner you get out of here, the better. Let the real vigilante have a chance . . .
>
> Yours thoughtfully, A Concerned Villager

'Jesus,' Adrian whispered.

Ellie stared at the letter, hands trembling so much it slipped from her fingers and floated down to the floor. For a moment, she couldn't move. She just sat on the sofa, blinking.

'Hey, it's okay,' Adrian said, picking it back up and putting an arm around her shoulders.

'It's definitely the same person,' Ellie said. 'The use of ampersands, the heart.'

'Do you have your mum's letters here?'

'Yes.' She went to the wall unit and got out the letters that had been sent to her mother, bringing them to the table where Adrian had laid the new letter out flat. She selected one of her mother's letters at random and placed it next to the one she'd just received.

'Yep, same writing,' Adrian said with a sigh.

'It's written in black biro on plain, white A5 paper too, like the others.'

'And yet it's been nearly thirty years between them.'

'I know, it's crazy. And look,' she said, pointing to the reference to the matches and fireworks, 'this means they've admitted to starting the fire at Tommy and Meghan's just now, and posting fireworks through Andrea's letterbox, right?'

'I'd say so.'

'Kitty did say fires can be an escalation from poisonous letters. There must be other clues.' She leaned down, sniffing the paper. 'There's a scent there, almost sweet.'

'Regular detective,' Adrian said.

She smiled slightly. 'I do like my puzzles.'

'True.'

Adrian got his phone out, directing the torch app on the paper.

'What are you looking for?' she asked.

'Maybe an indentation from another letter?' They both looked at it, but there was nothing. Same with the envelope, a plain white one. Nothing to give away who might have written it.

Adrian leaned back, raking his fingers through his light-brown hair. 'Was this here before we went to Tommy and Meghan's?'

'I don't think so. I'm pretty sure I would have noticed it, but I can't say for sure. We rushed out.'

'Is it okay if I take this?' Adrian asked, getting an evidence kit from his pocket. 'We might be able to pull some fingerprints off it.'

'Of course. Do you carry those kits around everywhere with you?'

'Life of a village cop,' he said with a wry smile.

He carefully picked Ellie's letter up with his sleeve over his fingers and slipped it into a clear plastic evidence bag before standing up. 'I'd better go, it's late.'

'How long will it take for the fingerprints to come back?' Ellie asked.

'Could be a couple of weeks. We're all pretty busy at the moment with the usual increase in crime in the summer over in Ashbridge. I swear it gets worse every day.'

'This should take priority though, right? Especially now this person has pretty much admitted they're behind the fires too.'

'Not really, Ellie,' Adrian admitted. 'It's bad for Forest Grove, but worse stuff happens in Ashbridge. Knife crime. Domestic abuse. Car theft. It's a battle I'm constantly having whenever I need to focus on any crime here in the village. Ashbridge takes priority. I'll keep you posted though.'

'Please do.'

As she led him back outside, she peered down the street, looking at the curtained windows.

Any one of Forest Grove's residents could be behind that spiteful letter. Worst of all, the fires too.

But which one?

Ellie couldn't sleep that night. She stayed downstairs, spreading out all her mum's old poison pen letters on the table alongside the one she'd received.

Surely she could find a clue *somewhere?*

But even after reading and examining all fifty of her mother's letters, one after another, she found no clues, she just had a feeling of nausea at the revolting things said about her wonderful mother!

Then something occurred to her. Maybe the *Ashbridge Gazette* had covered the poison pen campaign all those years back? They'd reported on the recent events in Forest Grove after all. Surely there would be old issues online?

Ellie got her laptop out and found the newspaper's website, clicking on the advanced-search option.

'Fab,' she whispered to herself when she saw the date search went back fifty years. She did a search for 'poison pen' and 'Forest Grove'. Only two results came up. She clicked on the first article, which revealed a scan of an inside page of the newspaper, a tiny story about the poison-pen letters from 16 May 1996 tucked away down the edge.

POLICE HUNT FOR POISON PEN WRITER

Residents of new 'eco village' Forest Grove have been subjected to a spate of poison pen letters over the past few weeks. The handwritten letters were addressed to a variety of residents and are posted through letterboxes. Ashbridge Police are currently investigating the letters to see if they can track down the culprit. Anybody with information must call Ashbridge Police Station.

Ellie clicked on the next link. This time, the story took up half a page of the newspaper, dated 1 June 1996, with a sad-looking Belinda Bell photographed holding a letter up to the camera. She may have been nearly thirty years younger, but she still looked very much the same, with her pinched face and tightly curled, short white hair.

FOREST GROVE WIDOW SUBJECTED TO VICIOUS LETTERS

After having lost her husband to cancer only last year, fifty-six-year-old Belinda Bell never expected to have to endure more heartache. But with the arrival of what she at first thought was an innocent letter two weeks ago, her already difficult days have been thrown into turmoil after she realised she was the latest victim of a poison pen campaign which is rocking the village of Forest Grove.

'I thought it was a note from the milkman at first,' Belinda told our reporter while sitting in her comfortable living room, a view of the forest beyond. 'But when I read it, I couldn't believe my eyes.'

Local police officer Tommy Mileham commented: 'These letters have caused great distress to the community and we are doing all we can to track the culprit down.'

Ellie bit her lip. She felt even worse now about what she'd done to Belinda. Yes, Belinda wasn't exactly the nicest of people. But then everyone had their reasons for being the way they were, didn't they? Belinda had clearly been through her own share of tragedies.

Her eyes homed in on the quote again. Tommy. He would surely have known about the poison pen letters. Reluctantly, she had to admit it: maybe she needed to talk to her ex-father-in-law.

Ellie approached the Milehams' large house in the morning to see Meghan standing at the front door, chatting to Rebecca Feine as she forlornly looked over at her burnt lawn. It looked even worse in daylight, black as coal and with holes in the ground where what remained of the rose bushes had clearly been torn out by Tommy.

Meghan smiled sadly when she saw Ellie. 'Hello, my love,' she said, giving Ellie a hug as Rebecca rubbed Ellie's arm.

'Sorry I didn't get a chance to chat last night,' Ellie said. 'What a horrible thing to happen.'

'I know,' Meghan replied with a sigh.

Ellie looked behind her down the hallway. 'Is Tommy around?'

'He's gone to the garden centre to get some stuff for the lawn.'

'Oh, I was hoping to talk to him, actually,' Ellie said, biting her lip.

'Anything I can help with?' Meghan asked.

Ellie looked at the two women. They had both lived in the village since the start. Maybe they knew something about the poison pen letters?

'I wanted to ask about the poison pen letters that went around the village all those years back,' she said.

Meghan frowned. 'That was a long time ago.'

'I know, but I just think it's interesting in light of the recent incidents,' Ellie said.

Rebecca nodded. 'Yes, I was saying to the hubby the other day how all this Facebook Vigilante stuff reminded me of those poison pen days. Why the interest, Ellie?'

Ellie paused. How could she explain?

'I'm helping Adrian by looking into this vigilante stuff,' she said impulsively, feeling uncomfortable. It was a lie in many ways, not to mention the fact that she was deeply involved with this 'vigilante stuff' herself. But it was all she could think of.

'Well, look at you, Detective Mileham,' Meghan said.

Ellie winced at the use of her married name, but didn't correct Meghan, instead giving a half-hearted bow. 'At your service. Anyway, the poison pen letters are just one lead I've been exploring.'

'Lead?' Meghan asked.

'It's complicated,' Ellie quickly said. She didn't want to mention the letter she'd received. 'But maybe I could ask you both some questions about what happened all those years ago with the poison pen letters? I found an article or two about it, but it would be good to fill in some gaps.'

Meghan's face brightened. 'I just suggested Rebecca come out into the garden for some lemonade and cakes. You can join us! I'm having a rare day off from the bakery.' She opened the door wide. 'Come through into the garden.'

Ellie walked through the house with Rebecca, feeling strange. The last time she'd been there was for Meghan's birthday dinner, just before Peter left her. Meghan led them out to a wrought-iron table on the large stone patio which overlooked the huge lawn Tommy had worked so hard to maintain. In the distance was the forest, a small gate leading from the Milehams' garden right into it. Ellie and Peter had often used that gate to sneak out into the forest when she'd stayed over all those many years ago.

As Meghan went back inside to get her home-made lemonade and cake, Rebecca talked about the poison pen letters.

'I remember when Mrs Wellings, a lady who used to live on this very street, received the first batch of letters that year,' she said with a sigh. 'She was so distressed. Such a lovely lady too, very popular in the village. I think that's actually why she and her husband eventually moved out.'

'Were there ever any suspects?' Ellie asked.

'Oh, there were theories. The finger of suspicion even pointed at Belinda after that splash in the *Ashbridge Gazette*. People said she was sending them to herself for attention.'

'Oh yes, I remember that,' Meghan said as she walked out with a tray in her hands. 'Belinda loved every minute of the attention, you have to admit.'

Rebecca laughed. 'Yes, indeed. But I don't think she would send them to herself. Ellie was just asking if there were ever any suspects.'

Meghan placed the tray on the table, pouring three glasses of lemonade from a translucent blue jug.

'Not from what I recall,' Meghan replied. 'Though there were rumours it was a bunch of boys from Ashbridge who'd cause trouble. Remember Richard Hague? He would bring his friends to the village and they were always up to no good. He ended up in prison a few years later for assaulting his girlfriend.'

'He couldn't string a sentence together though,' Rebecca said, 'so no chance he'd be able to write hundreds of letters. The arson incidents though. I could well see him being behind those.'

Ellie froze. 'Arson?'

'Yes, there were a spate of bin fires in random locations around the village,' Rebecca explained. 'Do you remember that, Meghan?'

'I do,' Meghan said as she handed Ellie a slice of cake.

'God, now I think about it, it is very similar to what's been happening here lately,' Rebecca continued. 'It caused a bit of a stir among residents at the time.' She took a bite of her cake and closed her eyes in joy. 'Delicious, Meghan!'

'Tell me more about these fires,' Ellie said, heart thumping.

'I think they happened later in the year,' Meghan said.

'The worst one was when the forest was set alight,' Rebecca added.

'The forest?' Ellie asked in surprise.

'Just one tree, Rebecca!' Meghan said.

'But that spread to three more,' Rebecca replied. 'Thank God it was caught before it spread further. That was the last fire, so clearly whoever did it realised they'd gone too far.'

'Wow,' Ellie said, trying to keep her cool. Could it be the poison pen author escalating to arson, like the man Kitty had referred to? 'Any suspects for the fires?'

Meghan shrugged. 'It could have been one of many, really, including Richard Hague, of course. You have to remember, this was before smartphones and TikTok videos. Kids got bored.'

'Yep, I remember,' Ellie said with a raised eyebrow. 'So Richard Hague doesn't live here any more? Does he have any connections with the village?'

'Nope,' Rebecca said. 'Do you think it's all connected somehow, Ellie?'

'I don't know. It just seems too much of a coincidence. Especially with the firework stunt and what happened here last night.'

'Wait a minute!' Rebecca said. 'I've just remembered something. The arsonist left something behind after one incident. Well, it was thought to have belonged to the arsonist anyway.'

Ellie leaned forward. 'Really? What was it?'

'A white lighter with what looked like a crown symbol on it,' Rebecca said.

Meghan nodded. 'That's right. Though, of course, it could have belonged to anyone. Lots more people smoked back then.'

'True,' Rebecca said, 'but the police seemed to think it might be significant.'

Ellie sighed. It really wasn't much to go on. 'Anything else?' she asked hopefully.

Rebecca shook her head. 'No, sorry, love. Tommy might be able to help more though.'

'I doubt it,' Meghan said. 'Only reason he was quoted in the paper was because that Karin journalist hounded him for a quote. He didn't really have much to do with the actual investigations; he was a serious-crimes detective, remember? He wouldn't have been involved in things like this.'

'True,' Rebecca said. 'Maybe Adrian can do some digging?'

'Maybe,' Ellie said, running it all over in her mind. She stood up. 'I'd better go, actually, I have a deadline.'

'You haven't even touched your cake!' Meghan said.

'I'll take some with me.'

'For the kids too.'

Meghan sliced three more huge wedges of cake and wrapped them in napkins, handing them to Ellie. 'Let me see you out. You stay here, Rebecca, you still need to tell me about that book you're reading.'

Meghan walked out with Ellie, linking her arm through hers. 'I wanted to grab a quiet word, actually,' she said. 'I felt *so* bad having Caitlin here last night.'

'Oh, Meghan, it's fine, really. She's Peter's girlfriend.'

'I know, but it's only been three months.'

'Well, longer than that,' Ellie said with a nervous laugh.

Meghan frowned. 'What do you mean?'

'It doesn't matter.' She just couldn't do that to Meghan. She'd figure it out eventually. 'Thanks for the cake,' she said. She gave Meghan a kiss on the cheek, then walked away, thinking about the poison pen letters and the arson attacks.

It occurred to her how the village was like an actual forest, a perfect veneer of trees hiding what lay squirming and rotting under the surface. To think Meghan had no clue what her son was like. But then Forest Grove was like that, it all lurked beneath and sometimes came out in the worst ways: poison pen letters, arson . . . Ellie's own little vigilante spree.

As she thought that, she noticed Adrian in uniform walking on the outskirts of the forest. She jogged over to him.

'PC Cooper!' she shouted.

'Inspector Nash,' he joked back.

She smiled. 'I thought you'd be interested in some stuff I've uncovered. Turns out my mum wasn't the only one who received poison pen letters all those years back. Other residents did too.' She told him what she'd discovered. 'Plus, there was a spate of arson attacks which occurred a few months after the poison pen letters.'

'Wow,' Adrian replied. 'That *is* interesting. Any suspects?'

'No. Though Rebecca mentioned that a lighter with a crown on it was left behind after one incident. Maybe you could look back at old records, find a photo of it?'

Adrian's face suddenly tensed.

'What's wrong?' Ellie asked.

'Nothing,' he said stiffly.

'I can tell that means something to you. What is it?'

'It's nothing, Ellie.' He looked at his watch. 'Look, I have to go. I'll look into it, but best to just leave the investigations to us, okay?'

Then he strode off into the forest.

Ellie frowned. It was clear that her mentioning the lighter had triggered something in him.

But what?

Vanessa stirred a second sugar into her latte and raised an eyebrow. 'So you really think the poison pen letters are connected to the recent fires here?'

'Yes, I do.'

They were sitting in the bakery café for lunch later that day. It had just started raining outside after a beautiful, clear morning, and people were scurrying back and forth with cardigans held over their heads as they attended to chores in the courtyard. In the distance the trees thrashed about wildly as though angry at the sudden change in weather.

'Have you mentioned all this to Adrian?' Vanessa asked.

'Yes, this morning after I saw your mum and Rebecca.'

'I saw him earlier, having a proper argument with Andrea. It was delicious to watch,' Vanessa added with a wicked grin.

Ellie tilted her head. 'Really? What time was this?'

'About ten? They were out in the courtyard.'

Ellie frowned. 'I'd just spoken to him then. What if he went straight to Andrea's after talking to me? He did react strangely when I mentioned the lighter.'

'What lighter?'

'Rebecca said a lighter was found at the scene of one of the arson attacks years ago with a crown on the front.' Her eyes widened. 'My God, something just occurred to me! You know how Andrea is into all things Disney?'

Vanessa wrinkled her nose. 'Yep. So gross.'

'I know Disney used to have branded lighters – totally wrong,' she added. 'Do you think . . . ?'

Vanessa's eyes widened. 'Disney princess *Andrea* could be the arsonist?'

'Yes! Adrian reacted *so* strangely when I mentioned the lighter to him. Maybe it clicked? Maybe he realised there was one person he knew who was into princesses and who used to smoke . . . still does, from what Adrian has told me. *That's* why they were arguing. As soon as I mentioned the lighter, he thought of Andrea so he went to confront her.'

'Now *that* would be a turn-up for the books.' Vanessa looked over to see a customer waiting. 'Better go, but keep up the work, Sherlock.'

As Vanessa jogged off to the counter, Ellie leaned back in her chair, thoughts running through her mind.

When the poison pen letters were going around and then the arson attacks took place, Andrea would have been fifteen, like Ellie and Vanessa. Kitty had talked about how poison pen writers sometimes moved on to arson. But if Andrea was behind it all, why would a fifteen-year-old Andrea send horrible letters like that, especially to Ellie's mum? But then someone like Ellie's mum was everything Andrea had strived to be as a teenager: a beautiful, blonde, stylish woman.

Another thought occurred to Ellie. That would mean Andrea posted a firework through her own letterbox. Unless she wanted to distract attention away from herself? It seemed a bit tenuous though. Was Andrea really that messed up?

Yes, a small voice said inside.

Ellie looked into the distance towards Andrea's house. Could she really be behind all this?

Ellie woke early the next morning and lay in bed with Stanley snoozing on her lap, staring at Andrea's Facebook profile on her phone. It was a photo of her at Disneyland Paris with Michael beside her. They were both in costume, Andrea as Cinderella, Michael as Prince Charming. It was pretty nauseating.

Ellie looked into Andrea's eyes. She certainly had that malicious edge that was evident in the poison pen letters, and she *did* love to attract attention. From her peroxide hair to her flashy clothes and the way she inserted herself into the community. Kitty had mentioned underlying issues and there was no doubt Andrea had had a challenging childhood: her parents had both been well off but had worked long hours, leaving her alone a lot. But did that make her capable of sending those letters when she was just fifteen . . . just for a little attention?

It really did all seem so very tenuous, but then it was the only lead Ellie had right now. She just needed some more clues to solve this puzzle.

She yawned. She really ought to get up. The kids were still asleep, but that was fine; it was Sunday, after all. Zoe was going to her friend Summer's house for the afternoon, and Tyler was planning to head into Ashbridge to visit a friend's new studio, so she'd have the day to herself. Even more reason to make the most of it and get up.

She dragged herself out of bed and flung the curtains open, then gasped.

Her car was on fire!

Chapter 24

Ellie screamed and ran down the stairs as Stanley galloped after her.

'What's wrong?' Tyler asked, coming from his room.

'Car's on fire, stay indoors!' she shouted.

She put her phone to her ear, calling emergency services as she ran outside.

Flames leapt angrily inside the car, black smoke billowing into the air. The acrid smell of burnt leather and steel filled the air. Ellie coughed, putting her hand to her mouth.

It was an old grey Mercedes. Not worth much – she'd bought it on finance and was still paying off the loan – but seeing it on fire made her feel sick.

Residents started to appear and Ed Piper darted towards the car with a bucket of water, throwing it at the flames which were now sparking out from the bonnet and exhaust.

'Be careful,' Ellie called over to him. 'It might explode. I'm calling for help.' As she said that, an operator came on the line and she quickly explained what had happened.

'Mum?' Tyler was at the front door, still in his pyjamas. Behind him was Zoe, watching with a frightened look on her face.

The poor kids, Ellie thought. To endure the fire at their grand-parents', and now this.

'What happened?' Tyler called out.

'I don't know, it happens to cars sometimes.' But as Ellie said that, she knew it had to be more than that and, from the look on Tyler's face, he felt that too. The firework, the rose-bush fire . . . and now this? It was just too much of a coincidence. She could tell that other people thought the same as they watched the fire with worried eyes, whispering to one another. 'Can you guys get back inside?' she asked the kids. 'Get yourselves some breakfast.'

Tyler nodded, leading his sister indoors.

'This has got out of hand,' Ed said, walking over to Ellie. 'We shouldn't have to put up with this bloody vigilante!'

'We don't know for sure it's the vigilante,' Sheila said as she joined them.

The vigilante, Ellie thought.

She was the vigilante . . . or had been.

'Of course it's the vigilante, Sheila!' Ed shot back.

'Did you post something on Tommy's group, Ellie?' Ed's wife asked.

'No, nothing.'

But I got a poison pen letter, she wanted to say.

That didn't explain why someone had decided to set her car on fire. It was different from the other attacks. It wasn't in response to a Facebook post.

It felt even more personal – just as the letter had.

Who was *doing* this? Ellie wrapped her arms around herself, feeling more vulnerable than she ever had.

She needed Adrian.

She quickly called him.

'Hi, everything okay?' he asked as soon as he answered.

'No, my car's on fire.'

'What?' There was the sound of glass breaking. 'Damn.'

'You okay?'

'Just dropped my water. I'm at the station, I'll be over as soon as I can.'

Adrian arrived twenty minutes later in his uniform, just as two fire engines flew down the road, coming to a stop in front of the burning car. He marched up to Ellie, directing her away from the car and pulling her into a hug, his police radio crackling. Ed raised an eyebrow and exchanged a look with his wife. But Ellie didn't care. It was just what she needed.

Everyone watched as the firemen got to work, directing their hoses at the car until the fire was out. Just a cage of a car remained when they had finished, wisps of grey smoke curling around black, charred and twisted metal.

'Who would do this?' Ellie asked Adrian.

'It could be random.'

'After the letter I received?' she said quietly. 'Unlikely.'

One of the firemen walked over to Ellie. 'Well, this is becoming a bit of a regular occurrence in Forest Grove.'

Ellie sighed. 'I know.'

'Any idea how it started?' Adrian asked the fireman.

'Can't be a hundred per cent sure,' the fireman replied, 'but my guess is it was deliberate. One of the windows was forced down and there seems to be an area in the back seat, beneath the window, where the fire might have been started.'

The fireman walked off and Ellie put her head in her hands, letting out a sob. 'This is too much. And it's *my* fault.'

'How's it your fault?'

She peered up at him. 'You know why,' she whispered. 'I started something with those pranks. I – I reawakened the poison pen author.'

'We can't be sure they're behind all this.'

'Oh, come on, they *have* to be. The letter on Friday night, then this morning my car's on fire? It's all connected.'

'Forest Grove, utopia of the woods,' a voice said. They looked over to see Detective Powell strolling over, her eyes on the car. Ellie's heart sank. 'A bit more like a dystopia, in my experience,' the detective said as she stopped in front of Ellie and Adrian. She eyed Adrian's arm, which was still around Ellie's shoulders.

He quickly removed it. 'I didn't realise this incident had been logged,' he said. 'I was about to call it in.'

'We had a call already,' the detective replied.

'Are you a detective, not just a PC?' Ed asked as Adrian's jaw tensed.

'I am,' Detective Powell replied.

'Good. Something needs to be done about all this,' Ed said, angrily gesturing at the remains of Ellie's car. 'It's out of control. That's seven incidents now.'

The detective tilted her head as she looked at Ellie. 'It is, isn't it?'

Ellie tried to keep her composure, but she knew what the detective was getting at. After all, Ellie had confessed everything to Detective Powell.

'The fire attacks seem different from the others,' Adrian said.

'An escalation,' the detective remarked, her eyes still on Ellie.

'They *are* different,' Ellie said, hoping to communicate her innocence to the detective. She also hoped more than anything that the detective didn't identify Ellie as being responsible for the other incidents in front of the villagers.

'Why don't you come into the station, Miss Nash?' the detective suggested. 'I think it's time we had a little chat.'

'Why do you need Ellie at the station?' Ed asked.

The detective smiled tightly. 'Miss Nash is—'

'The poor car,' Zoe said miserably. She was standing in the doorway, a piece of toast in her hand, Tyler behind her.

The detective looked at Ellie and Zoe, then sighed. 'We just need a little more detail about what happened with the car.'

'Yes, of course I'll go in,' Ellie said, grateful that Detective Powell hadn't unmasked her in front of the residents.

'Are you going to the police station then, Mum?' Tyler asked, walking up to his mum, suddenly seeming like a grown man as he protectively stood by her.

'Oh no, why?' Zoe asked.

Ellie's stomach did somersaults. She was getting a glimpse into how it would feel if Zoe found out she had been the original vigilante and she felt sick. It would come out though, it always did in Forest Grove.

'It's fine, darling,' Ellie said as she forced back the tears that were about to come. 'It's just so I can help the police figure out what happened.' She looked at Tyler. 'I don't know how long I'll be. Can you make sure Zoe is ready to go to Summer's by eleven? If you can walk her there, that would be great, then you can hop on the bus to Ashbridge. There's money in the bureau, take a tenner. Make sure you let Stanley out for a wee before you go too.'

'Yeah, sure,' Tyler said, brow knitted.

She gave Zoe a hug, then Tyler too, surprised when he didn't resist her for once, his worried eyes still on Detective Powell over her shoulder. As the children went back inside, the detective turned to Ellie. 'I can give you a lift if you want?'

'I'll come too,' Adrian said firmly.

Detective Powell frowned. 'There isn't really any need.'

'This is my patch.'

Detective Powell sighed. 'Fine.'

Ellie smiled at Adrian, grateful. She wasn't sure she could do this alone. She looked at the unmarked police car. At least it wasn't a marked car. But then she looked around at the dozens of residents now gathered on the street. They all knew it for what it was: a police car. And it was about to take Ellie to the police station.

Chapter 25

Sunday 1st August
9 a.m.

Andrea Simpson

I know it will be difficult for Tommy to post this as she's the mother of his grandchildren so I thought I would instead: why oh why was Ellie Nash taken away in a police car for questioning after the seventh – yes, *seventh* – vigilante incident this morning?

Rebecca Feine

You haven't mentioned what the incident was, Andrea. Ellie's own car was set on fire. They would have taken her to the station just to ask some questions about it.

Andrea Simpson

They didn't take me after my house was set on fire! That's a little more serious than a car going up in flames. No, there seems to be more to it than that.

Lucy Cronin

What are you saying, Andrea?

Andrea Simpson

I'm saying, if you put the jigsaw pieces together, it presents rather an interesting picture. Ellie becomes admin of the Facebook community group the VERY DAY after the first incident occurs. And then we end up here, with the police taking her away.

Vanessa Shillingford

You do talk rubbish, Andrea. Why would she set fire to her own car? And dog poo through a letterbox is a little different from setting lawns on fire.

Andrea Simpson

They're still acts of vigilantism.

Ed Piper

Andrea's right. As the detective who was at the scene said herself, it's an escalation. We all know how serial killers escape their crimes.

Sheila Leighton

Jesus, Ed, serial killers?! This is all ridiculous! Ellie simply isn't capable of such awful acts. I've been her neighbour for over twenty years and I've never seen any such evidence of behaviour from her to suggest her doing something like this. We must leave it to the police and fire service to investigate.

Belinda Bell

It's usually people like Ellie Nash though, isn't it? The seemingly perfect types. Weren't there rumours her mother was behind the poison pen letters years back? Wouldn't have surprised me.

Tommy Mileham

This has got out of hand. I'm closing this thread.

Chapter 26

Ellie couldn't believe she was back in the same interview room she'd been in a few days ago. Or maybe she could. Surely she had known this would come? She had played with fire, figuratively, and got burnt.

At least Adrian was there this time, even if he did look horribly uncomfortable sitting across from her in his uniform, pen and notepad in hand. As Ellie looked at Detective Powell, she wondered if she saw it as a game of sorts. Surely the detective had noticed the connection between her local police officer and Ellie? Was she going to try to play them off against one another?

There was nothing to play though. Ellie had told her everything. Apart from Tyler being behind the music prank . . . and the letter she'd received.

She also presumed the detective was aware Adrian knew after Ellie had reported it. But she needed to make sure Detective Powell didn't figure out Adrian had known before then, otherwise he could get into all kinds of trouble.

Maybe that was why he was there, to make sure Ellie didn't slip up?

'I think, first, it's important you know I got a poison pen letter Friday night,' she said.

'Yes, I'm aware of the letter,' the detective said, opening her folder to reveal she had it. 'PC Cooper logged it. This case has now evolved into an official investigation. Three fires now, combined with the . . .' She paused. 'The other *crimes*. It's essential we get to the bottom of who's doing this.'

Ellie swallowed nervously, her eyes flickering between them. Adrian gave her a reassuring look, but she could see in his brown eyes that he was worried too.

'They are very different from what I did,' Ellie said in as calm a voice as she could muster. 'The fires, they're not pranks.'

'But was what you did pranks, Ellie? You see,' the detective said with a sigh, 'I'm getting it in the ear from my boss about not arresting you the first time.'

Ellie's heart thumped against her chest as Adrian gave her a panicked look.

'But lucky for you,' the detective added, 'I don't always do what I'm told.'

Ellie let out a sigh of relief, looking down at her hands as she blinked back tears.

'The thing is,' the detective continued, 'on paper, it just screams *all* of this is you.'

'On paper?' Adrian asked. 'I wouldn't say Ellie's profile or history suggests she'd set fire to her own car and people's lawns and porches.'

'No, but then I wouldn't say she'd be the type to shove dog excrement through an elderly lady's letterbox either,' the detective countered, her dark eyes hard.

Adrian's jaw clenched. 'Well, you do have the doorbell camera footage to rule Ellie out of Andrea Simpson's fire.'

'Doesn't quite *rule* her out,' the detective said.

Ellie watched the two of them, silent, feeling as if she were on trial, watching the defence and the prosecution argue.

'What about alibis?' Adrian quickly said. 'I was with Ellie when the Milehams' lawn was set on fire.'

The detective raised an eyebrow. 'Were you now, PC Cooper?'

Adrian nodded, a look of determination in his eyes. 'Yes, it was clear the fire was started just before we turned up and I'd been with Ellie for at least twenty minutes.'

The detective looked down at her notes. 'After ten at night?'

Adrian sighed. 'Look, we're friends. And even if we were more than that, does it make a difference to all this?'

Ellie felt her face flush.

'It does when your ex-wife's porch is set on fire,' the detective shot back.

Ellie pinched the bridge of her nose.

Detective Powell leaned back in her chair, observing them both over steepled fingers. 'The more I think about it, the more I think it's probably not the best idea you're here, PC Cooper.'

Adrian nodded. 'You're right.' He stood up and looked at Ellie. 'We'll chat after.'

She gave him a grateful smile, then watched as he walked out.

'He's a good officer,' the detective commented. 'I could see how shocked he was when I told you'd confessed to the other incidents.'

Ellie nodded stiffly. Adrian was obviously a good actor.

'Good of him to forgive you,' Powell continued. 'But then, as you said, they were just pranks, right? Different from fires?'

Ellie sighed, raking her fingers through her short, smoke-filled hair. 'Look, I don't know what you're trying to get at here. I'll answer any questions you have. I just need you to know I had *nothing* to do with the fires.'

The detective was quiet as she watched Ellie for a few moments. Ellie held her gaze, hoping the detective could see the sincerity in her eyes.

'I know,' Detective Powell said eventually. 'Call it a police officer's gut instinct. But I know. And this letter,' she added, looking down at it, 'certainly adds a new dimension. You mentioned your mother was the victim of some similar poison pen letters last time we spoke. I did some digging. Turns out she wasn't the only victim back then.'

'Yes,' Ellie said, pleased the detective had done her own investigations. 'The same person who wrote those letters wrote mine, I'm sure of it.' She got her phone out to show the detective photos of the other letters. 'See the use of ampersands and hearts as dots?'

Powell examined the photos then nodded. 'What would make this person decide to pick up their pen again after all these years though?'

'I was wondering the same. Plus, there were arson attacks back then too.'

The detective looked at Ellie in surprise. 'Really?'

Ellie explained what she'd learnt.

'Now that *is* interesting,' said the detective. 'You should have let me know.'

'I told Adrian.'

The detective stared at the letter. 'I'm going to run this through the Forensics department. I think I can justify the resources now.'

'Great.'

'Can you think of anyone who might be behind this?'

Ellie paused for a moment. 'I did wonder about Andrea Simpson.'

Powell gave her a cynical look. 'PC Cooper's ex. Really?'

Ellie told her about the lighter that had been discovered at the scene of one of the arson incidents and the way Andrea was. 'I know it's flimsy, I'm kind of grasping at straws here.'

'A Disney lighter,' the detective said. 'Not much to go on, but it's certainly something we can look into.' She scribbled down Andrea's name. 'Anything else that comes to mind? What about your mother?'

Ellie looked at the detective in shock. 'My mother? What do you mean? She's in a retirement village!'

'I'm not suggesting she's behind it. But when I read the reports about the poison pen letters Belinda Bell received, something interesting *did* come up about your mother.'

Ellie's breath quickened. '*What* came up?'

'The detective in charge of the poison pen campaign all those years back told me that your mother was a suspect.'

Ellie's mouth dropped open. 'That's crazy! She *received* those letters.'

'She could have sent them to herself.'

'There's no way,' Ellie said, refusing to believe her mother would do that. 'No way at all. Why on earth would anyone think that?'

The detective fixed Ellie with her gaze. 'There was some indented writing on one of the letters sent to Belinda from something that had been written on a piece of paper on top of it.'

'What was it?' Ellie asked, temples throbbing.

'Your mother's signature.'

Chapter 27

As soon as Ellie got home, she found some letters her mother had written and compared the handwriting with the poison pen letters.

They were totally different styles of handwriting!

But still, she needed to look her mother in the face. So she headed straight to the retirement village. As she sat across from her mother, she just couldn't comprehend the idea that she was behind them. There needed to be another explanation for finding the imprint of her mother's signature on the letter.

Ellie pulled the letters from her bag now and with shaky hands spread them out on top of the Scrabble board that was still lying on her mother's table.

'Mum,' she said softly, leaning close to her mother, 'I've never needed your help more than I do now.'

'Oh, darling,' her mother said, putting her hand over Ellie's.

Ellie smiled at the feel of her mother's hand on hers. It was a rare occurrence but, lately, she felt like she was connecting more with her. 'Mum,' she said gently, 'I found the poison pen letters you received in your boxes in the loft, remember? Look, I've brought them with me.'

Her mother glanced at them, then her brow furrowed. 'Oh. Not those. Put them away.' She turned her face away.

'I know, they're horrible, aren't they, Mum? Did you ever find out who wrote them?'

Her mum's beautiful blue eyes lifted to Ellie's face. 'No. Did you?'

Ellie examined her mother's face. She seemed to genuinely not know who wrote them.

Ellie paused for a moment, gathering herself for what she was to say next. 'Something was found on one of the letters.'

'Oh?'

'An imprint from something that had been written over it. It was – it was your signature, Mum.'

Her mother's eyes widened. 'Signature? That's impossible.'

Ellie shuffled her chair closer to her mother. 'Yes. Do you know why that might be?'

Her mother looked her right in the eye. 'I didn't write them, Ellie, if that's what you're trying to say.'

She hadn't heard such clarity in her mother's voice for a long time. Her mother leaned forward, her other hand grasping Ellie's shoulder as she looked into her eyes. 'You have to find out who did though. You will, won't you?'

Ellie's eyes filled with tears. 'Yes, Mum. I'll find them.'

When Ellie got home, Adrian was waiting for her outside her house. He wasn't in uniform and was instead wearing a pair of jeans and a light-blue T-shirt. He'd texted her after leaving the interview room, telling her to call him when she finished. But she hadn't, too desperate to see her mum and talk to her about the signature.

'Hey,' she said, getting her keys out. 'Sorry I didn't call you, I went straight to see my mum.'

'Yeah, I heard about the signature imprint.'

Ellie let herself in, gesturing for Adrian to come in too when she remembered the kids had left already. Stanley jumped up at them both with joy, Adrian smiling as he stroked the dog.

'Mum didn't write those letters,' Ellie said. 'I just went to see her. She was so clear. Honestly, Adrian, I haven't seen her like that in ages. And she actually said outright it wasn't her.'

'I can't see it being her either, from what you've told me about her anyway,' he said, following Ellie down the hallway. 'Plus, I can't see her writing that recent letter to you.'

'Exactly! And anyway, the poison pen writer's handwriting is nothing like my mum's. Coffee?'

'Sure.' He sat at the kitchen island and Ellie set about making their coffee.

'Are you okay, Ellie?' Adrian asked.

'I'm fine, why?'

He gestured to the boiling water that was pouring from the machine, the cup she'd meant to place under the spout still in her hand. 'Damn. Damn, damn, damn.'

'Here, let me help.' Adrian got up, grabbing a tea towel, soaking the water up.

Ellie leaned her hands against the counter, taking in deep breaths. 'This is *such* a mess.'

'Hey,' Adrian said, opening his arms. 'Come here.'

She went to him, letting him wrap his arms around her as Stanley watched them from his bed. Adrian smelt so good and so pure, of washing power and toothpaste. And it felt so good and so pure to be in his arms.

'Do you think Detective Powell will be able to track down who's doing all this?' she asked, peering up at him.

'Maybe,' Adrian said, tucking a stray lock of hair behind her ear. They were still holding each other, and Ellie was happy about that. 'She's bloody good at what she does.'

'But do you think it's really a priority for her? You said there's loads of issues in Ashbridge at the moment.'

'It's definitely moved up the list of priorities, and I'll make sure she keeps on it. I'm good at pestering people. I know it's scary, but we will figure this out.'

Ellie sighed. 'It's not just that. I still feel I need to prove I didn't start the fires.'

'I think Powell is pretty convinced you didn't.'

'And you?'

Adrian looked at her in surprise. 'You think I'd be here with my arms wrapped around you if I thought it *was* you? My kid was in the house when the first fire was started.'

Ellie sighed. 'I guess not.' She bit her lip. 'As for the arms being wrapped around me bit . . .'

Adrian quickly unwrapped them and stepped away. 'Sorry.'

'No, I liked it.'

'Yeah, but . . .' He sighed, shuffling awkwardly. 'I shouldn't have.'

Ellie frowned. It was so sad, how they both clearly liked each other, but Ellie had ruined it all. She just needed to accept that chance had flown out of the window and try to make the most of them being friends. 'Let me try that coffee again,' she said, putting the cup under the spout. 'Another thing that worries me is other residents finding out. What if they begin to suspect me? They did see me taken away in a police car this morning. I'm sure word has got around. I can't even bear to look at Tommy's Facebook group.'

'Anyone who knows you knows you're not capable of setting fire to things.'

Ellie laughed bitterly as she brought over Adrian's coffee. 'You suspected me, didn't you?'

'Yeah, but that was in a moment of madness. The more I get to know you, the more I see how passionate you are about protecting the people you love, especially your kids. I don't approve of what you did, but I kind of get it, now I know about those letters.'

'But I was wrong,' Ellie said as she sat across from him with her own coffee. 'So wrong. And I feel a duty to find out who's behind the other stuff.'

'Don't get involved, Ellie. Let us do our job. I promise you, I'll take this fight on. I have the resources, the training. I don't want you getting hurt.'

'Why would I get hurt?'

'That letter to you wasn't nice. And arson isn't nice either. Clearly, whoever is doing this wants to hurt people.'

Ellie rubbed at her tired eyes. 'It's like history repeating itself. The poison pen letters, the arson attacks.'

'But this time, we're going to find out who's behind it all.'

Ellie nodded. 'We are. I just hope we do before it's too late.'

The rest of the week was unusually uneventful, especially with it now being the school summer holidays, the kids wanting to laze about in the garden or see friends while Ellie did her work, grateful for this period of calm to catch up on the puzzle book she was due to submit by the next Monday. While Zoe was at her friend's one afternoon, Ellie headed to the bakery with Stanley to meet with Vanessa and Meghan during their lunch break.

As she walked in, maybe it was her imagination, but she sensed a frosty tone in other villagers' usually warm greetings. She was pretty sure something nasty about her had been posted on Tommy's Facebook group after she'd been taken away in a police car, but she couldn't bring herself to read it.

Vanessa seemed unusually quiet. Ellie hadn't seen much of her the past few days, she had been so busy with her work deadline.

They had spoken on the phone though, about the fire and the letter Ellie had received. Vanessa had been her usual angry self about it all, but Ellie had sensed something else bubbling underneath. When she'd asked what was wrong, Vanessa had claimed it was 'just that time of the month' and she was being a 'moody git'.

'Did you manage to sort a replacement car, love?' Meghan asked as she placed some rolls and cake on the table, taking a seat beside Vanessa as their assistant manned the till.

'Yes, it arrived yesterday,' Ellie said.

'Presume your car is a write-off then?' Vanessa asked, dropping a treat on the floor for Stanley.

'Yep,' Ellie said with a sigh.

She began eating, the three of them subdued.

'I popped in to see your mum earlier,' Meghan said. 'She seemed more anxious than usual.'

Ellie frowned. That was her fault, bringing up the past. But she'd had no choice.

'What did she say?' Ellie asked.

'Kept talking about some letters?' Meghan replied. 'I wondered if she meant the poison pen letters we were chatting about with Rebecca the other day?'

Ellie sighed. 'I haven't told you, actually, Meghan, but I found out recently that Mum got some of those poison pen letters too.'

Meghan's mouth dropped open. 'Really? But she never said anything!'

'I know, she didn't tell anyone, as far as I know, she just kept them all hidden away . . . until I found them.'

Meghan shook her head, brows knitted. 'Why would she not say anything to me?'

'Pride?' Vanessa suggested. 'Maybe she was embarrassed?'

'Maybe,' Meghan agreed. 'Your mum didn't like to make a fuss. What did the letters say?'

Ellie got out her phone and showed Meghan the photos she'd taken.

As she did, an email notification popped up and Ellie realised with a jolt that it was from Karin Hawkins.

'Isn't that that annoying journalist?' Vanessa asked.

Ellie quickly swiped the notification away. 'I dread to think what she wants.' She found the photo of a letter her mum had received and showed it to Meghan.

'How horrible,' Meghan whispered, shaking her head.

'It helps explain a lot,' Vanessa said.

Meghan peered up at her daughter. 'Like what?'

'Like why Ellie's mum is the way she is,' Vanessa explained.

'Yes, maybe,' Meghan said, handing Ellie's phone back to her.

'Those letters chipped away at her,' Ellie said. 'They broke her spirit.'

'But they're just words,' Meghan said.

'Really, Mum?' Vanessa replied. 'Just words? It's more than words. Letters like this can really get to people.'

'And now it's all starting again,' Ellie said.

'What do you mean?' Meghan asked as Vanessa and Ellie exchanged looks.

'I got a letter,' Ellie said with a sigh.

Meghan's eyes widened. 'You did?'

'Do you have a photo of it?' Vanessa asked. 'I haven't seen it yet.'

'Yep.' Ellie showed them both the photo she'd taken of the letter on her phone.

'Oh my,' Meghan said.

'Oh my indeed,' Vanessa said, shaking her head.

'Surely it's not the same person writing them?' Meghan exclaimed. 'It's been nearly thirty years!'

'Once a psychopath, always a psychopath,' Vanessa said.

Meghan tutted. 'Psychopath? Honestly, darling, you do exaggerate.'

'I'm thinking whoever's behind the recent fires *must* be behind the letters,' Ellie said.

'And all the other stuff too, like the dog mess and breaking poor Pauline's arm?' Meghan asked.

Ellie's face flushed. 'It was a sprain, I think.'

'The fires are a completely different ball game, Mum,' Vanessa quickly said, casting Ellie a look. 'Somebody else *has* to be responsible for the fires.'

'I don't think so,' Meghan said. 'They've all harmed villagers in some way. It's just escalated now.'

'Have the police had any luck trying to figure out who's behind the fires?' Vanessa asked Ellie.

'That was why I was at the station the other day,' Ellie said in a loud voice so others could hear her. 'They want my help in tracking down the vigilante.'

'And what exactly are they doing to track them down?' Meghan asked.

'They've got Forensics involved to look at any possible fingerprints on my letter,' Ellie said. 'And the car too.'

Vanessa looked impressed. 'Very *CSI*. Any luck?'

'Not yet,' Ellie lied. She didn't want to tell them about her mum's signature imprint. She couldn't risk word getting out about it and people gossiping about her mum even more than they were already. She trusted Vanessa and Meghan, but she also knew to be super-careful.

Ellie closed her eyes and leaned back in the chair.

'Hey, let's not talk about this any more,' Vanessa said. 'How about we talk about what on earth we're going to do to entertain the kids over the summer holidays?'

Over the next hour, the three women chatted and joked, and Ellie tried to enjoy herself. But her mind kept straying back to everything that had happened . . . plus, she was aware of the unfriendly atmosphere around her. Not to mention the email awaiting her from Karin Hawkins!

As she walked back home, she reluctantly read it.

> Hi Ellie!
>
> I hope you don't mind me emailing but I suppose you could call us colleagues, considering you do puzzles for us (I had NO idea!). So I heard your car was set on fire . . . and yet I can't see any posts from either the archived community group or Tommy Mileham's new one to suggest the Facebook Vigilante would want to target you. Maybe we can have a chat. My number is in the signature below. Always best to get your side of the story in!
>
> Take care, Karin x

Ellie shook her head, deleting the email in anger. There was no way she'd talk to Karin bloody Hawkins!

As she drew closer to her house, she was surprised to see Peter waiting outside in his flash car. Maybe he was coming to check on her after the fire? She had received a rushed text from him, checking in, but nothing more.

He got out of the car, slamming the door shut behind him.

'Where are the kids?' she asked as she let Stanley in.

'Sleepovers.' Peter was very keen about arranging sleepovers for the kids so he could palm them off on others' parents.

'You're supposed to check with me first.'

'It's no big deal, Tyler's at Aaron's for his birthday, Zoe's with Summer.'

'Next time, tell me. I got a replacement car by the way,' she said, gesturing to the red Peugeot she'd been given.

'Right,' Peter said, his jaw flexing and unflexing, something she knew he did when he was angry.

'The police are on the case,' she continued, 'Forensics and everything.'

'I'm not here about that.'

'Oh, right. Everything okay?'

'Not really,' he snapped.

Ellie nervously pulled the sleeves of her cardigan over her knuckles. Had he found out what she'd done?

'Mum told me what you said to her,' he said.

'What do you mean?'

'Calling me useless, saying I'm a crap dad,' he seethed.

Meghan had told him about a conversation they'd had? She supposed Meghan *was* his mother. But still, Ellie was surprised.

'Look,' she said, 'I didn't mean for it all to come out, but she was talking like you were the Messiah and I couldn't help it! I had to say something. I mean, come on, Peter, you're no Mr Perfect.'

'And you are?' he shot back. Ellie realised then she could smell beer on his breath. Was he drunk . . . and if so, what the hell was he doing driving?

'Not unless I've had a sex change,' she shot back.

'This is *serious*, Ellie. You going around accusing me of being a bad dad when you're no mother of the bloody year.'

'How so?' Ellie asked, putting her hands on her hips. 'Who's the one who went to parents' evening when you were "working late"?' she said, using her fingers to make quotation marks. 'Who cooked dinner every night, made sure the kids' uniforms were ironed? Who checked their homework and drove them to dance classes and band practice? Who nursed Zoe for days on end when she had tonsillitis? Or marched down to the school when Tyler was getting bullied? What exactly haven't I done, Peter? Do tell me.'

'Him, that's what!' he said, pointing down the road. Ellie followed his gaze to see Adrian striding along the street. He hesitated when he caught sight of Peter.

'Don't worry, mate!' Peter called out, curtains twitching now as residents sensed drama. 'The coast's clear, the kids aren't staying tonight so you can fit in a quick shag.'

Ellie's mouth dropped open. 'How dare you.'

Adrian continued walking, stopping in front of Peter. 'What did you say?'

'I said you two can have a quick shag,' he shouted. Graham and Malorie Cane walked by, whispering to each other. In the distance, two mums walking with their young children paused, having a good look.

'We're friends, Peter,' Adrian said calmly. 'That's all. I think you should calm down.'

'Nah, it's fine, I'm cool,' Peter said, stumbling slightly.

'You're drunk,' Ellie said.

Peter shook his head. 'No, I'm not.'

'You're a liar,' Ellie shot back.

'I'm the liar?' Peter said. 'You're the one who's been at it with the local bobby. Don't worry,' he said, lowering his voice as he looked at Adrian. 'I know what she's like in the sack. All pristine on the surface, but a dirty little minx when you get her between the sheets.'

'Peter!' Ellie shouted.

Adrian gently put his hand on Peter's arm, trying to steer him away as he got his phone out. 'Let's call a taxi. Or maybe your father? Best you don't drive in this state.'

Peter shoved him away. 'Get off, you twat.'

Adrian took in a calming breath.

'Seriously,' Peter said, shoving Adrian's shoulder. 'Get off.'

'Stop doing that,' Adrian said in a low, warning voice.

'Peter, you're being a dick,' Ellie hissed as she sensed people watching from their houses. 'Just go.'

'Oh, whatever, you useless cow, you're not worth it,' Peter said, walking off. 'You're an embarrassment.'

Adrian marched up to him. But Ellie got there first, smacking Peter in the face with the flat of her palm, making contact with his cheekbone.

'That,' she said, flinching as she nursed her hand, 'is for being a cheating, lying scumbag who's spent the past twenty-five years treating me like crap. Yeah, did you hear that, everyone?' Ellie added, shouting at the people watching from their windows. 'Peter Mileham cheated on me with Caitlin Cohen. He's been cheating on me for years and he walked out on me and the kids. Now you know it all.'

'What the *hell* is going on?' Tommy was storming down the street, heading for his son.

'He's drunk,' Adrian said. 'He drove here drunk too. You're lucky I'm not doing him for drink-driving. Get him home, get him sober.'

Tommy grabbed his son's arm. 'What happened to your face?'

'Her!' Peter hissed.

Tommy looked at Ellie, eyes narrowing. Then he pulled Peter away.

'Come on,' Adrian said. 'Let's get you inside, away from prying eyes,' he added as people emerged from their houses.

Ellie let Adrian lead her inside, now in shock at what she'd done too. 'I can't believe I did that,' she said.

'He deserved it. He's lucky you got there before I did. Or maybe not,' he added, raising an eyebrow as he looked at her red palm. 'That was quite the slap.'

'What if he reports me?'

'And risk being done for drink-driving? Nah.' He made Ellie sit at one of the stools in the kitchen and got some pieces of paper towel, soaking them under the tap before coming back to Ellie and pressing them against her sore palm.

'I guess that was twenty-five years of resentment all expressed in one slap,' he said.

'Yep. And it felt soooo good.' As she said that, she suddenly burst into tears. 'Sorry, I just can't believe I slapped him in front of people. But the things he said! It was just so – so disrespectful.'

'Because he's a disrespectful idiot,' Adrian said, holding her hand and looking into her eyes. 'You deserve so much better than him. It makes me sad you wasted twenty-five years on that fool.'

'I guess we both wasted so much time with fools.'

'Tell me about it.' He was quiet for a moment, then he got an intense look on his face. 'You know what? I don't want to waste any more time. Sorry, I just can't resist wanting to kiss you.' He leaned down, putting both his hands on the armrests of Ellie's chair, and pressed his lips against hers.

Relief and joy mixed with a deep yearning inside her as she wrapped her arms around his neck, kissing him back. He lifted her from the seat and wrapped his arms around her waist, their kisses growing more urgent. He lifted her up, and she wrapped her legs around his waist. He stumbled as he tried to carry her to the sofa in the conservatory, and they both laughed.

As they sunk on to the sofa, Adrian's lips trailing down to her collarbone, his fingers fumbling with the buttons of her cardigan, she felt as if the trees were watching them through the window, judging them.

She thought about getting up and closing the curtains, but then Adrian was slipping his fingers beneath her blouse, then her bra, and all thoughts other than being there, with Adrian, left her.

That night, as Ellie lay in bed with Adrian sleeping beside her, she couldn't help but think how only four months before she'd been in this very bed with Peter. It was so different though. Adrian's smell was different, the feel of his skin . . . the fact she was *feeling* his skin. She and Peter had barely touched in the last months of their marriage. It had been devastating when Peter had walked out on her, but she now understood that he had been right to leave. Their marriage had been empty and loveless for a long time. Being with Adrian had shown her what it really meant to *be* with someone. It had felt so natural. Completely different from the way things had been with Peter, who had insisted on manipulating her into all sorts of strange positions to copy some adult video he'd watched.

Adrian took his time, waiting to see how her body reacted when he touched her. She was still aching in a way that had been different from when she was with Peter. Her aches with him were the kinds of aches you'd get after a gym session. But with Adrian it was the ache of how her body had reacted to his soft, focused touches.

She looked over at Adrian's face as he slept, taking in the contours of his nose and his cheeks beneath the moonlight glowing in through the window. She smiled to herself. For the first time, she welcomed the idea of divorcing Peter. It wasn't just because of what she and Adrian had done, nor the argument she'd had with Peter earlier.

It was just her mind finally understanding that her marriage was over, for good. And for the first time, she found she fell asleep almost instantly.

It didn't seem long though before she was being shaken awake.

'Ellie, Ellie, wake up!'

She peered up to see Adrian standing over her, eyes alight with worry.

'What's wrong?' she said, still groggy as she struggled to sit up.

He pointed out of the window. Ellie let out a gasp.

Bright orange flames lit up the night sky, devouring the tree-tops in the distance.

'The forest is on fire!'

Chapter 28

Ellie raced down the street with Adrian, watching in horror as flames leapt angrily towards the dark skies above. Around them, other villagers ran towards the forest too, mouths agape with terror, eyes wide as they took in the scenes of devastation ahead of them. The horizon, which was usually just black at night with brief hints of the forest, was dominated by a sail of bright orange that rippled and gaped, growing larger and larger with every second.

Ellie felt the shocking burn of the heat coming from the blaze as she drew closer. Now she could see individual trees on fire, barely trees any more, just thin, black columns, their sides crawling with orange flames. New sounds emerged above the roar of the fire, as the creak and thud of falling trees combined with the wail of distant sirens and the panicked cries of villagers.

Adrian instantly headed for a group of people close to the fire, and Ellie followed, desperate to help.

Ed Piper shoved past her, in his hands a garden hose straining as it ran taut from the closest house.

'It won't reach!' he shouted.

'We can use it to fill buckets,' Ellie said.

'Got them!' another voice shouted, running past her. It was Tommy, with two large buckets dangling from his hands, Peter walking groggily behind him, an ugly bruise now prominent on his cheek.

Thank God the kids were on sleepovers in houses on the outer rings of the village, away from the forest.

Around Ellie, more people ran towards the fire with buckets.

'Form a chain!' Adrian shouted. 'Two of them!'

Everyone did as he asked, quickly moving into two long chains. Ellie joined Adrian's chain and peered over her shoulder, watching as Ed filled bucket after bucket with water, each bucket then passed down the line. Ellie nearly buckled under the weight of the first bucket that was handed to her, but she forced herself to find the strength, passing it on to the next person.

When the first bucket got to Adrian at the front of the line, he ran to the edge of the forest with Ed and threw the water towards a nearby tree. But it scarcely made a difference.

Still, they continued, buckets passed from villager to villager, and Ellie found tears running down her face as she helped, other people around her crying too.

Who had *done* this? The beautiful, lush, green forest was the beating heart of this village. It was evil, pure evil.

You played your part though, a small voice inside her whispered. *You play with fire, you get burnt.*

It was true. Her pranks as the Facebook Vigilante had ignited this blaze. Deep down, she knew it. She was implicated in this devastating fire sweeping through the forest – the forest she had lived beside for so many years of her life. Sure, she hadn't struck the match, but she may as well have passed on the matchbox like a baton.

Ellie felt immense relief when two fire engines appeared. The crowds moved back as firefighters jumped from their vehicles, rushing towards the forest with jets of water. Ellie noticed Vanessa was there now, and Meghan too, the two women helping to clear the way for the firefighters.

'Move back!' a fireman yelled. 'All the way back!'

Ellie retreated with the other residents, finding Meghan and Vanessa.

'This is awful!' Vanessa said, shaking her head as she looked at the blazing forest.

Meghan put her arm around her daughter's shoulders. 'It'll be all right. The fire engines are here now.'

The three of them watched as the firefighters fought to beat back the flames. At first, it looked impossible, the blaze remaining as defiant and horrifying as it had when Ellie arrived. But eventually, flames that had a few minutes before danced in defiance began to die down, leaving behind a pall of grey smoke.

'This was no accident,' Andrea said, joining them. She was wearing jogging bottoms, her nightdress tucked into them, her hair all over the place. 'Someone tried to burn down the forest.'

'You really think so?' Meghan asked. 'I mean, fireworks and rose-bush fires are one thing. But *this*? Maybe it was an accident, a barbecue still alight.'

'Of *course* somebody did this,' Andrea hissed.

'But who?' Rebecca asked as she came over, soot on her cheek.

Lucy Cronin was there, too. 'Myra Young's the newest resident to move here,' she whispered. They all looked over to where Myra was watching the firefighters tackling the blaze, her baby in her arms.

'That's not fair, Lucy,' Rebecca said. 'Being the newest member of the village doesn't make her guilty.'

'Plus, we all know why you want to blame Myra,' Graham said as he stood nearby. 'I heard about your little falling-out from my daughter. Can you keep a friend for longer than five minutes, Lucy!'

'How rude of you, Graham!' Lucy said.

'I think it's Andrew Blake,' Belinda said, sidling up to them in her dressing gown. 'He's always been a bit odd, living in the forest with his mother.'

'*Or* it could be Neve Morgan,' Andrea said. 'That hair of hers is very odd.'

'She's a teacher, Andrea!' Rebecca said, shaking her head.

'Teachers can be psychopaths too, you know,' Andrea retorted.

Graham nodded. 'Very true, and that Neve woman is a bit of a hippie really. I can imagine her posting dog poop through someone's letterbox. Haven't you noticed how—?'

'Shut up!' Ellie screamed.

Everyone looked at her in surprise, including Peter, who raised an eyebrow, his hand instinctively going to his bruised cheek.

'Neve Morgan did not post dog poo through your letterbox, Belinda,' Ellie said.

'You can't say that for sure,' Andrea retorted.

'I can, because I did it.'

Chapter 29

Everyone went quiet and Ellie wrapped her arms around herself.

'Oh, bugger,' Vanessa said under her breath.

Ellie didn't regret it though. Even with the looks of recrimination being aimed at her, she felt a weight had lifted off her shoulders. She knew this village; she knew she'd eventually be unmasked as the Facebook Vigilante, so better to take control and admit to it.

'Did you hear that?' Andrea shouted out, looking around her to make sure others were listening. 'Ellie just admitted that *she's* the Facebook Vigilante! Someone call the police!'

'She didn't say she was behind the fires, you moron!' Vanessa hissed back.

'Not the fires,' Ellie quickly said. 'I would never do that.'

'What exactly did you do, Ellie?' Belinda Bell called out, her wrinkled face grey with soot.

All eyes turned to Ellie and she felt as though she were on fire, buckling and melting under the heat of their gazes.

'Yes, I shoved dog poo through your letterbox, Belinda,' Ellie said in a trembling voice. 'Ed's green bins,' she said, gesturing towards him as he shook his head in disgust. 'The guns . . .' Then she hesitated. 'I was behind the loud music too.'

'And breaking Pauline's arm?' Peter asked as he walked over, shaking his head in disapproval.

Ellie took in a deep, shaky breath. 'It was a sprain, but I didn't mean to hurt her, I lost control of the bike.'

'I suppose you never meant to hurt me when you set fire to my porch, or Meghan and Tommy when you set fire to their lawn?' Andrea yelled.

Ellie looked at Meghan and Tommy, who were watching her with hooded eyes. 'I didn't do any of that. Nothing related to fire, not this either,' she said, pointing to the smouldering forest.

'I don't believe you! Clearly you're lying to save your skin!' Andrea said. 'Adrian, you need to arrest her!' she shouted over to Adrian, who was walking slowly over towards them now, confused as he took in all the villagers forming a circle around Ellie.

'What's going on?' he asked, pushing his way through them to stand with her.

'The dork told them all about what she did,' Vanessa said. 'But she didn't have anything to do with the fires, okay, everyone?'

'Oh, Ellie, why'd you tell everyone?' Adrian asked.

'You knew?' Peter said in an outraged voice.

Adrian took a deep breath and turned to the villagers. 'Yes, the police know.'

'Then why isn't she under arrest?' Ed asked.

'She was let off with a caution,' Adrian replied.

'Let off to set fire to our forest!' Graham shouted.

'I did not set fire to the forest!' Ellie said.

'Then why do all the other stuff?' Peter asked, crossing his arms. He was obviously enjoying this.

Ellie tensed her jaw.

'Why, Ellie?' Peter pushed again. 'Why do any of it?'

'You heard the way people were gossiping just now,' Ellie replied, 'accusing different people of being the vigilante, throwing in little insults along the way.' She looked around at everyone. 'You're *all* guilty. Guilty of poisoning the village with your gossip, just like my mum was poisoned by the letters she got all those years ago.' There were a few raised eyebrows and whispers. 'Yes, my mum was a victim of the poison pen author all those years ago. And let's face it, there's no difference between some of your Facebook posts and those poison pen letters. Nothing has changed about this village, that's the problem.'

'So is that what the fire is about?' Tommy asked as he glared at Ellie.

'Tommy, don't,' Meghan whispered.

But he ignored her, stepping towards Ellie. 'Well, Ellie? What reason do you have for setting fire to my – your children's grandfather's – rose bushes?'

'I've already said, I am not behind *any* of the fires,' Ellie said.

'Are you sure you didn't sneak out earlier and start this fire?' Peter asked, gesturing to the singed trees.

'Yes,' Andrea chimed in, 'you seem to be very good at creeping around and causing havoc.'

'She didn't start the fire,' Adrian said.

'How can you be so sure?' Peter asked.

'Because I've been with her all night.'

Andrea's eyes widened as Peter shook his head in disgust. 'I knew it,' he hissed.

'Everyone should go home,' Adrian called out. 'The fire's under control now.'

'But we have the culprit right here, Adrian!' Andrea shouted out. 'Why aren't you arresting her?'

Adrian clenched his fists in frustration. 'Ellie has already told you—'

'No!' A scream rang out. Everyone turned to see Sheila running through the crowds, her face twisted in torment. She darted towards the forest, but two firemen stopped her, holding her back from the withering flames as she battled against them. 'Let me get in! He's in the forest! I have to save him!'

Ellie's blood turned to ice.

'Who's in the forest?' Tommy asked.

'Aaron,' she replied. 'Aaron *and* Tyler!'

Chapter 30

'Why the hell are they in the forest?' Ellie asked as Peter ran over, looking as frantic as Ellie felt.

'I gave Aaron a video camera for his birthday,' Sheila said, her hand to her mouth as she shook her head. 'They decided to do a video for their new song, a video with the sunrise in the background. Something about it turning the sky red, like fire. They – they were so excited, planning it after the party. I just called Terry after I saw the fire,' she said, referring to Aaron's mum, 'and they're not in their rooms, so they must be in there.'

'No!' Ellie screamed, looking into the forest, imagining her boy caught among the flames. She went to run towards the blackened trees, but Adrian grabbed her. 'No.'

'Jesus Christ, we have to get in there!' Peter said.

'What's going on?' Meghan asked as she and Tommy ran over.

'Tyler's in the forest,' Peter said, pacing back and forth.

'No!' Meghan cried, looking into the forest in horror as Vanessa stood still, in shock.

'We're going in,' Tommy said as he grabbed Peter's arm and they started running towards the forest. Ellie pushed away from Adrian and ran with them, but firefighters blocked their way.

'My boy's in there!' Ellie shouted at them.

'There are kids in the middle of the forest, two teenagers,' Adrian explained.

The firefighter nodded. 'We'll go in. But you must stay here, you'll only hinder our search.'

'Nobody knows the forest like us,' Tommy said.

'And nobody knows fire like us,' another firefighter replied. 'You have to stay here.'

All the fire crew headed into the forest. Though the outer perimeters of the fire had eased, flames still shot up from the middle.

Ellie crouched down, her head in her hands as Vanessa put her hand on her back.

'He'll be fine,' Vanessa said as she stared into the woods. 'He *has* to be fine.'

Meghan started crying into Tommy's shoulder as Peter raked his fingers through his hair. Adrian paced back and forth, eyes darting from Ellie to the forest. Around them, the villagers were quiet now, on silent watch. Ellie realised Karin Hawkins was among them with a photographer, taking photos as Ed tried to shove her away.

'My God, was she here when I – I confessed?' Ellie asked Vanessa.

Vanessa followed her gaze and shook her head. 'No, hon, I saw her just turn up.'

Finally, there was a sign of movement and two firemen appeared, a boy limping beside them . . . and another on a stretcher, an oxygen mask on his face.

It was Tyler.

Ellie ran towards him, Peter following.

'He should be fine,' one of the firefighters said. 'Just some smoke inhalation.'

'He saved me,' Aaron said to his grandmother as he looked up at her, his face dark with soot. 'Pushed me away from the flames into a ditch.'

'Darling, oh, Tyler,' Ellie said, walking beside her son as she held his limp hand. She could hardly see his face beneath the mask but could make out the streaks of soot on his cheeks and a burn on his shoulder.

She felt him squeeze her hand as his eyes fluttered open. 'Mum,' he moaned.

'I'm here, darling, I'm here.'

Chapter 31

Sunday 8th August
9 a.m.

Tommy Mileham

I hope I speak on behalf of the whole village and my grandson, Tyler, who is currently in hospital, when I say we are all in a deep state of grief following the near-destruction of our beautiful forest. As I look out of my window now, so used to seeing the forest in all its glory, instead all I see are the black, charred remains of trees which once stood tall and proud. If it weren't for the heroic efforts of this wonderful community and, of course, the Ashbridge Fire Service, there would be no trees left at all and my grandson might not have been here today.

Rebecca Feine

Absolutely devastating.

Myra Young

I haven't lived here as long as others, but I still share all your pain. Am gutted.

Andrea Simpson

Beautiful words, Tommy. But as it says in the Bible, there is a time to grieve, then there is a time to find blame. And I think it's very clear to many of us who were there earlier that we know who the culprit is now.

Rebecca Feine

She said she didn't do it.

Belinda Bell

Ellie is our Facebook Vigilante, Rebecca, she admitted to it. And no doubt she is behind last night's forest fire. I've already called the police about it. I've always found her to be a strange one anyway. A bit too perfect for my liking.

Nero Patel

That's ridiculous. Ellie is one of the nicest people I know! I'd do the same as she did if I found out my mum had got letters like that. And she said she didn't start any fires!

Graham Cane

It's the nice ones you need to look out for. I said to Malorie how she reminds me of a Barbie doll. All pristine and perfect on the surface, but there's nothing inside.

Pauline Sharpe

Totally agree, Graham! Now I think about it, it doesn't surprise me. Pretending she's a good citizen with her game days at the retirement village when we all know it's just so she looks charitable and kind when the truth is, she's a cold fish.

Andrea Simpson

Who else can be behind the fires? Ellie openly admitted to being the Facebook Vigilante. It came right out of the horse's mouth. So who else would be behind the worst kind of vandalism – setting fire to a forest and, in turn, unwittingly harming her own child – than the person who has recklessly been targeting villagers with similar acts the past few weeks?

Rebecca Feine

How many times do I have to say that Ellie denies being behind any of the fires. There's a difference between silly pranks and setting fire to a forest. And aren't you all just proving exactly what she said about the viciousness of the words you all fling about? The poor woman is at her son's bedside now. Thank God he's going to be okay, but still.

Graham Cane

Vicious? Vicious is setting fire to our beloved forest. You say there's a difference between silly pranks and fire, but criminals have a progression in their acts, from small – say, injuring wildlife – to, eventually, the big, like full-on murder.

Rebecca Feine

Jesus, Graham, we're not talking about murder! And anyway, who's to say the forest was set on fire on purpose?

Tommy Mileham

It was. I spoke to the man in charge of the fire service. They found evidence of where the blaze was started, at the foot of a tree. Remains of a crude DIY contraption with party sparklers attached to weights. Somebody did this on purpose. I can't bring myself to say that somebody is Ellie, but the signs aren't looking good . . .

Andrea Simpson

See, her children's grandfather is saying so. I have turned over all my evidence to the police about Ellie. She can hide all she wants behind her curtains but, eventually, she'll need to come out of hiding and tell the truth.

Chapter 32

Ellie sat beside Tyler's bed, holding his hand. He was sleeping now. The doctors said that although they were pretty sure he would be fine, he had inhaled a lot of smoke, so they wanted to keep him in just in case. Luckily, the burn to his shoulder was minor.

The fact was, it could have been a *lot* worse.

At first, as Ellie sat there, watching her son sleep, she felt as still and as bereft as the charred trees she'd glimpsed from the hospital window when she'd dared to look out towards Forest Grove.

But then she began to feel anger. At herself, yes. But mainly at the person who had started that fire.

She would not *let* them get away with it.

Peter walked in then, after going back to his parents' to take a shower. They'd taken it in turns to watch over Tyler as Zoe stayed with Meghan and Tommy. Peter looked more alert . . . and more angry.

'Can we talk?' he asked.

Ellie peered at Tyler then sighed. 'Yes.'

They got up and walked out into the corridor.

'We haven't really talked about this,' Peter said, 'but are you really the Facebook Vigilante?'

'Yes. But I was *not* behind any of the fires. Someone else did those.'

He shook his head. 'You've lost it.'

'No,' Ellie replied as calmly as she could. 'I was stupid to play those silly pranks, but I had a reason. This,' she said, looking through the open door towards their son, 'this is different.'

Peter's blue eyes sparked with anger. 'Is it really so different?'

'Yes. You *know* me, Peter,' Ellie said, lowering her voice. 'I would *never* do that.'

'I do know you, Ellie. I know you did this to me,' he said, gesturing to the bruise on his cheek.

'Because you're an arsehole,' Ellie said, unable to help herself.

Peter's nostrils flared.

A shadow fell across the room. Ellie looked up to see it was Detective Powell.

Her heart beat accelerated.

She was surprised Detective Powell hadn't turned up already. After all, according to the Facebook posts she'd seen as Tyler slept, half the village seemed to have gone to the police with their suspicions about her. At least Adrian had been with her all night when the fire was lit, her alibi again . . . but then that didn't mean she couldn't have crept out into the forest while he slept, striking the match.

She shuddered as she remembered her first sight of the trees on fire. It was just too horrific! Who would *do* that? The same person behind the other arson attacks, obviously. The same person who wrote those poison pen letters.

'Must have been pretty scary for him out there,' the detective said as she peered in at Tyler.

Ellie held back her tears, nodding.

'We need to talk,' Detective Powell said.

'Yes, you bloody do,' Peter said. He walked back into Tyler's room, glaring at Ellie over his shoulder.

'Amicable separation then?' Detective Powell asked Ellie.

'Not quite.'

'There's a side room we can use.'

Ellie followed Detective Powell to a room down the corridor. The detective shut the door and they sat opposite each other on two small sofas.

'This is becoming quite the regular meet-up, isn't it?' Detective Powell said.

'Yes,' Ellie said. She caught sight of herself in the reflection of the window, her shocked eyes staring out of her soot-coloured face.

Who cared? What did it matter how she looked? Maybe this was more suitable than any make-up, a reflection of the chaos and horror she felt inside.

'I went to see the forest just now,' Detective Powell said. She took out some photographs of the crime scene and spread them on the coffee table in front of Ellie. 'It's quite something.'

It was so horrible to see, the buckled trees and charred ground.

'It's awful,' Ellie said. 'And I didn't do it.'

'We'll see. The fire inspector said that five fires were set around the perimeter of the forest.'

Ellie shook her head. 'I can't believe it. Five?'

'Yep. Clearly whoever did it wanted to burn the whole forest down. *Luckily*, the wind was blowing in the wrong direction, which meant only two of the fires spread. Maybe two-thirds of the forest was spared.'

'Thank God.'

'We need to search your house,' Powell said sadly. 'Can you give us permission?'

Ellie sighed. 'Sure. I didn't do it though.'

'You're the best lead we have.'

'What are you hoping to find?'

'Anything to connect you to the fire.'

'You won't find anything.'

'Maybe.'

'I presume half the village called to report me now they know everything about me?'

'Not quite half.' The detective watched Ellie for a moment. 'That took balls, publicly admitting to your "pranks", as you call them.'

'I'm starting to regret it.'

'I bet you are.' She looked in the direction of Tyler's room. 'I bet you have *lots* of regrets.'

Ellie looked down at her hands. 'I do. I may have not lit the match that caused the fire, but I may have inspired it.'

'Very true.'

The detective leaned back on the sofa, smoothing her slim, brown hands over her tight hair bun. She looked exhausted; no doubt the added pressure of dealing with the incidents in Forest Grove as well as the crime in Ashbridge was wearing on her.

'It was interesting talking to the fire investigator, actually,' the detective said. 'I've never had to deal with an arson case before, believe it or not. He gave me an interesting insight into what it takes to be an arsonist. Or pyromaniac, as he calls them.' She was watching Ellie closely as she talked and Ellie wondered if she was trying to drag some kind of confession out of her. 'He described how the act of setting something on fire is a form of relief after a build-up of tension. People who deliberately start fires usually don't cope very well when it comes to dealing with stress. It's all that pent-up tension rising to the surface.'

'Yes, someone I know said the same,' Ellie said, thinking of Kitty.

'I believe you and your ex-partner split up just four months ago.' The detective leaned forward. 'How did you deal with that stress, Ellie?'

'I drank wine with my best friend, ate lots of chocolate and watched stupid films,' Ellie said, looking the detective in the eye. 'What I didn't do is set fire to anything.'

'If not you, then who?'

'I really don't know.'

The two women stared at each other, then the detective's phone rang. She slid her eyes away from Ellie's and stood up. 'Give me a moment,' she said, leaving the room.

If not you, then who?

Ellie thought of the other villagers. Were there any who had been through a traumatic experience recently? She couldn't think of anyone, bar the people she'd targeted with her pranks and the ones who'd been victims of arson.

Ellie looked through the photos in front of her, staring glumly at the scorched remains of the forest. Then she realised not all of them were of the forest. In the pile was a printout of the article about the poison pen letters written to Belinda Bell from all those years before. Attached to it with a paperclip was a grainy photo of the lighter.

The lighter found at the scene of the arson attacks at the time.

Ellie picked the photo up, looking closer at the symbol on the lighter. 'That's not a crown,' she whispered to herself.

She turned it upside down, realising that rather than a crown symbol, it was a bridge.

A bridge . . .

Ellie suddenly jumped up.

Vanessa had used a bridge in her logo for FKAPS, the Forest Grove Kids Against Pollution Society she'd set up, its slogan *Creating a bridge across the world.*

Was it *Vanessa's* old lighter?

And what did that mean? Was Vanessa the Forest Grove arsonist?

Chapter 33

Sunday 8th August
3 p.m.

Andrea Simpson

I just heard word that the police have been searching Ellie Nash's house. I think that's confirmed it, Ellie is behind this reign of terror that's been inflicted on our village. And now, thankfully, it will be over.

Rebecca Feine

Hold your horses, they're just searching the house. There's no suggestion she's a suspect or has been arrested.

Graham Cane

You need to take your rose-tinted glasses off, love. It's obvious. Ellie is the arsonist.

Vanessa Shillingford

How do you know they're searching the house?

Ed Piper

I told Andrea.

Lucy Cronin

Will be a horrible surprise for the kids when they find out.

Belinda Bell

Especially after what they went through with the marriage break-up. Makes you realise now why Peter left her.

Vanessa Shillingford

Okay, I just called my brother. Ellie hasn't been arrested, nor is she a suspect. So everyone chill out. And as for why my brother left her, he's a jerk, that's why.

Graham Cane

Hmmm, you seem to be a little too defensive, Vanessa.

Rebecca Feine

Ellie's her best friend, Graham! Of course she'd defend her.

Andrea Simpson

Maybe you're involved, Vanessa? The lights were seen on in the bakery just before the fires were lit, after all.

Andrew Blake

How do you *know* all this information, Andrea?

Graham Cane

Didn't you know? She's the all-seeing, all-hearing heart of Forest Grove.

Andrea Simpson

I have my sources. Hmmm, interesting how Vanessa hasn't replied, isn't it? It wouldn't surprise me if she and Ellie weren't in on it together.

Chapter 34

Ellie didn't mention her suspicions concerning the lighter to Detective Powell. Instead, she let the detective wrap up her interview and leave, then told Peter she was going to head home for a shower and check the police hadn't made a mess during their search.

But instead of heading home, she drove straight to Vanessa's house, running through everything in her mind.

Vanessa had always been the feisty one, more prone to taking risks and showing her disapproval through action . . . even if it led to her being arrested. Like Ellie, she too hated the way Forest Grove could be a hive of bitchy gossip.

There had been one time, too, when Vanessa had set fire to a bin when they'd been drunk. Ellie remembered the way she'd talked about it as Ellie, horrified, got a bottle of water from her bag to put out the fire.

'Wait,' Vanessa had said. 'Isn't it beautiful? Look at it!'

But no! That would mean Vanessa was behind the poison pen letters . . . including the letters to her mum and to Ellie herself! Not to mention the fact that it would mean Vanessa had set fire to her own parents' lawn. But then Vanessa had said in the past how fed up she was with her father's obsession with his rose bushes. Maybe it was more of a statement . . . and a way to throw everyone off the scent. That might explain why she wrote a letter to Ellie too, to divert police attention away from Ellie. Vanessa *had* been rather excited when Ellie confessed to her after Tyler's gig.

'No,' Ellie whispered. It just all seemed too much. Vanessa couldn't be behind it all, she just couldn't.

She needed to talk this through with someone. She called Adrian, using her hands-free.

'Ellie, how's Tyler?' he asked as soon as she answered.

'He'll be fine.'

'Thank God.'

'Look, Adrian, I'm going to run something past you and I do *not* want you acting on it. Promise?'

'You know I can't promise that, Ellie,' he said in an unsure voice.

'Please?'

She heard him sigh. 'Fine. I promise.'

'It kills me to say this, but I think Vanessa might be behind the poison pen letters . . . and the arson.'

'What?' he exclaimed.

She explained why and Adrian was quiet for a few moments.

'Adrian?'

'That's interesting in light of what I've just learnt,' he said.

'What have you learnt?'

'There was activity at the bakery before the fire was lit. Someone unable to sleep saw the lights on there around three in the morning. The fires were likely to have been lit just after.'

Ellie banged the steering wheel. 'No!'

'I know Vanessa's your friend,' Adrian said, 'and I think she's great,' he quickly added. 'But she does always seem a bit . . . angry.'

He was right, Vanessa had always been a bit angry with the world, whether it be with large polluting companies or the village gossips. But she'd mellowed a bit as they got older. Maybe a 'sleeper rage' of sorts had been ignited by Ellie's pranks?

'Do you want me to talk to her?' Adrian asked.

'No!' Ellie said. 'I'll – I'll go around and chat to her. I know it's not her; deep down, I know.' Ellie swallowed. Was it more a case of, deep down, she didn't *want* it to be her best friend? 'But I'd like to just look her in the eye when I mention the bridge symbol on the lighter, see her reaction? I know her so well.'

'I get it,' Adrian said. 'Call me after, yeah? And be careful. I know she's your friend but, ultimately, if what you're saying is true, she started a fire that harmed your son . . . her *nephew*.'

Ellie sighed. 'I know.'

She drove into Forest Grove, heading towards Vanessa's house, stomach in knots at the idea of bringing this up with her friend. She knew Vanessa would be in; she'd texted Ellie to say they'd closed the bakery for the day and would be at home if Ellie needed her. But when she got to Vanessa's house and rang the bell, Vanessa didn't come to the door.

Maybe she was in the garden?

Ellie walked to the side of the house, calling her name out. 'Ness! Are you there!' But she wasn't in her garden either.

As she was about to turn away, Ellie paused.

There was a collection of rubbish bins down the side of the house and, through the clear plastic of one of the bin bags for recycling, Ellie noticed something.

Packaging for sparklers.

She thought back to what Tommy had written in the group about what the fire service had found at the scene of the forest fire.

Remains of a crude DIY contraption with party sparklers attached to weights . . .

'No,' she whispered as she peered back at her best friend's house.

That confirmed it. Vanessa really was the arsonist!

Ellie ran back up the path, banging on Vanessa's door, desperate to see her. 'Ness! Let me in, Ness!' She leaned down, opening her letterbox. 'Vanessa, please let me in. I want to talk.'

Still nothing.

'She's gone for a walk, Ellie!' a neighbour called over. 'Or should I say run, she was doing a Usain Bolt towards the forest.'

Ellie looked at the remains of the forest and her stomach turned over.

She knew where Vanessa must be heading: to the forest, to finish the job she'd started in the early hours when she'd set it alight.

Chapter 35

The smell of ash lingered in the air as Ellie approached the forest, the scorched ground ahead of her still smoking in places. It couldn't be a coincidence that the most-burnt trees were close to the bakery where Vanessa worked, it just couldn't. About a hundred square metres of forest were a desolate, ashen graveyard of ash, solitary, scorched trunks reaching helplessly into the sky. Beyond, the untouched forest stood healthy and beautiful and Ellie felt an aching grief for the trees that had gone.

As she drew closer to the edge of the forest, she saw police scene-of-crime tape had been placed around the black, skeletal remains of the outer trees, and there were fire-service notices warning people not to pass.

But ahead of her, in the distance, Ellie could see Vanessa running towards the surviving part of the forest.

'Vanessa!' Ellie called.

Her friend paused, turning to look over her shoulder.

Ellie lifted the police tape and slipped beneath it, her loafers sinking into the thick layers of ash, the black soot staining the yellow leather.

'Wait!' Ellie called.

For a moment, she thought Vanessa would wait. But instead, she turned and continued running towards the trees, even faster now, her leather backpack bouncing up and down with each hurried step.

'Nessa, please!' Ellie said, running after her. 'This isn't the answer. *Please!*'

But Vanessa just ran faster and, with each step, memories ran through Ellie's mind from their friendship.

That first meeting, in the classroom, Vanessa's lopsided grin and mess of red hair.

The smell of her Body Shop Peach Fuzz perfume as she hugged Ellie when Ellie first got her period.

The sight of her handing leaflets out in the school playground, a look of defiance on her face.

The smile of pride she gave Ellie when she saw Ellie in her wedding dress, ready to marry her brother.

How could she have not realised all that rage was hiding inside?

Ellie quickened her step. It was up to her to stop Vanessa. She had ignited that rage, after all. She had a duty to put a stop to this, to save Forest Grove.

As she drew closer, though, she noticed another figure.

It was Meghan.

And in her hand was a packet of matches, a pile of sparklers and wood before her on the ground.

Chapter 36

'Mum,' Vanessa said, out of breath as she stared at her mother. 'Please don't.'

Ellie looked on in shock. How could it be *Meghan*? Ellie hadn't seen Meghan angry in her whole life.

It's all that pent-up tension rising to the surface.

'How did you know?' Meghan asked Vanessa.

'Dad's post about the sparklers,' Vanessa said. 'It took me a while to figure out, but then it hit me: you asked to borrow some of the extras I had left over from Dad's party. When I went to talk to you, Rebecca said she saw you heading to the forest.'

'You did this, Meghan?' Ellie asked, shocked. 'Your grandson is in hospital because of this!'

Meghan's eyes jerked to Ellie. 'I – I never meant to hurt Tyler. But it makes me more determined. It can't be a waste. I need to finish what I started.'

'But why?' Ellie said. 'I thought you loved this place.'

Meghan's face twisted. 'Love it? I *hate* it,' she spat.

'Mum, *please*,' Vanessa pleaded.

'This place *ruined* my life,' Meghan continued. 'Everything was perfect before we arrived here, but then this village ruined everything.'

'How? How did it ruin everything?' Ellie asked, trying to keep her talking. Anything to stop her lighting that fire!

'It's not this village, Mum. It's Dad! Dad ruined everything,' Vanessa said with a sigh.

'Tommy?' Ellie asked. 'What are you both talking about?'

'Dad had affairs. *Lots* of them,' Vanessa said. 'It was just too tempting, living in a close-knit village like this, getting so close to its residents . . . especially its female residents.'

Ellie's mouth dropped open. 'You never said. We – we tell each other everything.'

'Not everything, Ellie. Some things I keep for my own lucky self,' Vanessa said sarcastically.

Ellie looked at the two women. The clues were right in front of her and yet she had never quite put them together.

'What about the poison pen letters?' Ellie said. 'Did you send those too, Meghan?'

She nodded.

'But . . . my mum was your best friend!'

'She was until I found Tommy and her kissing.'

'My *mum*?'

'More like Dad trying to force himself on to her,' Vanessa replied. 'I saw it too, Mum, at the party for the pub opening. Ellie's mum was *not* interested!'

'Oh, come off it,' Meghan said. 'She loved the attention. Sorry, Ellie, but she really did.'

'That's why you sent her those poison pen letters?' Ellie asked.

Meghan's jaw tightened. 'I thought it might help her see what a slut she was. How *tempting* she was for the men in this village, going out without her husband.'

'Do you realise how old-fashioned you sound, Mum?' Vanessa said. 'How *sexist*. She was just sociable, her husband wasn't, that doesn't make her a slut!'

'You modern women, you miss so much with your politically correct views,' Meghan said, shaking her head.

'She was your *friend*,' Ellie said again.

'Even more reason she shouldn't have come around to dinner with those fancy dresses on, making eyes at Tommy!'

'Mum, come on!' Vanessa shouted. She turned to Ellie, eyes filled with tears. 'I'm *so* sorry, Ellie.'

'Why did you send me that letter, Meghan?' Ellie asked. 'Am I a slut too?'

'Yes, maybe. The way you slagged off my Peter! I even felt sorry for you!' Meghan exclaimed. 'And then he goes and tells me you were seeing Adrian before you had even split up . . .'

'What?' Vanessa said. 'That's ridiculous.'

'Vanessa's right! I barely knew Adrian before Peter and I split up,' Ellie said.

'But that's what Peter said,' Meghan insisted.

'Peter would say *anything* to carry on looking like the golden boy with you,' Vanessa snapped. 'Let me guess how he said it. *Well, Mum, who's to say Ellie wasn't seeing Adrian while we were married?* Anything to take the blame away from him.'

Meghan didn't say anything, and it was clear from her face that Peter had said something similar.

'So you did send all those poison pen letters?' Ellie said, running it through in her mind. 'Which, now I think about it, targeted the women in the village. What about the fires? Were you behind all those arson attacks from all those years ago too?'

'Tommy found out about the letters,' Meghan said. 'He caught me writing one so I needed to change my method.'

Vanessa shook her head in shock. 'My mum, the arsonist. So Dad knew then? Didn't he get you help?'

Meghan looked down at the match in her hand. 'You know how he is. Told me to pull myself together. He had no idea about the fires I started.'

Ellie sighed. 'You used one of Vanessa's lighters too.'

Vanessa's mouth dropped open. 'What?'

'It was your lighter that was found at the scene, Ness,' Ellie said. 'It wasn't a crown, it was a bridge! I – I thought you were behind the fires. Obviously, I know now you're not.'

Vanessa shook her head at her mother. 'I can't believe you risked me being implicated.'

'I didn't mean to drop the lighter!' Meghan insisted. 'Someone was walking by and – and I panicked. I would never have let you take the blame, I would have admitted to all of it.'

Ellie thought of Tyler and how she had taken the blame for him.

'And the recent fires?' Ellie asked. Of course, she knew Meghan was behind those too, but she just needed to know for sure.

Meghan nodded.

'Your own *garden*, Mum?' Vanessa said.

'Your dad's precious rose bushes! He thought more of those things than he did me.'

'What's the deal with Andrea's porch?' Vanessa asked.

'Oh, she's always throwing herself at Tommy during their weekly gardening club meet-ups,' Meghan said.

'So you attack anyone who takes Tommy's attention away from you,' Ellie said. 'With nasty letters and arson.'

'It's pathetic, Mum!' Vanessa cried out.

'Vanessa,' Ellie said in a low voice.

'No, no, she's right, Ellie,' Meghan said matter-of-factly, the matches still in her hands. 'I am pathetic. I can't even get this right,' she said, gesturing to what remained of the forest. 'Nearly killing my grandson, not even burning half the forest down in the process.' Her eyes flashed with anger. 'I will now though.'

As she said that, she lit the match.

'Mum, no!' Vanessa screamed. 'Think of your grandkids!'

Meghan hesitated.

'You can't burn it all away,' Ellie quickly continued. 'It's just a forest, a symbol. But the people will still be here.'

'Ellie's right, Mum,' Vanessa added. 'You know what this place is like, they'll use it as a chance to show how bloody amazing they are. I can see it now, Belinda digging holes for new trees. Andrea in her flashy Joules wellies, raising money for some new forest revival charity she's set up.'

Ellie nodded in agreement as Meghan looked at them both. 'As Vanessa said once,' Ellie added, 'there's something rotten at the core of this place. Burning down a few trees – the whole forest! – won't change that. All it's doing is burning *you* away. Just like it burnt away at my mum. She kept it all inside, it made her have a nervous breakdown. You talk of this place being corroded, but that's what's happening inside *you*.'

'Ellie's right, Meghan,' said a deep voice from behind them.

Ellie turned to see Tommy and Adrian striding towards them, Detective Powell and two police officers close behind.

'Give me the matches, Meghan,' Tommy said when he got to them, holding out his hand.

But instead of doing what her husband asked, Meghan threw the lit match towards the sparklers.

Chapter 37

Sunday 15th August
1.32 p.m.

Andrea Simpson

Welcome back, everyone. I'm pleased to say I've taken back control of the group. It's also a great opportunity to announce the Forest Grove Regeneration Fund, which I've launched to raise money to restore the forest to its former glory. There's a Just Giving link in the bio of this group and, each week, a number of activities will take place to help us raise money. I very much hope you all get involved!

Rebecca Feine

Didn't they say only thirty trees were destroyed in the end?

Andrew Blake

It would have been more if Adrian hadn't put out Meghan's fire with the bottle of wine in Vanessa's backpack. Lucky she'd just been to the shops.

Lucy Cronin

Isn't wine flammable?

Vanessa Shillingford

Wine isn't flammable, actually, not enough alcohol in it. Anyway, it was Adrian's coat that did the real work.

Ed Piper

Good old PC Plod, saved our forest with his coat.

Adrian Cooper

PC Plod isn't so ploddy after all, is he?

Ed Piper

You know I've only ever meant that as a term of endearment. Seriously, mate, we appreciate it.

Sheila Leighton

How's your mother, Vanessa?

Vanessa Shillingford

Thanks for asking. She's fine. We're all relieved she was only charged with third-degree arson in the end instead of aggravated arson. She'll likely get a fine and the chance to see out a two-year sentence at a low-security institute, making her one lucky woman. And for those nosier among you, my interview with Karin Hawkins will be in the Ashbridge Gazette next week.

Belinda Bell

Sorry, Vanessa, but it really should be more. Not only for the fires but the letters too. As the recipient of one, I can say they caused irreparable damage.

Rebecca Feine

What's done is done, Belinda. Can't we just all live and let live? Meghan was clearly going through a lot.

Ellie Nash

Live and let live? As if! This *is* Forest Grove, Rebecca!

Epilogue

Ellie placed the sapling in the hole Adrian had dug as the kids watched from nearby. Andrea had given each household in the village the chance to plant their own tree – paid for with the generous funds raised by the whole village – contributing towards making the forest even bigger and better than it was before.

'How will we even know it's our tree?' Zoe asked. Behind her several other residents were digging holes and manoeuvring saplings into place.

'It'll be the wonky one if you leave it like that,' Vanessa called over from where she was planting her own tree. Ellie smiled at her. Somehow, they'd grown even closer after all that had happened. Maybe it helped that Vanessa was the only original Mileham left in Forest Grove. Tommy had sold their house to cover the legal fees of the overpriced solicitor he'd hired to try to get his wife off. Peter was moving even further out now, getting a house with Caitlin in a town forty miles away.

As for Meghan, she had just started her sentence and had already sent Ellie a letter, asking Ellie to visit her. But Ellie just couldn't bear to be anywhere near Meghan after all she had done and the terrible effect that her poison pen letters had had on her mother. She couldn't face Tommy either, who hadn't even bothered trying to make contact or apologise, proving what a spiteful man he was. So it was left to Peter to arrange meet-ups between the kids and their grandfather, to send letters to their nan.

Ellie looked over to her mother now. She was sitting on a chair nearby, a blanket over her legs as she smiled at her grandchildren. Her mum had changed after discovering it was Meghan who was behind the letters. When Ellie had sat down and explained it to her the day after Meghan's confession, her mother had surprised her with her response.

'Poor Meghan,' she'd said. 'Now it all makes sense. What a horrible man Tommy was to make his wife like that. I forgive her.'

Ellie wished she felt the same. But she was proud of her mum for being so forgiving . . . and if it meant her mother now felt some resolution, which she clearly did, judging from the way she grew brighter and cheerier each time Ellie saw her, she was fine with that.

Ellie noticed someone watching her as she thought about her mother.

It was Karin Hawkins.

After hearing Ellie was behind the initial pranks, Karin had threatened to expose her. So Vanessa had offered Karin an exclusive interview in exchange for not printing a word about Ellie. For a while, after not hearing back from Karin for days, Ellie had expected her to say no. But in the end, Karin had agreed. Maybe it had something to do with the fact that Karin had finally decided to take up a job at a national newspaper? She was happy to leave the petty crimes of Forest Grove behind.

'Why's it so wonky?' Ellie asked as she crouched down, investigating the soil for clues. Stanley attempted to help her, pushing his wet nose into the mud.

'It's fine,' Adrian said. 'Who cares if it's wonky anyway?'

'But yours is perfect,' she said, gesturing to the tree Adrian had planted. His son, Carter, was standing nearby, looking thoroughly bored.

'Yeah, well, I had one of your frothy coffees before I planted it, so I had precise planting skills,' Adrian quipped back.

Ellie smiled. He'd stayed over the night before, the first time with the kids there. It had been six months since Peter had walked out on her, two months since Meghan had set the forest ablaze. And yet it felt like a lifetime ago.

Ellie had thought she'd be out of the village by now. But a small house had cropped up on the outskirts and Ellie had put in an impulsive offer. She had got the job as entertainment editor at the *Ashbridge Gazette* after all, meaning more of a regular income.

'Maybe there's a stone pushing it to the side,' Ellie said, prodding her gloved fingers in the soil.

'Not everything is a puzzle to solve, remember, Ellie?' Vanessa said.

Ellie took a deep breath and stood back up. She was right. Finally, Ellie had learnt that.

'Fine, let's plant it as it is then,' Ellie said.

The kids walked over, kneeling down and throwing fistfuls of soil into the hole.

Ellie watched them, her arm around Adrian as what remained of the forest rustled around them, the autumnal trees swaying in the distance.

It would take years for these young saplings to catch up with the others. But that was fine. Not everything had to happen at once.

As Ellie thought that, she felt very aware that the soles of her boots had sunk deep into the soil.

Forest Grove's soil. *Her* soil.

Maybe this place wasn't so bad after all?

Her strength during challenging times over the years will always be an inspiration for me to carry on even in the toughest of times. It's just a shame this will be the first novel of mine she won't read . . .

. . . or will it? As I write this, I imagine her sitting in her sunny spot in her new garden, wherever she is now, reading this book. Here's to you, Mum. I love you. x

AUTHOR'S NOTE

And there you have it, my third book set in Forest Grove! I hope those of you who have read my other two Forest Grove books – *Wall of Silence* and *Circle of Doubt* – enjoyed returning to this claustrophobic village. I really loved returning to it and particularly enjoyed giving characters like Belinda and Graham a piece of their own medicine!

It was such an easy book to write at the start, despite the challenges of having to write during a pandemic. I just knew so clearly what would happen. When I think about me as a debut author, I never would have dreamed I'd have two books published in the midst of a pandemic. I never dreamed I wouldn't have my mum by my side as I did either. Sadly, my dear mum passed away from lung cancer recently.

As many of my regular readers know, she played a huge part in my reading and writing life. She was the reason I became an author, her love of words seeping into my soul from a very early age. My most abiding memories are of visiting the local library each Saturday with her, coming away with a pile of books. Or sitting with her in a sunny spot in the garden, both engrossed in our books, which we'd swap when we'd finished. I loved scouring her bookshelves, filled with the greats from Danielle Steel and Barbara Taylor Bradford to Stephen King and Dean Koontz, and all my books, of course! Whenever I think of her, I feel the warmth of the sun on my head and feel the pages between my fingers. She was my sunny spot, my reading companion. I'm bereft she is gone, but each time I write, each time I read, I feel her here with me, her influence so profound.

I know many of you reading this understand the pain I'm feeling, maybe also the strange couple it makes with joy too when we think of all the times we shared with those we love and now miss. Big hugs to you and feel free to get in touch, whether it be about your own loved ones or about anything at all to do with my books. You can find all the details you need at www.tracy-buchanan.com. And for lots of exclusives, from me and other authors, head on over to www.facebook.com/groups/thereadingsnug too.

Until next time (and let's hope the next time I write an author letter, it will be in better times).

Take care, Tracy

ACKNOWLEDGMENTS

Many thanks, as ever, to the people who helped me weave this novel from start to finish: my awesome agent, Caroline Hardman, and the team at Hardman & Swainson. To the Lake Union team, including Sammia Hamer, Ian Pindar, Victoria Oundjian and Nicole Wagner, not to mention the host of copy-editors, proof readers, cover designers and more. Thank you all for your support and understanding over a difficult few months.

To the constants in my life, my 'oak tree' husband, Rob, always there to lean on, and my daughter, Scarlett, always there to make me giggle and inspire me to make her proud. Oh, I mustn't forget my dog, Bronte! Useless as an assistant but fabulous as a cuddle companion and background music maker (if you count snoring as background music).

To the friends who make lovely walls for bouncing ideas off. Liz Richards, of course, plus Robyn Slingsby, Emma Cash, Angela Cranfield and Tamsin Petty.

To my wonderful family, the biggest cheerleaders in the world, especially my dad and brother, who harass their work colleagues to buy my books!

And finally my mum, who passed away while I was writing this novel. People ask how I managed to finish this book in the midst of enduring her diagnosis in the middle of a pandemic. SHE is why.

ABOUT THE AUTHOR

Photo © 2018 Nic Robertson-Smith

Tracy Buchanan is a bestselling author whose books have been published around the world, including chart toppers *Wall of Silence, My Sister's Secret* and *No Turning Back*. She lives in the UK with her husband, their daughter and a very spoilt Cavalier King Charles Spaniel called Bronte.

Before becoming a full-time author, Tracy worked as a travel journalist, visiting and writing about countries around the world. She has also produced content for the BBC and the Open University, and rubbed shoulders with celebrities while working for a London PR firm.

When she isn't spending time with her family and friends, Tracy now spends her days writing with her dog on her lap or taking walks in forests.

For more information about Tracy, please visit www.facebook.com/TracyBuchananAuthor and www.tracy-buchanan.com.